VALHALLA STATION

DAVID BRUNS

CHRIS POURTEAU

SEVERN RIVER
PUBLISHING

VALHALLA STATION

Severn River Publishing
www.SevernRiverBooks.com

ISBN: 978-1-64875-546-0 (Paperback)

ALSO BY BRUNS AND POURTEAU

The SynCorp Saga

The Lazarus Protocol

Cassandra's War

Hostile Takeover

Valhalla Station

Masada's Gate

Serpent's Fury

Never miss a new release! Sign up to receive exclusive updates from authors Bruns and Pourteau!

severnriverbooks.com/series/the-syncorp-saga

I pledge allegiance to the star
Of the Syndicate Corporation of Sol.
And to the bylaws for which it stands,
One compact under law,
Irrevocable,
With service and security for all.

1

KWAZI JABARI • MINERAL EXTRACTION AND PROCESSING FACILITY 12, MARS

The explosion ripped through the refinery.

A sudden, hot eruption of sound overwhelmed Kwazi Jabari, drowning the white noise of tools and machines and the small talk of routine. The regolith walls of Mars's underground tunnels shook; the artificial gravity hiccupped. Rock and metal and human flesh smashed together. Bone, as always, surrendered to physics.

The first shockwaves passed. It was like a giant was running through the tunnels, smaller blasts like footsteps rumbling away deeper, ancient cannons firing in quick succession, one after the other against an enemy battle line. Dust and twisted metal rained down around Kwazi. He wrapped his arms around his head for protection. Stunned oblivion wrapped around him. The dull thud of the giant's footsteps echoed in the dusty rock beneath his cheek.

Kwazi's awareness began to return. The red emergency lights flashed, casting the familiar lines of Extraction Station 16 in the foreign shadows and broken angles of wrecked machinery. Dust floated everywhere, visible currents of ruddy air stirred by the atmo recyclers.

Blinking hard, Kwazi tried to raise himself from the ground. The artificial gravity was unstable, making his stomach heave. His heart thudded like one of the sluice pumps, swelling and receding in his head. A single, piercing note stabbed inward from his ears. His right arm hurt from a long, red gash along his forearm. Blood flowed freely. A familiar thing among chaos, it was sort of hypnotizing, his own blood. His eyelids felt lazy, heavy.

Kwazi shook his head to clear it, grabbing on to the pain that followed, a lifeline to awareness. He ripped the torn sleeve free of his uniform, wrapped it twice just below his elbow, and tied it off. The triage had come from muscle memory, something taught to him by a grandfather who'd had little patience for a grandson who'd rather be doing anything else than learning first aid. The pain in his forearm faded to a dull throb, and Kwazi wiped the grit from his eyes. He could hear sounds beyond his own skull again.

Deeper inside the facility, past a score of extraction stations like his, the giant's footsteps were awkward, the stumbling destruction of a drunken goliath. There was the screech of machinery bent and broken, still trying to work, thrashing itself to pieces. And there were other sounds now.

Grunting. Screaming.

The sounds of people dying.

Amy!

Kwazi dragged himself into a kneeling position. He ignored the Martian rock biting into his knees. She'd been working right next to him. They'd been talking about nothing at all and everything, the way future lovers do when they know that's what they'll be. Conversation as intimacy, an aphrodisiac of words, the beginnings of mutual exploration.

"I don't know," she'd said once she'd accepted his offer for dinner together after shift. "Maybe we could try Polynesian?"

I hate Polynesian, he'd thought. What he'd said was: "That sounds wonderful."

The facility shook again, the gravity hiccupped again, and Kwazi let the quake pass before attempting his feet. His knees felt made of jelly. Placing one hand against the control panel he'd been working on, Kwazi steadied himself.

He traced his way along the panel. Everything seemed to be where it shouldn't be. He'd been talking with Amy, checking the chemical composition levels for the leaching process. Optimizing the liquefaction of the metals extracted by his team from Shaft 16. A process he'd done with Amy a hundred times while the rest of Team 16 pulled the rocks from the tunnel. Aika and Mikel on the laser drills, Max and Beren moving the cuts from the holes to the conveyor belts. And he and Amy, the crew's exochemists, keeping everything tweaked to peak performance.

The air processors had made progress. The red haze was thinning, the fog clearing as Kwazi's mind had started to clear. A harsh Klaxon sounded. The hole in the refinery's protective dome was breached. Atmosphere was leaking to the Martian surface.

Amy!

Kwazi's heart began to race again. Where was she? They'd been standing together at the control panel. How much farther could—

A low moan stopped him breathing. He followed it, straining to hear through the noise.

"Amy!"

She lay on her side on the rough ground, one hand grasping at nothing. The top knot of her blonde hair hung loose. Kwazi knelt beside her, took her hand in his. He should evacuate her, get her to safety. And the rest of the team...

The strident Klaxon flooded the tunnels. Particulate matter in the air funneled upward with a reddish tail toward the surface.

Next to Kwazi, Amanda Topulos groaned. Ignorance of the right thing to do paralyzed him, wrestling with the certain knowledge that doing nothing was the worst of bad choices. He needed to act, to *do something*, or Amy might die. He might die. The other four members of their crew-family might die.

Vac-suits. The voice of Qinlao Manufacturing's safety trainer told Kwazi to help himself first, then help others. *You can't help anyone else if you're dead.*

He needed to get into a vac-suit, then get Amy into one. And then he'd find the others.

Kwazi forced himself to release Amy's hand, which flicked at the air again, a reflex. She seemed to be begging him to stay.

Leaving a silent prayer behind, a ward to watch over her, Kwazi staggered against the shifting gravity toward Station 16's emergency locker. Thunder roiled from farther down the line, thrumming the ground. He stumbled over something solid—a human arm holding a tool, a wrench he recognized, stamped *T16*. The fingers gripping it were African like his.

Jesus.

Kwazi traced the arm to the torso and the primary crushing machine lying over the body. Stepping carefully, he found Max Okafor's head twisted, his neck hyperextended. Kwazi swallowed hard, pushing down the quick bile of loss in his throat. There was a hard place behind his breastbone, a desire to stop, to process, to mourn.

On Mars, your crew was your family—that's what QM taught its workers. The safety chief had emphasized it during training, over and over again, along with the meme meant to make it stick: "Family Is Safety at QM."

Max was dead, but Amy was still alive. Maybe the others were too. He didn't want to lose them like he'd lost Max. The feeling in his chest morphed from sadness to determination. He *wouldn't* lose *her*.

Kwazi felt his path along the wall until he found the emergency locker. Spitting on the keypad, he wiped the dust off and typed the access code. Gears ground as the panel slid aside, revealing six vac-suits. He slid quickly into one, tested its seals, then grabbed a second one for Amy. He couldn't carry three more all the way down into Shaft 16. They were too heavy and bulky. So Kwazi detached three rebreathers from the other suits. They wouldn't protect from vacuum if the breach in the plastisteel dome around the refinery's entrance gave way, but they'd keep people breathing when the air got too thin. Maybe long enough for the rescue crews to arrive.

Static scratched at him from his helmet.

"Mayday, mayday, this is Crew Sixteen, anyone out there?"

Beren?

It'd been a long time since Kwazi had worn a vac-suit. He'd worked the Martian mines so long, it took a moment to remember how to engage comms.

"Beren?" he whispered.

There was a pause on the other end. "Jabari? Holy Christ! Aika, it's Kwazi! I told you we'd be okay!"

Aika was muttering in the background. She sounded odd, more than just distant from Beren's mic. Kwazi had a sudden impulse to tell them about Max, to let them know that Amy didn't seem to have serious injuries. They were family. They should know those things—the good and the bad.

"Hey, Kwazi, we're trapped down here," Beren said. "We're behind about twenty tons of rock. Halfway down Shaft Sixteen."

"Okay."

"Aika is injured but can walk. I'm fine, except for a little red lung from all this dust."

"Okay." Maybe he should wait with the news about Max. "Amy's alive but unconscious. How's Mikel?"

Another pause. Kwazi wasn't sure he'd engaged the comms correctly, then remembered they were voice activated.

"He didn't make it, bro," Beren said.

A keening began, a primeval sound that wasn't language. Kwazi thought it was feedback over the channel.

"I know, Aika, I know," Beren said. "But we'll do right by Mikel. We just need to get out of here first."

Kwazi began to move. "I'm coming," he said, refusing to look at Max's body as he passed.

"Sending you the specific coordinates," Beren replied, Aika's mourning a low murmur of loss in the background.

Aika and Mikel had been lovers since before he'd joined Team 16. Their relationship had inspired his courage to finally approach Amy. They were professional on shift and playful off. They'd been perfect together, balancing Mikel's Russian bravado with Aika's Japanese reserve. Now Mikel was dead and Aika alone. The thought that he might lose Amy forever made Kwazi's chest ache with the regret of wasted time.

There was a red dusting around her form, outlining her body. Kwazi shook that thought from his head, ignoring the still-pounding pain in his temple. Her restless hand clawed weakly at her throat.

Kwazi hurried his step, glancing at the readouts on his arm. Breathable atmo had fallen by thirty percent. He knelt beside Amy again, gently controlling her hand and fitting the rebreather over her nose and mouth. She resisted it at first. Then as the air began to flow, her struggles calmed. Kwazi held her hand and watched her breathe.

"What's going on up there, Kwazi?" Beren asked. He sounded bright and forced, despite the itchy background noise in the comms. "You've gotten awfully quiet."

"I'm here. Getting Amy into a suit." He shook himself from the trance of watching Amy be alive. Kwazi unfurled the second vac-suit next to her, hesitating. If she was injured, he could make it worse by moving her. "Give me a few minutes."

"We might not have a few minutes, bro," Beren said, his voice edgy. "We're losing atmo too fast. If you don't break those rocks pinning us in—"

"Don't leave her, Kwazi!" Aika shouted. "You stay right there beside her. Don't you leave her alone!"

Static and the heavy sound of one pair of coveralls rubbing against another.

"Leave me alone! Just leave me alone!"

"Aika?" Kwazi said, concerned.

The tense flesh of an open hand smacked skin.

"Jesus!" yelled Beren. "Aika, settle down!" More scuffling and exasperation filtered over the fuzzy channel.

"Guys!" Kwazi pulled the second leg of the vac-suit to Amy's thigh, then lifted her torso up to fold her inside. It was slow work, careful work. "I'm coming, but I can't just leave Amy here."

"Stay there! Don't leave her!"

"Aika, shut up!" Beren was more than angry now; he was scared to death. Scared *of* death.

Does he really think I'll leave them buried in a Martian mine shaft?

Kwazi sealed her vac-suit and brought the monitoring system online. A steady one atmo of pressure bloomed inside. Exterior read point-five. It'd dropped another ten percent of nominal in less than a minute. What was happening up top? Why weren't the seal protocols kicking in?

Kwazi gazed down on Amy, leaned over her. Somehow, with them both behind the plastisteel visors of their vac-suits, it didn't seem a violation of her space to be so close. He brought his helmet in contact with hers, their visors touching.

"I love you," he said, knowing the sound carried through the plastisteel. "Don't leave me alone—forever. Ca va?"

Amy loved it when he spoke French.

"Jabari, for God's sake, quit dicking around!"

"I can't leave her, man," Kwazi said, realizing he'd neglected to mute comms. "The rescue teams are coming. I can't leave her."

There was a hissing in his ears.

"You listen to me, noob—"

The screeching tone of the emergency broadcast signal overrode them both.

"Citizen-workers of Facility Twelve, this is Captain Li of Qinlao Faction. We have mobilized multiple rescue teams. Follow standard emergency protocols. Don your vac-suits and shelter in place. Stay off comms—"

"Captain Li! My team is trapped in Shaft Sixteen!" Kwazi heard the frenzied relief in his own voice, tried to rein it back. "Atmosphere is bleeding fast. We have less than half atmo. I'm sending you their location now. We have injured!"

"Whoever the fuck you are, get off comms!" Li blasted back. "Follow my orders and stay put. We have things under control again."

Kwazi looked around him. Things didn't seem to be under control. The air was moving faster up the tunnels, the blood-red dust trail racing to the surface. He had the absurd thought that if enough dust clogged the hole in the refinery's dome, it would act like a plug.

A flood of responses from other teams up and down the line overwhelmed comms. Details of injuries, cries of hope, pleas for rescue.

Kwazi tuned it all out. He'd provided Li with Aika and Beren's location. He would stay put and watch over Amy, make sure she was one of the first out. She didn't seem seriously injured, but she hadn't woken up either. She could have internal injuries, a potential death sentence in low-g because blood couldn't coagulate, wounds couldn't heal. He gazed down at Amanda Topulos, admiring his handiwork in keeping her alive, thinking how proud his grandfather would have been. Then the plodding steps of the angry giant marched through the refinery again, this time beginning in the deeper quarters, moving toward the upper tunnels and Shaft 16.

A second round of explosions.

2

RUBEN QINLAO • LANDER'S REACH, MARS

"How long will production be down?"

Modulated electricity hummed beneath Ming Qinlao's question. The inflections were still her own, as was the impatience in her voice. Concern for quota, the reason for the question, was hers too. But without the vocal enhancer, her ability to speak was like a whisper on the wind.

"Unknown," Ruben said. "We're still assessing. But we should know something soon."

His cheek ticked once before he could stop it. He'd recognized too late the tone he often used now without thinking. Captain Li's report made it clear that such an assessment was impossible in the near term. There was far too much damage to the plant to even begin to estimate repair time. That would come days if not weeks from now, after damage control crews had dug past the debris and extracted the dead. Ruben had just briefed the other three people in the room on that very point. But as was the case so often lately, Ming seemed not to have absorbed any of it.

Another sign of her mental decline, which had accelerated over the past year. Like her muscles before, Ming's mental acumen seemed to ebb and flow as frequently as her moods. Ruben hated watching his sister's deterioration. She seemed to be losing pieces of herself, one at a time. The worst part? Ming didn't even seem to notice. At fifty-eight, she was far too young to seem so old.

"Our emphasis now is on search and rescue," he said. Again.

"As it should be," Daniel Xiao confirmed from the other end of the conference table. His virtual form shimmered slightly, a momentary hitch in the Company's subspace relay network. The skyline of Shanghai rippled behind him. Ruben found himself missing Earth as he always did when confronted by its images. "Remember the long term, Ming," Xiao said. "Remember the optics."

Ming's modulator burped a grunt of disdain, or perhaps it was her cough coming back. Ruben sometimes couldn't tell one from the other. "I suppose the workers *are* corporate assets," she said. "Worth preserving, when possible."

"Training is expensive and only earns out its worth over time," Tan Huan observed, nodding to Ming. As usual, his contribution was trite and meant to curry favor with Ming. As Regent of Mars and head of the Syndicate Corporation's Qinlao Faction, she was the very definition of power here. Ming's word was Martian law.

She took no notice of Huan, who effected a cold smile to her non-response. Ruben reflected on the old aphorism about how generations decline over time. Tan's father, Dong, had served on the board of Qinlao Manufacturing for decades. When Dong had died, Tan had taken his seat on the board. But unlike his father's insightful advice, Tan's contributions were most often inane expressions of the obvious.

"Li speculates sabotage by the Resistance," Xiao offered, swiping the air in front of him. He tossed information into the shared feed. It hovered above the conference table. Still images showed bent, twisted plastisteel where clean, load-bearing infrastructure had been. With thumb and forefinger, Xiao zoomed and enhanced the image. "See here? And here? The results of carefully placed charges at the connectors." Daniel Xiao knew what he was talking about, having run one of the largest manufacturing companies of his own before QM had absorbed it, part of Earth's corporate consolidation under SynCorp. Xiao looked meaningfully around the table from behind his Shanghai desk. "We've got a major problem, Ming. And I don't just mean the saboteurs."

Ruben focused on his sister. She seemed mentally present and carefully considering Xiao's words. Ming resembled her mother Wenqian more every day, Ruben thought sadly. Stricken by a gene-hopping virus and confined to a maglev-chair much like the one her daughter now inhabited, Wenqian had lived her days out as a broken woman. And now Ming was following in her mother's fated footsteps: broken physically and heard only with the assistance of vocalizing tech.

More than that. Ming Qinlao was *alive* only with the assistance of technology, her current state the long-term legacy of radiation poisoning. Even the medical implant SynCorp had recently installed in all its citizens couldn't keep up with the progressive damage she was suffering. Her own body had turned against her, its cells mutating and murdering one another. Early therapy had retarded and even reversed the effects of the radiation for a time, but that time was long past. At least Wenqian, unlike Ming, had kept her faculties to the end. Ruben's heart was heavy. He could already feel the loss of his sister's inevitable conclusion.

"Ruben?"

His mind snapped back to the present. "I'm sorry, Daniel, it's the middle of the night here. What were you saying?"

Xiao sat forward, placing his virtual elbows on his desk more than a quarter billion kilometers away. "I asked if this incident has shown up on CorpNet yet? And if so, where? What form?"

Ruben engaged his sceye to check one last time before speaking. The SynCorp implant projected media images and headlines from CorpNet onto his retina. "Helena Telemachus is on top of things, as usual. She's cast the headline on CorpNet as a mining accident. She's already crafted the standard thoughts-and-prayers message for the public."

"She's good at that," Tan Huan said. "But it's not the top level of the 'net we need to worry about. It's the Basement and the Undernet."

Again, the obvious masquerading as wisdom.

"Of course," Ruben replied, speaking to Xiao's image rather than the flesh-and-blood Huan across the table. The Basement, the virtual traffic channel just below the publicly consumable, sanitized top level of CorpNet, was beyond the means of most citizen-workers. It was strictly pay to play for such delicate consumables as taboo pornography and ahead-of-the-curve investment advice. And one level below that was the Undernet, where the real business of the Company happened. Where backroom deals were brokered and conflicts among the Five Factions resolved. That's where the unvarnished facts about factory explosions on Mars would be analyzed. Which meant the Undernet—because it presented the truth of life under SynCorp—was where the real damage to the Company could happen. Fears stoked, relationships fractured, trust broken. "Our QM communications people are crafting a message now. We'll frame the narrative by presenting it first."

"I want to see it within the half hour," Ming said, looking straight at Ruben. "*Before* the formal board meeting."

"Of course," Ruben replied, glancing down deferentially. The three of them—four, he reminded himself as Xiao's image flickered again—had come together quickly. QM's formal board meeting was scheduled for three hours from now.

Daniel Xiao rapped his knuckles on his desk three times. It was his way of emphasizing a point before he made it. "Tony Taulke will blow a gasket when he hears the Resistance is behind this. He'll think we're not doing our part to keep the peace on Mars."

Ruben's eye ticked again. *And I wonder how he'll get that impression?* It was an open secret that Xiao was Tony's man on QM's board of directors.

"Don't be surprised if he sends Taulke operatives here," Xiao said. "Maybe even Fischer."

"Like hell," Ming said. She seemed to grow in her chair, become more substantial. It made Ruben's heart ache again with memories of the formidable woman she used to be. "Tony Taulke can—"

"But perhaps it won't be necessary," Xiao continued. "Not if we handle this the *right* way."

"Quickly, without mercy," Tan Huan supplied, receiving a nod from Xiao.

"Once we've saved those workers we can," Ruben said. All eyes turned his way. "We have two missions here. The first is search and rescue."

"Each team is to have an investigator present," Ming said, banishing any suggestion of her previous mental void. She looked straight at Xiao. "I want it all vid-documented and stored on an encrypted server. I won't give Tony an inch of sunlight to start wedging a toe in here."

There was a slight delay as Xiao held her gaze. Had he noticed her slipping lately too? Ruben wondered. Did he sense an opportunity that, with Tony's help, he could exploit?

Over my dead body. What Ruben said he directed to Ming: "Of course, an investigator with each S&R team. I'll see to it personally." He leaned back from the table. "We're planning to convene a full meeting of the board in three hours. If you could attend, Daniel?" Ruben avoided Huan's gaze but said, "You too, of course, Tan."

"Of course," Tan said.

"Contact my assistant," Xiao said. "If there's a conflict, I'll clear it."

"Thank you—"

"Yes, thank you, Daniel," Ming said. "Your presence is always reassuring."

The iron in her voice might have been refined in the plant that had just suffered sabotage. Ruben assumed it was directed at him. He'd overstepped again, run the meeting with her sitting right there at the head of the table. Didn't she realize he was doing that to protect her?

The virtual Xiao smiled. His image faded in silence.

"Well then, if there's nothing else for now," Huan said, already rising. "I was having a lovely dream that involved three geishas and a—"

"I also want to thank you, Tan," Ming said. Her attempt at a smile was twisted by the scarred skin that even the most delicate surgery seemed unable to restore. "It's like seeing your father every time I see you. Such a pleasant memory."

Ruben stopped the laughter before it left his throat. She was having a really good day today. Sometimes his sister flared brightly with lucidity, as she had with Daniel Xiao—became a sunspot of the old Ming despite the mechanical monotone of her voice, the sweetness of her chosen words sprinkled over a tart bed of sarcasm. Only those who knew her well knew her well enough to catch it.

Which meant Ming's subtle jab was lost on Tan Huan.

"So kind of you to say," Huan replied with a slight bow. He turned and left the two of them alone in the board room.

Ruben allowed himself a small chuckle.

"Such an imbecile," Ming said.

"Yes, sister. As long as you know it."

Despite its cockeyed affect, her smile for him was warmer, more intimate. A knowing forgiveness of Ruben's having run the meeting. Somewhere behind it, overlain by years of physical and mental suffering, was the Ming Qinlao who'd held his hand in the caverns beneath the Moon when he was just a boy, who'd protected him from the men hunting them in LUNa City. When Ming had been more than his older sister. When she'd been his heroine. His protector.

And now he was determined to repay that debt. To be hers.

"Ruben," she said, "one more thing."

"Yes?" he said, smiling with memories.

"How long will production be down?"

She regarded him with the open face he remembered but with little awareness evident in her eyes. He forced the smile to stay on his face, though it was a falsehood now. That was the thing about sunspots, he realized. They flared quickly, brightly ... but they always burned out.

"We're still assessing," he said. His sceye pinged him a reminder: it was time for her meds. "But we should know something soon."

"That could have gone better," Ming said. Her eyes focused on something across the conference room. Ruben followed them and found half a bottle of Jameson's whiskey, her favorite brand. It was the last bottle left of the case Tony Taulke had sent for her birthday last year. The aftereffect of staying mentally present for the board meeting, hyped on stims, had left her shrunken in her chair. Ming seemed a generation older than she had just a few hours before.

"They can always go better," Ruben replied. He rose to fulfill her unspoken wish.

To say the full board meeting had been rough was like comparing a hurricane to a gusty breeze. But at least the board wasn't in open rebellion. Not yet, anyway. Daniel Xiao had helped them there, sidelining a motion by

Elise Kisaan, Regent of Earth, that would call for a vote of no confidence in Ming. The last thing Qinlao Manufacturing needed after the bombing, Xiao had argued, was more public embarrassment.

Ruben still didn't trust him.

"They think I'm weak," Ming said. "There was a time I would've encouraged that."

Ruben considered adding ice to the glass, a sometimes preference of his sister's. Maybe neat was the way to go today. He brought the glass to her and set it down on the tabletop, a black volcanic agate mined from Olympus Mons, the tallest mountain in the solar system.

Everyone who sat around the table recognized it for what it was: Ming Qinlao's statement of power as Regent of Mars. At least that's what the pitch-black tabletop had once symbolized. Now it seemed just so much compacted, lifeless rock. The cast-off refuse of a dead planet's dead past.

He wanted to say something, to make Ming feel better. But the ping of her private channel saved him the effort.

Tony Taulke was calling. Not answering wasn't an option.

Ruben shared a look with his older sister, whose expression hardened despite her fatigue. With effort, she sat up straighter in her maglev-chair. One never showed anything but strength to Tony. The chime rang again.

She nodded, and Ruben accepted the call. The CEO of the Syndicate Corporation's Five Factions filled the screen.

The first thing you noticed about Tony Taulke was the vertical line of bone framing either side of his skull. Each arched upward sharply, like they were standing guard on either side of his forehead. His skin looked stretched over his brow, flattened to perfection, free of worry lines, which was oddly perverse on a man cresting sixty. Tony's smile, when it appeared, never seemed to reach his eyes. His teeth seemed imported from a cosmetician's catalog.

Taken separately, his features were almost comical. But their combination presented the finely crafted face of a man born to rule others.

Here we go, Ruben thought.

3

TONY TAULKE • SYNCORP HEADQUARTERS, LOW EARTH ORBIT

"Ming," Tony said without preamble. The first-name basis came from earned intimacy. He and the other leaders of SynCorp's Five Factions had spent the past quarter century carving up the solar system together. That bred a certain claim to closeness. "I trust the QM board meeting went well? Danny Xiao has already briefed me on the security situation."

"That was fast," Ming Qinlao replied coolly, a bit of the old bitterness in her voice. Love was not a commodity lost between the Qinlao and Taulke Factions. And especially not between Ming and Tony. "I hope his information was complete and accurate."

The subspace network somehow enhanced the mechanical tone of her vocal amplifier. The vital, whip-smart engineer Tony had watched decades earlier reclaim her company from her aunt, Xi Qinlao, seemed as far away in memory as Mars was from Earth. The broken woman before him hadn't weathered time well, especially over the past year.

"Oh, it was full of disturbing detail," he said, pushing aside his pity. "The kind of explosives used, for instance. The kind the Resistance favors, yes?"

Ming sat up straighter in her maglev-chair, her face betraying inner conflict. Perhaps she was deciding how much of the truth to admit. "That's what we believe. We're still investigating."

Tony nodded and let the distance breathe between them. The subspace network of satellites was a wondrous thing. It allowed instantaneous communication from anywhere in the solar system, though when you got as far away as Titan, there was an annoying, multi-second lag. But Earth to Mars was like talking to someone in the next room. Letting that wonder of technology lay fallow for a few moments ... well, that was just another way to punctuate a sentence.

"We've already got the Marshals Service moving on suspected Resistance cells," Ruben Qinlao offered. The camera displaying the image of the QM boardroom focused its digital shutter on him. "We're making sure footage of the raids is top news on CorpNet."

Though she was out of focus, Tony noted a sharp, annoyed gesture by Ming. She knew as well as he did that the first party to break the silence in a negotiation was the party destined to lose. And every discussion with Tony Taulke was nothing if not a negotiation.

Yes, Ming knew that. She might be faltering, but she'd been dealing with Tony a long time. Ruben was still learning.

Tony raised his chin and addressed the younger Qinlao directly. "A good start. But here's the thing, kid..." The head of the Syndicate Corporation leaned in. His head swelled in the preview image of his own viewscreen. "The factory's already blown up. Those cells should've been exterminated *before* the fact ... not after."

Ruben glanced away from the camera. Tony offered the screen a flinty smile.

"Do you know Tan Huan?" Ming asked. The image zoomed in on her again.

"I know *of* him, of course," Tony said. "Don't think I've ever had the pleasure."

"Ah. Well, like you, he has a penchant for saying what everyone else in the room already knows."

Though he quickly covered it up, Ruben's gasp could be heard all the way to Earth.

"Perhaps I should send Galatz and the corporate fleet to Mars," Tony said, opening his hands in a supportive gesture. "Anything I can do to help speed up the investigation."

Ming's mouth slit sideways, one corner sweeping upward. Tony recognized her attempt at a catbird's seat smile. Like so much else about her these days, it manifested as crooked and sad.

"Isn't Admiral Galatz running down those pirates in the Belt?"

Tony let subspace breathe. "They were the biggest problem I had until those Ghosts bombed your refinery." Calling members of the Resistance *Ghosts* had been Helena Telemachus's idea, a reflection of her wicked sense of humor. The Resistance, she'd argued, were the ghosts gumming up the works of the corporate machine. "Now, *you're* the biggest problem I have."

Ming waved a withered hand. "We don't need the fleet, and we don't need you meddling in Mars business. We'll deal with the threat ourselves, as we've always done. We'll have the refinery back up and running within two standard days, or we'll increase production in the other facilities to fill quota until it is. Agreed?"

He weighed pressing the issue against letting the Qinlao Faction clean up its own mess. Threatening Ming's sovereignty over Mars and, more to the point, her faction's manufacturing charter—even if only in the short term—would send ripples across the entire Syndicate Corporation. Always in tension with one another, always jockeying for advantage, but in the end, each faction was a master of its own domain. The Qinlao Faction had mastered manufacturing. Elise Kisaan was queen of agriculture on Earth. Gregor Erkennen, innovator and technology king, reined over Titan's R&D labs. Adriana Rabh, keeper of the corporate purse, managed SynCorp's finances from the Jovian moon of Callisto. And the Taulkes, from the penthouse of SynCorp HQ more than three hundred kilometers above Earth, controlled distribution of all that, fueling the Company's economic engine by keeping traffic flowing along the system's Frater Lanes. The balance among all five, the tenuous tension of the status quo, was something Tony held sacrosanct above all else.

Disruption—disharmony—could torpedo profits, and that would stir up discontent among the factions. The refinery's being offline was, of course, its own threat to the status quo, but overreaction would only make matters worse. Still, Ming needed to know he was serious, if there were any doubt at all about that. After all these years, there really shouldn't be.

"Agreed," Tony said. "Two days."

"Fair enough," Ruben said quickly. The camera's eye found him again. Then, perhaps still anxious over his sister's nerve: "We'll do better."

In the background, out of focus, Ming's body language grew agitated again.

Never take the kid to a poker game, Tony thought. *You'll get cleaned out.*

"Ming," he said, pausing until she was center image again. "I'll remind you once: there's a one-to-one relationship between production and profit." He spoke deliberately, with steel. "As Regent of Mars—"

"Qinlao Manufacturing is aware of its responsibilities under the Corporate Compact," Ming stated. "We don't need a lecture from you."

Sitting back in his chair, Tony regarded his old partner and adversary. If he were being honest with himself, he was glad to see this side of Ming Qinlao. It reminded him of his own youth and all they'd accomplished together, and despite one another. Her arrogance, her defiance genuinely touched him. And to think he'd tried to have her killed before they'd ever really gotten to know each other.

"I miss you, Ming," he said, displaying his perfect teeth. "I miss your fire."

Her expression was curious. Her eyes narrowed.

"Miss me? What does that mean?"

Ruben sat forward. "It's been a long night, Mr. Taulke. Is there anything else?"

More irritation from Ming in the background. Tony knew what Ruben was doing. It had taken him a while to notice Ruben's interventions after first observing Ming's recent decline. But now the SynCorp CEO easily recognized them for what they were. Despite how it no doubt appeared to Ming, Ruben's attempts at protecting her were admirable in their loyalty. But the Company couldn't afford an invalid in charge of Sol's manufacturing mecca. Ming's obvious decline was something Tony would have to keep tabs on.

"I'm glad you asked," Tony said, addressing Ruben directly. "Helena will arrive in Lander's Reach in two standard days. Just in time to celebrate meeting your repair deadline, in fact. I want her personally directing the public narrative on this, and I want her on Mars to do it. You'll provide her every courtesy and cooperation." He stretched his arms wide along the edge of his English oak desk. It was a favorite gesture meant to seem inclusive and expansive at the same time. Tony knew exactly how wide the camera lens captured him. "I'm depending on you, Ruben."

To his credit, Ruben held fast Tony's gaze. Not many risked doing that, not even among the faction leaders. "Of course, Mr. Taulke. Every courtesy and cooperation."

Tony ended the call with as little ceremony as he'd begun it.

"Where does she get off talking to you like that, Pop?"

Regarding his son, Tony pursed his lips. The boy had an entitlement problem. Part of that was being a teenager and, like all teenagers, a heretic against the Galilean notion that the universe did not, in fact, revolve around him. Part of it came from being the oldest and only son of the most powerful man in the solar system. Tony sometimes wondered what his heir might have been like if Junior's older brother hadn't died in utero.

"She's a faction leader, just like me," Tony said. "In one sense, my equal."

"Yeah, but you're—"

"Shut up and listen, son."

Tony the younger, called Junior behind his back, clamped his mouth shut. Had anyone else addressed him so, he likely would have leapt up and punched the person in the face. Junior's having grown up in the lap of luxury had imbued him with an impulse-control problem. It had also spoiled him. Not just materially but morally. Being a good leader required a broader view, a flexibility in one's perspective. One day, Tony knew, his son would be sitting in his chair, leading the solar system. It was his obligation to educate the boy.

"She's leader of the Qinlao Faction, like I'm leader of the Taulke Faction. Like Gregor Erkennen leads his family's faction. Like Elise Kisaan leads hers. And Adriana leads the Rabh Faction."

"God, what an ancient bitch," Junior said. "Won't she ever die?"

Tony released a silent breath through his nose. "Interrupt again and see what happens."

Junior's expression went stiff for a moment, and Tony thought he might actually have to make good on the threat. Then the fire burned back to embers in his son's eyes.

"As faction leaders," Tony continued, "each of us is exactly equal to the others under the Corporate Compact. But when we implemented business rules to make sure the arms of this giant octopus we created together actually work together, we knew there could be only one leader. You can't sail a ship across the ocean with five captains at the helm. I put the Taulke at the top, and the other factions agreed because each got its own piece of the pie. The syndicate is a balancing act, son, a high-wire walk with crosswinds blowing in every direction. When the wind whips up, like with this sabotage business, a steady course becomes even more important. Too big a hiccup and the whole body shakes. Understand?"

"Yes, sir."

Tony doubted Junior really understood the life lessons he was trying to teach him, or that he cared much about them if he did. If only his first son hadn't died before being born.

"Pop, you've told me all this before. I get it. But I've seen you go off plenty of times. Like what just happened with Ming. You were gonna send the fleet to Mars. You said so."

"No, I did not."

"I heard you!"

"You heard your interpretation of what I said. What you wanted to hear —which is another problem for another day, by the way—but not what I actually said."

Junior seemed confused.

Was I this dense when I was his age? Tony wondered.

"I *threatened* to send the fleet," he said. "I suggested it *might* be necessary."

"What's the difference?"

"The difference is the gray between the black and white, son. That's what you need to learn if you're ever going to run things."

His son's face pinched. A juvenile's reaction to being frustrated and out of his depth.

Tony threw him a line.

"I told Ming, without saying it, that if she didn't get her house in order, I'd get it in order for her. Could I send the fleet? Sure. Could I even replace Ming Qinlao or overthrow the whole Qinlao Faction? Sure. But either one of those things, especially the second one, would throw the whole Company out of balance. Others might even try to exploit the chaos and take out the Taulke Faction altogether."

"Like Ra'uf Erkennen did a few years ago," Tony Junior said.

"Right. Like Ra'uf Erkennen did a few years ago."

"But you made a deal with his brother Gregor—"

"And Ra'uf went bye-bye. And now Gregor leads the Erkennen Faction. And the Company survived. Thrived, in fact."

"And so did we," Junior said.

"And so did we."

"I think I get it, Pop."

Tony smiled. "Good," he said, "now hit the road. I've got other business to attend to."

Junior made no attempt to rise. "I can't stay and learn? Someday—"

"Not this time," Tony said. "And don't be in such a hurry to take over. You'll make your old man paranoid."

Returning a nervous version of his father's smile, Tony Junior rose from the chair. "Aw, Pop, you know me better than that."

Do I?

Tony knew part of his paranoia stemmed from his own method of taking power. He hoped committing patricide didn't run in the family.

After Junior left the room, Tony counted to ten to clear his mind, then pinged his receptionist.

"Kesh?"

"Yes, Mr. Taulke?"

"Send in Fischer."

4

STACKS FISCHER • SYNCORP HEADQUARTERS, LOW EARTH ORBIT

I walked into Tony Taulke's office, my eyes lingering on the new receptionist in the anteroom. She was a looker. And she knew it, too.

The door slid into the wall, cutting off heaven.

"How's life in the killing business?" Tony asked.

"Tolerable," I said.

That's our way of saying hello, a kind of password of greeting between the head of the Syndicate Corporation and his top enforcer.

"What happened to Mai?" I asked, tossing a look to the sealed door behind me. X-ray eyes, where are you when I need you? "Not that I'm feeling particularly nostalgic."

"I'm sending her with Helena. Special media tour to Mars. Kesh is her temporary replacement."

"Kesh?"

"Marakesh."

I thought about the exotic name. And what else about her might be exotic. "I think I'll call her Mary. Safer that way."

"For you, maybe."

"Right."

Tony Two-point-oh and I went way back. No one ever calls him that to his face because it reminded him there'd been a Tony One-point-oh—his father, Anthony. Tony ascended the throne the old-fashioned way, by killing Papa Bear and taking control of Taulke Industries and the entire corporate conglomerate most people nowadays just call SynCorp. Sometimes I feel like the only person in the solar system Tony can relax with, but even I don't call him Tony Two-point-oh to his face. I've pulled Tony's ass out of more scrapes than I can count if I used my hands *and* my feet. That makes me the closest thing Tony has to a friend.

Then again, nobody's friends with Tony Taulke. I'm more like a comrade in arms. He's SynCorp's top dog in a pack of dogs, the one the other dogs let eat first from a fresh kill. I'm his right hand for getting the seedier side of business done. I'm a problem solver. I'm the guy you call when you want it done quick, quiet, and without a mess for the press. Unless, of course, you want the mess front and center for the press. Then I'm still the guy you call. Every faction has its top fixer. I'm Tony's.

"Heard about Mars?" Tony asked.

"Who hasn't? *The Real Story*'s full of feeder content. Lots of video of pulling bodies out, that kind of thing."

The Real Story ... 'round-the-clock, real-time streaming vids of whatever infantile, in-flagrante clickbait happens to get captured in high def. The offerings can sometimes be schizophrenic, five- or ten-second snatches separated by flash ads of corporate propaganda. An algorithm determines the seediest thing the public wants to see based on past, popular clicks, then pops it to the top of the queue: a famous entertainer's uncensored sex vid, a murder in progress on a backwater moon. Sometimes SynCorp even seeds content to shape whatever story it wants out there. Tony tolerates *The Real Story*, figuring it feeds the public's darker angels and keeps them from thinking too much about more important things. Critical thinking is the death of empires.

Mentioning the program brought a dark cloud over Tony's features. When he gets that look, it's like the humanness has left him, and all that's left is the cold, calculating CEO. Soulless Tony. Patricidal Tony.

"Resistance?" I ventured.

"Seems like."

"And Helena is off to manage the message? With Mai as backup?"

"More or less. Mai's my eyes and ears on the ground," Tony said.

"Isn't that Helena?"

"Mai's my eyes and ears on Helena."

That was a surprise. Helena's been Tony's mouthpiece for decades. The Queen of All Media. And one hundred percent loyal. Or so I'd thought.

"Don't tell me Helena's looking for greener pastures."

Tony shrugged. "I've got no reason to suspect Helena," he said, raising a hand. "But I'm in a careful mood. Mars is only the latest problem on my plate. Things are starting to pile up, Eugene. Coincidences are starting to seem too coincidental."

Whenever Tony uses my given name, I know he's getting serious. It means he wants my attention. And he doesn't like repeating himself.

"Such as?" I prompted.

"Such as the pirate problem between Jupiter and the Belt."

That one was new. "I hadn't heard."

"Officially, only the five faction leaders know about the problem."

"Pirates, though. Sounds like something for the fleet."

"It does, doesn't it?" Tony leaned forward, doing that arm-stretch-across-the-desk thing he does. "Blowing them out of space, yes. Finding who set them loose in the first place? Admiral Galatz isn't that subtle."

"An infiltration op, then. What about the marshals?"

"Too corrupt. Too tied into the public domain. If I needed a headline on CorpNet about shutting down a run-of-the-mill black marketeer, I'd call them. Having them run to ground whoever's feeding shipping schedules to the pirates—well, that's as likely to net them a payoff from the prey as help me catch them."

Understandable. The marshals—formally an arm of the United Nations when LUNa City was the only off-world colony Earth had—were the tin-star-wearing keepers of law and order most citizen-workers looked to for protection. Fact is, the marshals are bought and paid for by the Company like everything else in the system. They enforce SynCorp law but only when SynCorp wants them to. Like the corporate navy, they wear a uniform and perform a function. But they're Kama Sutra'd with local bosses, who pay them off to look the other way. Some even employ marshals after hours as local muscle. The Service would do what SynCorp told them to, but there was no guaranteeing they'd keep quiet about it.

I thought that through. Sounded like Tony wanted me to deal with the pirates in a way the marshals and the fleet couldn't. That meant surgical work. As in cutting out a cancer.

My specialty.

"You think this is more than a space-based black market? A faction making a move?"

Again Tony shrugged.

After Ra'uf Erkennen's ballsy move five years earlier, I had to ask. The elder Erkennen brother had innovated Molecularly Enhanced Synthetic Hemp, or MESH, which acted like a shield against stunner tech when woven into clothing. Without it, a stunner lives up to its name in spades: your own EM field, enhanced and focused by the weapon, fries your nervous system. Shocking, I know! Ra'uf hoped to topple Tony and set the Erkennen Faction atop the SynCorp totem pole. I stopped him—permanently. Things had been relatively quiet since then.

We were due for another coup.

"Someone's siphoning helium-three and deuterium from the tankers coming out of the Jovian system," Tony said. "I want you to go out to Callisto and sniff around. Find out who's behind it. Find out why."

"Okay," I said. A colony barely ten years old, Callisto was the coordination point for what the Company took off Jupiter. The tankers moved from there into the Frater Lanes headed for the switch rings orbiting the Moon, their cargo offloaded or redirected from there. "The Belt is full of asteroidal hidey-holes," I said. "That's where I'd work from too."

"The working theory: the pirates match course and speed, hook up to the tankers, and drain off amounts so small, they seem like margin-of-error losses," Tony explained. "Do that a hundred times and you've got a lot of fusion fuel."

"That seems labor intensive, not to mention inefficient. How'd you ever figure it out?"

"My margin of error is zero."

His voice was crypt-like. The Taulke Faction does more for SynCorp than just give the orders. They run the distribution network. Nothing moves in the solar system that isn't tagged and tracked by them. On the books, there probably was a legit margin of error—allowable loss from whatever cause, mechanical or human slipup. But Tony Taulke keeps closer watch on the numbers than he leads others to believe.

"Think the pirates and the refinery explosion on Mars are linked?" I asked.

"Coincidental, maybe," Tony said. "*Maybe*. But like I said—I'm in a careful mood."

"Am I catching or killing?"

Tony considered my question. If I caught a big enough fish, he'd want the flapper brought back and gasping for air. Public trial, lesson for the masses, that kind of thing. But if things were getting hinky across the system, keeping things quiet on the home front might be smarter. Take care of business, make sure only those who needed to see the endgame saw it. I like to get my orders straight before executing them.

Pun intended.

"Use your discretion, Eugene," he said finally. "There's a ship leaving for Callisto in the morning, the *Cassini's Promise*. Settlers, migrant workers, supplies. Be on it."

I prefer the Hearse, my own personal ship. That's not an official designation, of course—she doesn't have one. The Hearse is off-network, unregistered, which comes in handy in my line of work. I like the closeness I feel wrapped inside the Hearse's cocoon, the isolation on the front end of a job. Sitting alone, inside my own head. Even on six-day hard burns like getting to Callisto required. Without the Hearse, I'd be entirely reliant on the Company to be mobile.

"I'll have the Hearse shipped separately," Tony said, guessing my thoughts. To my raised eyebrows, he said, "I want you integrating with the people heading out there. Lose the MESH coat and fedora. You're an over-the-hill migrant worker spooked by the explosion on Mars. I want you thinking like they think. You might even scare up a lead or two on the trip."

Doubtful, but possible. I hated losing my longcoat and hat. An enforcer without MESH is like a soldier without armor—damn-near defenseless. But Tony's the boss. I'd keep 'em packed away and close at hand, just in case.

"Understood. I'll leave the keys to the Hearse with K—Mary."

He nodded. "Good hunting, Stacks."

"Good luck with Mars," I replied. The door disappeared into the wall, and Miss Exotic turned her smile my way from the front desk. It felt like sunshine.

At least I was getting a warm send-off.

Exotic Mary booked passage on the *Promise* for me before I reluctantly left her presence. The ship wasn't scheduled to depart for twelve hours, so I headed to Mickey Stotes's place. The Slate's located on the main docking ring of SynCorp Headquarters and the first stop for anyone wanting a quick drink soaked in atmosphere. It's done up like an Old West saloon, which makes it stand out among the higher-tech, slick shops around the ring.

Marketing! Mickey's smart like that.

I passed through the squeaky half doors (marketing!) and into a slurring murmur, the common language of regular drinkers. Uniformed Taulke employees at one table, a couple of corporate fleet stripers at another, three blue-coveralled worker-citizens at a third. Each sitting with their own kind. Mickey caught my eye and nodded me over to the bar. I mounted the stool that fit my butt best.

"Same ole?" he asked like always. I seem to have salutation ruts with people—I realize this.

"Just don't make it shit." Same ole answer.

He drew a lager from the tap, tilting the mug to cut the head off. Then he poured me a shot of scotch.

"Heading out?" Mickey asked.

I shot the scotch and stared hard at him. "Why do you ask?"

Who's been talking?

"You have the look," he said with a soft leer.

"Maybe I'm just getting in."

"No, that's a different look."

"Ah."

I was probably just being paranoid about Mickey. He knows my ins and outs, I guess. In my business, paranoid's not a bad thing to be. Maybe Tony's allergy to coincidences was catching.

The lager tasted good. Everything's better chasing scotch.

In the corner I noticed a kid, maybe twenty-two, sitting alone. He stuck out among the tribes I'd seen when I came in. He sat up arrow straight, like his momma had just corrected his posture, looking at nothing. He had a rictus smile on his face like someone had pinned his lips back.

"What's up with the kid?"

Mickey turned around to look.

"Hackhead," he groused. "It's the latest thing." That was a new one on me. I guess Mickey knew my ignorant look too, cuz he started to explain. "Those new troubleshooters? The ones that are supposed to keep you young forever?"

"Yeah?"

"Latest thing—timed algorithms. They're selling like crazy. Dealer can tailor it to the DNA signature of the medical implant. No two algorithms are alike. Sends the user off to La-La Land. Better than sex. Better than gorging on chocolate ice cream. Better than gorging on sex in chocolate ice cream."

"Huh," I said, my vocabularic acumen on full display. "How does the dealer ever have a repeat customer?"

"Did you hear the part about the algorithm being *timed*? The effect lasts as long as the addict can pay for. Then it locks up again. Their implant goes back to its day job of keeping them cancer free and such. Want it unlocked? Pay again to play."

"Huh. A subscription to ecstasy."

"Something like that," Mickey said, giving the stoned kid the eye. "I think I'll name my autobiography that. Mind?"

"Give me ten percent off the top, and it's all yours."

Troubleshooters—a common name for the SynCorp implant. I don't understand the SCI down to the studs, but it's basically a DNA-tailored medical implant that keeps tabs on a person's health. Cholesterol, cardiac function, genetic markers for a hundred-and-one physical and mental degradations—all at the genome level. It's like a built-in mechanic and extended warranty all in one for the human body. If the troubleshooter spots a problem—narrowing arteries, say—it actively works from the *inside* to fix it before there's a *real* problem, like a heart attack. The SCI is SynCorp's way of ensuring a healthy and efficient workforce.

Some people even call it a Fountain of Youth. If you can repair cells, why not regrow hair? Recover the pigment from age spots. Smooth out skin like you've lived all your life in low-g. But none of those wishes-come-true had proven out, at least not yet. The tech was still new.

I'd refused to have the implant installed because it's also trackable, the Company's second reason for requiring its citizen-workers to have it. Since I'm Tony's main man, I can get away with saying no. Someone gets access to my signal, it can be a bad day in Black Rock for Stacks Fischer—and Tony Taulke.

And here someone had gone and figured out how to hack it already. Humans are nothing if not innovative opportunists.

"Hackhead, huh?" I said.

"Yeah." Mickey's face twisted like he'd just stepped in something. "The hacks are undercutting the old standards."

"Less money for booze, eh? Gambling? Ladies of the night?"

"Yeah, those standards," Mickey said.

Fair enough. Booze, gambling, and prostitution were all legal diversions under SynCorp law. The Company even encouraged them, as long as they didn't undercut productivity. Hell, some vices even made citizens better workers. Regulated them, controlled them through their appetites. Drugs, though—the return rate on those was low, so penalties for druggies were stiff. For suppliers, stiffer—as in morgue stiff. This smelled like something new. While technically not illegal, hacking the troubleshooters sure walked and quacked like a drug duck.

"It's getting so a man can't make an honest living around here," Mickey said.

"Maybe not an honest one," I said, watching the twentysomething experiencing the best sex or chocolate ice cream or sex in chocolate ice cream he'd ever had. "But someone's making a killing of a living, all right."

5

EDITH BIRCH • VALHALLA STATION, CALLISTO

Market Day was always a treat for Edith Birch. Once a month, when the new ships dropped fresh cargo, she set out on a treasure hunt to find the juiciest fruit, the most vibrant vegetable. Fresh meat was a luxury most citizen-workers couldn't afford, relying on the much cheaper dehydrated bags of amalgam proteins easily reconstituted by adding water from Callisto's vast underground reservoirs.

Besides the chance to buy spices for cooking, it gave her a chance to interact with other people in a way her husband Luther would allow. She glanced backward to find him talking with Sam Madden about something or other. The expression on his face seemed half amused and half irritated.

Probably grousing about the seven-day work schedule this week, she thought.

Luther's prediction had come true, and Sprague's mining crew was being forced to work the scoops tomorrow on what would have been their day off, just to make quota. If they missed that, SynCorp might reassign their crew to lighter duty, which meant pulling in less of a percentage for the gases mined from Jupiter's atmosphere. And nothing put Luther in a foul mood faster than taking SynCorp dollars away from him.

Her basket in hand, Edith pushed aside worries she couldn't control and returned to the bustling marketplace. She paused in her meandering among the bazaar's vendor stands to appreciate the bubbling of life around her. Its sounds filled her ears. The happy haggling over this or that, handshake bartering of labor for food, a young girl's first attempt at catching a young boy's attention. Wafting across the market, the scents of luxury meats tempted Callistans to spend more than they should to sample a taste of the Old World. Exotic fragrances made the antiseptic scent of recycled air barely noticeable.

Market Day brought Valhalla Station's residents together. Vendors lined one side of the thin corridor called Erikson Street. Station residents walked among them, sampling and talking. No one hurried. Today was a day to be savored, to be enjoyed through negotiation or the sudden discovery of a treasure from Earth or Mars among the wares.

Overhead, the clear plastisteel of the Community Dome shone with a faint, yellow glow. Jupiter hung in the station's sky ever present and watchful, like a mother planet guarding her rocky child. The glow came from Jupiter's natural golden hues and the solar mirrors in orbit above Valhalla Station, reflecting light and heat down to Callisto's surface.

The colony's name was a clarion call to the adventurous who didn't mind leaving behind the more pampered life of the inner planets to carve a new one out for themselves beyond the Asteroid Belt separating Mars and Jupiter. But it was also a disclaimer, a notice to the more casual colonist: only the courageous of spirit need apply. This was the new frontier, where deals were sealed with a handshake and a promise of fulfillment, one party to another. Residents of Valhalla Station said what they'd do and did what they said. Those who failed to live up to that simple and sometimes inconvenient standard didn't stay long.

A passing Callistan bumped her arm.

"Apologies, ma'am," the young girl said, distracted. She moved away quickly, and Edith couldn't help but smile at the back of the young boy following and not quite catching up. It stirred a vague memory in her of a similar pursuit not six years earlier. The memory stirred only sadness now, and a thick kind of depression that sat heavily behind her breastbone.

So much of her life here, though, felt comfortable, familiar. The plain clothing, the cordial manners, the enthusiastic, easy conversations all reminded Edith of the small Southern community she'd grown up in. The

United States had been spared much of the catastrophe of the previous generation's Weather War, especially the states insulated by coastal states. Her father was a local pastor in Medina, Mississippi, and Ephraim and Enid Mason's church had served as an overground railroad for climate-crisis refugees.

Some of Edith's earliest memories were of playing with other children, the names of which she'd barely have time to learn.

Then the Company had taken over, and the planet had seemed to breathe a collective sigh of relief—like humanity's burden of being responsible for itself had finally been lifted from Atlas's shoulders. The Syndicate Corporation took care of everyone, offered everyone a chance to make a life. And she'd taken hers on Callisto.

Edith hadn't realized she was still watching the young couple until the young man turned and, baiting his prey, began moving back toward the heart of the bazaar. The girl, flustered, debated her own pride for a heartbeat or two, then became the pursuer.

And so Edith's life had gone. When the call had gone out for miners to populate the moons of the outer planets, Luther Birch had been one such willing soul. He'd charmed Ephraim Mason with his deference to her father's calling and God, and he'd charmed Edith with near-constant attention and kindness. The thought of leaving Earth, of following such a good-looking, attentive man not just into marriage but to the stars, had bloomed in Edith like a flame kindling dry wood. Her father, with tears in his eyes, had married them. Their honeymoon was a whirlwind, condensed by the departure demands for third-tier colonists. Luther's skills had earned them a berth to Callisto.

Six years and a lifetime ago. It was only after they'd been married a while and settled on Callisto that things had changed so drastically. Luther's abiding attention became a kind of grudging surveillance. His kindness before—so solicitous and full of wonder at how lucky he was to have her in his life—was spoken now as harsh compliments spiked with sarcasm. Thinking back, Edith had no idea how or when it had all changed, the transition had been so subtle, so unnoticed. What moment had that been when she'd gone from being a young wife, happy and on life's adventure, to the most prized possession Luther Birch owned?

"Hi, Edith," said a familiar voice, pulling her out of her mixed-emotion stew. "Guess what I've got?"

She turned her eyes on a market stand done up in an Indian style, festooned with brightly colored fabrics hanging loose in the station's breeze of manufactured atmosphere. The fabrics were for sale, of course, as was everything else, but their real purpose was to brand the booth as Reyansh Patel's, the man of a thousand recipes. His booth was always a must-stop on Market Day.

His eyes begged her to make at least one guess. Engaging with your neighbors was half the fun of Market Day.

"Curry," Edith said, playing along.

His smile dipped. "*So* culturalist. Come on, you can do better than that!"

She darted her eyes at the bins, but he was too smart to have it sitting out. Knowing Reyansh, he'd set the prize aside knowing she'd be stopping by his booth.

"Mint? Basil?"

Patel rolled his eyes. "Now you're just being uncreative."

With mock frustration, she stamped a foot. "Just tell me!"

His smile returned. "Cumin," he said. "And ginger!"

The smile was catching. "Oh, that's wonderful," Edith said, moving her basket around in anticipation. "How much?"

Looking from right to left as if passing a secret to a spy, Patel said, "For you? Free."

Edith blinked, her expression curious. "Free? Oh, Reyansh, I can't—"

He held up both hands. "No, no, I insist. You are one of my best customers. Every Market Day for four years"—he counted them off on his fingers—"you come here and purchase items from me. This is my gift to you."

Not knowing what to say, Edith smiled nervously as he reached behind him and produced two small, brown bags. They were tied with string, like always, Patel's personal touch.

"What's for free, now?"

Luther's hand found the small of Edith's back. She tensed, an involuntary reaction.

"Reyansh has fresh cumin and ginger," Edith said, the words racing each other to leave her mouth. "We can make your favorite chili tonight, work on it together if you like, before you have to go back out tomorrow."

Luther's hand trailed by the index finger up her spine until his palm rested at the back of her neck. It slipped with the ease of practice around her shoulder.

"Why, that sounds fine!" Luther said. His voice seemed to clamp them all together in goodwill. His right hand squeezed Edith's shoulder. "We haven't had chili in, hell, I can't remember when."

Patel lifted the bags in his hand, preparing to put them in Edith's basket.

Luther's hand intervened. "But what's this about free?"

"Oh, Luther," Edith said, "it's just that—"

"I was asking Reyansh." Laughter and good-natured bartering up and down the bazaar crested, forcing Luther to speak up.

The Indian vendor's smile was back but flatter, like a flower that's been pressed into a book.

"I was just telling your lovely wife that she's such a good customer that I wanted to reward her loyalty," Patel said. "I know how much you like your chili, Mr. Birch."

"Do you?"

Edith's insides seemed to settle within her. As if her body were securing her organs like furniture before a storm.

"Yes, she's always asking after spices for the meals she cooks for you. Black pepper for breakfast eggs, mint for your bourbon coffee in the evenings. All sorts of things."

He probably thinks he's helping, Edith thought, her insides tied down and taut. *Please, Reyansh, stop helping.*

"You know quite a lot about our eating habits and what my 'lovely wife' likes to cook for me," Luther said. His face was friendly, unlike the undertow of his voice. "But I guess that's to be expected, given your business here."

Another squeeze of Edith's shoulder.

"Yes, exactly so," Patel said.

"But I can't take your stock for free," Luther continued, trying to sound magnanimous. "Nothing's free on the frontier ... isn't that right, Edith?"

She nodded, forcing herself to avoid eye contact with Patel.

"Yes, there's always a price for something," Luther said. His inflection made it suggestive. "Even if it's bartered in trade."

Patel stood still, staring Luther in the eye but saying nothing. He seemed to be debating the idea of giving ground or standing tall on it. The tiny, brown bags of spices hung in the air between them.

"How much?" Luther asked.

"I'm sorry?"

"How much for the cumin and ginger?"

"Oh, well..." Patel's eyes shifted, doing some calculations. "They were small amounts, tokens only really. Two dollars for both?"

"That sounds like a steal," Luther said, looking down at Edith. "Doesn't it, honey?"

"Yes," she said mechanically. "Thank you, Rey—Mr. Patel."

"We'll take them." Luther offered Patel his wrist syncer to pull the two Company dollars out. Patel scanned it, completed the transaction, and handed him the small bags. Luther dropped them in Edith's basket.

"Enjoy your chili, Mr. Birch," Patel said. Edith heard something in his voice, an attempt at encouraging a better mood in her husband, perhaps. She loved Reyansh for it.

"Oh, I plan to," Luther said as they moved off, his arm guiding Edith away from the booth. "My lovely wife is nothing if not a good cook!"

Walking among the giggling fun of the crowd, Edith's body was hard and inflexible. Her back ached, roped by a spider's web of constricted muscles.

"I have more things to buy," she said as they walked. "For the chili. And a dessert I was going to make."

"Of course. We'll buy them together. It'll be a fun thing to do. A couple's thing to do." His voice turned somber, regretful. "I need to make it up to you, honey."

Make it up to me?

That's the first time she'd ever heard those words come out of Luther's mouth. It couldn't mean anything good. But better to know now, in the crowded marketplace.

"What do you mean, Luther?"

Luther grinned amiably, nodding at the folks passing. He even threw a half salute with his free hand to one of the mining supervisors. "Clearly, you have a preference for dark meat. And all you've got is lily-white me."

Approaching a booth abounding in vegetables grown in the local hydroponic dome, Luther engaged its owner in polite conversation.

A lightness settled over Edith, a feeling of complete lack of feeling. Her insides seemed to float free of gravity. Untethered, insecure.

Not much longer, she told herself. *It won't be much longer, and I'll be free.*

But not before tonight.

6

Li was late.

Ruben could hear his own labored breathing in the vac-suit. It was like
the air was too heavy, and his lungs had to work to pull it in. The nervous
awareness that this was no quick fix, whatever Ming had promised Tony,
was like a solid thing in his throat.

The blast—*blasts*, he reminded himself—had caused cave-ins up and
down the line. Qinlao Manufacturing had drilled tunnels far past the hard-
scrabble dermal layer of Mars—deep into the planet's vitals, where the
richest mineral deposits waited to be mined, crushed, and leached of their
precious metals by QM machinery.

It was the devastation in front of Ruben that made him labor to breathe.
The mangled equipment. The lost lives.

The lost production, a voice whispered in his head. Was it Ming's? Tony's?
My own?

The voice of Medina Li crackled over comms. "Coming up now, Mr.
Qinlao. Apologies for the delay."

"It's all right, Captain," Ruben replied. "Gave me time to—" Take stock?
Feel regret? "—think."

A shadow formed on the other side of the semiopaque, plastisteel
barrier the damage control crew had erected around the refinery's main

entrance. The barrier served as a temporary bulkhead against depressur-
ization until the outer dome sealing the underground facility from the
surface was completely repaired. Some of QM's engineers argued they'd
need to rebuild the dome entirely to ensure structural integrity. Domes
weren't something you built half assed.

But the regent's orders were clear: get the refinery back online ASAP.
And so the patchwork process to make that happen was under way.

The bulkhead hatch opened. Li bounced quickly toward him in the
half-g.

Afraid he's upset his employer, Ruben surmised. He took the gloved hand
Li extended.

"Pleasure to meet you in person, Mr. Qinlao."

"Ruben, please. Let's not waste time here, certainly not on
formalities."

"Yes, sir." Li's voice, crystal clear now without interference from the
surrounding cavern walls, audibly relaxed. "I still think this is a bad idea,
sir."

"I appreciate your opinion, and I respect it," Ruben said. "But I want to
see the damage for myself. Regent's orders."

"This way then, sir."

They passed through the bulkhead's hatch into a small, waiting
antechamber. Locks cycled behind them until the outer seals showed
green. The door on the other side depressurized with a hiss of atmosphere
before sliding aside.

It's an anthill that's been kicked over.

Ruben took his first steps into industrial anarchy. Engineering crews
were moving everywhere, dismantling useless slag that had once been
working mining equipment, bracing load-bearing walls with temporary
columns. The constant activity had elicited the anthill image. But that
wasn't quite right, either. It looked like someone had taken a gigantic collection of enormous tools, dumped them on the ground, and then randomly
scattered them around.

There were no bodies evident.

That was something anyway, he thought, embarrassed at himself.
People had died here, QM employees doing the jobs they were paid to do.

His distaste at the thought of seeing a corpse or two seemed disloyal to their memory somehow.

"All twenty-four extraction stations were hit," Li was explaining. "This was an extremely well-coordinated attack. Made in two phases for maximum damage."

"Are you sure?" Ruben asked. Those details weren't in the official report he'd read. But that wasn't a surprise. Official reports had a way of being leaked to the Undernet. No one put anything into an official report they didn't want seen by the other factions.

Li nodded. It was an odd, almost non-gesture inside the captain's vac-suit. "The first round of explosives targeted strong points. Once those were compromised, the second round hit them again. The mouths of the mining tunnels were a principal target. Millions of SynCorp dollars in damages. It'll take weeks just to clean up. Engineering is still trying to make it safe enough to work in here—the cleanup work, I mean. Restarting the facility? Not even on the radar."

They walked a ways, Ruben fascinated by the ballet of engineers bringing order to anarchy.

"How many people died here, Captain?"

"About a hundred."

About?

"More than half of those were the crew personnel down the shafts," Li said.

Ruben watched as two workers wearing loader exoskeletons each clamped on to the ruined end of a massive machine. A compactor, he thought, what the crews used to crush extracted rock to make it easier to liquefy its precious metals before chemically reconstituting them into their pure form.

"It sounds like the point was to cause maximum casualties," Ruben said.

"That was part of it. Hey! Watch your angle over there! You're about to hit that temporary pylon." Following Li's pointing finger, Ruben saw one of the cleanup crew stop, look, and adjust what he was doing. Or she. In the suits, it was hard to tell. "But the biggest impact, long term, is the hit on productivity. The ripple effect across the Company. It's only one facility, but still..."

"Your report was very specific about the explosives used," Ruben said.

"C-4B, old military grade stuff," Li confirmed. "I'd only ever read about it before this. In the reports on Graves's Rebellion."

"What's that? Machine lubricant?" Ruben pointed at a wide splash of brown streaking the gray of a reinforcing wall. It looked like someone had dipped an enormous brush in Martian red paint and dragged it along the wall. Only, it had dried to a dull rust color, almost indistinguishable from the wall itself.

"It's blood, Mr.—Ruben."

Ruben stared at the wall, his imagination filling in the details of how the blood came to be slung so high. How could one human body contain so much of it? Or had it even been *one* human body... The inside of Ruben's stomach fluttered. He had the sudden epiphany that throwing up in a vac-suit might not be the best idea.

"We've removed the bodies," Li said, "at least the ones we can get to." His tone held a patient sympathy for a civilian's lack of familiarity with violent death. "The rest of the cleanup, well, we have to make the place safe first."

"Right. I understand." But he didn't. Not really. Not any of it. "Everyone that could be evacuated...?"

"At Wallace Med."

"Right."

"You know," Li began, "it wasn't all tragedy. There were heroes too. People who helped before the rescue crews arrived." He sounded like he was trying to make Ruben feel better. Which only made Ruben feel worse.

"That's good to know. Sometimes the worst in people brings out the best in people. I guess."

"Weeks?" Ming's modulator burbled with disbelief. "We can't wait weeks to get that plant back online."

Ruben sat across from his older sister, absorbing her anger as he usually did, especially lately. He glanced at the 3D motion image behind her on the bookshelf. Her favorite, the one of her as a young girl with her father, Jie, on a worksite in Japan. She rose in the image, trying to catch a butterfly. Reminding himself of that younger Ming saddened him, but it also gave him strength.

"That's just to make the facility safe again," Ruben said. The truth was the truth. "Bringing it back online will take much longer."

The silence of the room was broken only by the antigrav whir of his sister's maglev-chair. Ming was taking in the facts, thinking through their ramifications. At least, he hoped she was.

"So far we've been able to keep up with the quota," she said. "But that will get harder with time."

Ruben nodded. "We've done that by bringing more crews into the other refineries. More bodies in the mines, more processors on the line. But many of those workers are green, the product of rapid recruitment. Accidents are happening more frequently."

"Incentivize them," Ming said.

He wasn't sure he'd heard her right. Sometimes the vocal enhancer seemed to hinder, not facilitate, understanding.

"I'm sorry?"

"Incentivize the workers. We'll pay higher wages for extra hours." Ming's eyes became animated. It warmed Ruben's heart to see it, until she spoke. "Run a lottery—we'll give the most productive crew a week's paid leave to Vegas-in-the-Clouds. Hell, we'll even stake them. QM can write off the losses next quarter. If any of them have families—"

"Not many do," Ruben interjected. Training loners for crew work was a corporate strategy. Workers came to love their crews as their surrogate family. Productivity benefited when crews felt they weren't just working for the Company, but also for each other. And they looked out for one another.

A safe worker is a long-term investment paying off, every day.

One of Tony Taulke's pearls of wisdom.

"I said *if* they do. We'll set up vacations here for the entire nuclear unit. Up to six people. That allows crews without blood kin to qualify too, increasing competition. Trench diving in Valles Marineris. A week's chaperoned scaling of Olympus Mons. By yourself? No partner to speak of? We'll find one for them in Lander's Reach. You can rent those by the hour, I believe."

The warmth in his heart withered.

"I'm not sure that would help much in the long run," he said.

Ming's eyes focused. Yes, this was the most present she'd been in a long time. Ruben found himself wishing it wasn't the case. And hating himself for wishing that.

"What do you mean?" she demanded. "People always want more luxuries—"

"We've already suspended the safety protocols to get more bodies working more hours," Ruben said. He could hear the edge in his own voice. "Offering more money, more luxuries, for ramping up production—especially with the greener crews—it'll just increase the likelihood of accidents."

"So what?" Ming said. "There are always more workers. I'll contact Elise on Earth—there are always dreamers looking to move off-planet, out of her factory-farms."

The tension between Ruben's shoulder blades became painful, as if his muscles were drawing his scapulae together to meet at his spine.

"As I said," he began deliberately, not trusting himself to maintain calm, "the accidents are adding to the problem. Multiplying those can only—"

"What's *your* solution then, little brother?"

He took a moment to breathe. "We should be up front with the other factions. Adjust our output so they can adjust their need for manufactured goods and distribution quotas. No one can blame us for being victims of the Resistance."

The sound of a croaking frog came from Ming's vocalizer. Ruben recognized it as laughter.

"*Everyone* will blame us. They'll take their cue from Tony, and we know where he stands. We have to clean up our own mess, little brother."

I wish she'd stop calling me that.

"Tony Taulke knows that the power of the Company is in its unity," Ruben said. "He might grouse privately, but publicly, he'll accommodate the situation. He has no choice."

Ming guided her maglev-chair around the desk slowly until she'd settled next to Ruben. "Never believe you know what Tony Taulke is or isn't capable of. Give him an inch of his foot in the door on Mars, he'll take the whole goddamned planet."

That makes no sense, Ruben thought. *Taulke has decades invested in QM. He'd never put that at risk over something like this.* He was about to speak when the chime sounded.

"Yes?"

Ming's ill temper seemed to fuel the speed of her chair as she moved back behind her desk.

"Ma'am, Helena Telemachus has arrived for her appointment."

"Send her in," Ming said. Then, to Ruben: "The spider is here."

Ruben shared a look with his sister. If there was one thing that could end an argument between them, it was Helena Telemachus showing up. Family unity. Faction unity.

"Regent, so good to see you again," Helena said as she entered. She was careful to offer her left hand for Ming to shake, Ruben noticed. "And Ruben, always a pleasure."

"Ms. Telemachus," he replied.

"H, it's been a long time," Ming said. *Not long enough* hung in the air between them.

"Please, I prefer my given name these days," Helena said. "Not that juvenile affectation I used to go by."

"All right, then."

Helena turned. "Let me introduce Mai Pang, my assistant for this little media trip."

Mai smiled at them both. Ming ignored her.

"I suppose Tony wants an update on the situation?" Ming said.

"Yes, let's get right to business." Helena took a seat next to Ruben, who stood and offered his own to Mai. She demurred, standing formally a polite distance from the other three. "Please brief me on the situation. Leave nothing of consequence out."

Ming turned to Ruben, who gave Helena the latest. Confirmation of the C-4B explosives used, the apparent emphasis on causing the greatest death and damage possible, and Medina Li's prognosis of weeks of cleanup before reconstruction could begin. Ming offered her idea for inspiring increased productivity. At first intrigued, Helena asked Ruben's opinion. He gave it honestly under Ming's glare.

"No, I think you're right," Helena said, "and Tony would agree. We've got enough of a narrative to shape as it is. No need to add to it with more accidents on Mars. So, there's no good news? Only inconvenient facts?"

The room was silent. Then Ruben remembered the one positive thing Li had shared with him.

"There were heroes too," he said, "not just victims."

"Heroes?" Mai asked. It was the first time she'd spoken.

"Yes," Ruben said, flashing her an unconscious smile. "Even amid all that confusion, all that death. I guess you never really know what you're made of till tragedy strikes."

After a moment's contemplation, Helena's face lit up. "Did any of these heroes survive?"

Ruben shrugged. "I'm sure some did. I can ask Captain Li—"

"Do that," Helena said, her tone distracted. "I want a list of three or four, if that many are still alive." The way she said the last bit made Ruben wince.

"Okay," he said.

"Regent," Helena said, turning to Ming, "maybe we can't get your refinery back online any faster. But we can distract the public narrative. And crucify the Resistance in the process."

"Oh?" Ming said. "And how do we do that?"

Helena's smile was thin. Her green eyes sparkled.

"Leave that to me."

7

KWAZI JABARI • LILLIAN WALLACE MEDICAL COMPLEX, LOW MARS ORBIT

"Fee-fi-fo-fum, I smell de blood of a Kenyan mon!"

The bass-drum voice boomed in the blackness, reverberating off invisible walls. Rastafarian in accent, English fairy tale in cadence. The rhythm embraced the stride of a giant who enjoyed the game of stalking his prey.

Kwazi stood frozen in the darkness, able to move but terrified of moving. The giant's voice was everywhere.

"Hide in de tunnels, hide in de rocks, I'll strain your blood to make my stock!"

Where is Amy?

He had to find her. That's why he was here. They were trapped down a hole in the underbelly of Mars. He had to find her and cut her golden hair and weave a rope out of it to lift them out.

Whenever he inhaled, red dust clogged Kwazi's lungs. The giant had ceased his incessant pacing, was listening. A cough threatened to give Kwazi away, but he stifled the impulse. How long could he hold his breath before passing out?

Amy!

"Don't you move," Aika Furukawa said, coalescing from nothingness in front of him. She bit at her thumb, looked up at him from beneath arched eyebrows. She was almost coquettish, which fit not at all with her words. "Don't you leave her like Mikel left me."

I don't know where she is. I'm trying to find her.

The giant couldn't hear his thoughts.

Right?

A silver light appeared far across the cavern. The dust blocking his lungs evaporated. Kwazi moved toward the light, careful to step lightly. The sharp edges of the Martian rock sliced the soles of his feet. Each step cut his flesh.

But Amy was in the light. Kwazi knew it.

"I smell you, Kenyan mon," the giant mused in the shadows. His tone smiled. "I smell your bloody feet."

The ground upended, cast itself sideways. Kwazi fell backward, sliding toward the light. The rock cut through the loose, white hospital gown he was wearing, lacerating his backside.

"There you are!" the giant roared.

Kwazi ignored the pain. Amy was in the light.

"Find her," Aika encouraged him. Her whispered voice was somehow as loud as the giant's.

The ground pitched more sharply, gravity pulling him faster.

The light grew brighter, its silvery blaze starting to burn.

The giant's feet *boom! boomed!* in pursuit. Their thudding became the heartbeat pounding in his ears.

"Kwazi!" Aika called.

The giant's hand reached, and he was sliding now too, laughing at the game.

"Kwazi!" Another voice, not Aika's.

He lifted a hand to shield his eyes from the searing silver light.

"Amy?" His voice was feather light.

A stark, white ceiling replaced the dark void of the mining tunnel in his dream. A persistent, metronomic pinging replaced the giant's heavy stride. Kwazi recognized the sound as a device registering his pulse.

He tried to clear his eyes. The leering face of the giant receded. Aika too had vanished.

"Where's Amy?" he asked.

"Amy?"

A woman in white stood over him, framed in the overhead light. Her complexion was olive, her smile open and comforting. Red piping lined her white uniform, and a red medical caduceus adorned her left breast. When she leaned over him, the pleasant scent of rose petals pushed aside the antiseptic hospital air. Her hair, brown streaked with black, reminded him of Amy's, though it looked nothing like Amy's. It wasn't even the right color.

"She's my..." Kwazi began. But no, Amy hadn't become that yet. He was superstitious, unwilling to risk fate punishing him later for such presumption now. "She's my friend. My ... family. A member of my team. We were in the refinery, and a giant walked through..." He realized he was picking at the sheet. A little embarrassed at mentioning the giant from his dream, he asked, "Where am I?"

"Wallace Med," the woman said. "We've been taking care of you. My name's Milani Stuart." She pointed at the name badge opposite the caduceus. Her smile widened. "I'll be your doctor today. Pleased to meet you, Mr. Jabari."

"Kwazi," he replied automatically. He latched on to the conversation to settle himself. "Milani is a pretty name. I've never heard it before."

"My mother's parents came from Italy," she said, turning her attention to the readouts on the monitors. "I was in the crop of kids that got named after places on Earth that don't exist anymore. Remember when it was like every newborn got named after some place like that?" She paused, looking down at him. "Kind of a morbid memorial, when you think about it."

Attempting to sit up in the bed, he found himself too weak to do so. "Uh..." Kwazi swallowed the sick feeling rising from his stomach.

"Slow down. The Med creates gravity the old-fashioned way in this unit, by spin. It takes a little getting used to."

He sat back. "How long have I been here?"

"Three days," Stuart said, sitting down on the bedside. Her hand found his forearm. "Take it easy. Coming out of a coma can be disorienting."

"Three days?" Panic began to rise inside him, replacing the nausea. "Coma?"

She squeezed his arm. "We had to induce a micro-coma to treat your injuries. You had significant head trauma, and the low-g on Mars didn't help. They got you here quick as they could, but to avoid brain damage...” Stuart turned her head to one side. “I’m dragging you into the weeds with me. Sorry about that.”

“No, it’s okay,” Kwazi answered, reaching up to find a bandage around his head. “I don’t remember any of that. The last thing I remember is...” Kwazi levered himself up, ignoring the warning from his gut. “Amy—is she here too?”

Stuart’s expression became solemn. “I don’t know of an Amy that was brought in, I’m afraid.”

“Amanda Topulos. She was a member of Team Sixteen, like me. We were together when the second round of explosions hit. I was sitting with her, holding her hand, and I’d just gotten her into a vac-suit, and she was fine really, no serious injuries, but Aika, she’s another member of our team, Aika told me not to leave her, and I couldn’t even if I’d wanted to, and Beren—”

Kwazi realized he’d been sitting up toward her, running his words together. Her hands on his chest were kind but firm. He looked down to find himself sitting straight up in bed.

“You have to take it easy,” Dr. Stuart said. “I’ll ask around. They’ve had everyone here on deck, literally, since the event. Your Amanda might be in another room or another ward altogether. Every section here was converted for triage and trauma. I’ll see what I can find out.”

“Thank you,” Kwazi said, closing his eyes. He snapped them open again and looked around, trying to engage his sceye. “My CorpNet link isn’t work-ing. Is something wrong—?”

Standing, Stuart shook her head. “We disconnected your implant when we put you into a coma. Once we run some more tests, I can hook you back in. For now, how about that monitor?” She tossed a hand at the wall behind her.

Kwazi forced himself to calm down. Amy was here, somewhere. She had to be. It sounded like everyone from the tunnels was here somewhere. If he was here, she was here.

“Sure, thanks.”

Stuart switched on the monitor. “I’ll be back in a few. I have to check on other patients, and I’ll look for your friend. Okay?”

"Okay." As the door sealed behind her, he said, "Volume: ten."

The Real Story was streaming over a headline that read:

CITIZEN-WORKERS MURDERED BY RESISTANCE ATTACK ON MARTIAN REFINERY

"Volume: twenty."

He'd said it so softly, Kwazi had to repeat it for the command to register.

A corporate spokesman with SynCorp's five-pointed star prominent on his jacket appeared, speaking in cryptic tones of barely contained fury. Behind him, Kwazi recognized what was left of the outer dome that had sealed off the mining-refinery complex of Facility 12. No wonder the air had bled out so quickly. The breach in the dome wasn't the finger hole Kwazi had imagined. The reinforced plastisteel that remained looked like the mouth of a massive see-through jack-o-lantern. Jagged and random, cut without care by someone in a hurry.

It looked like a giant had thrown rocks through it.

Amy. Where are you?

And Aika. Beren. Don't forget them.

Max and Mikel. Try not to remember them.

Not yet.

The camerabot over the spokesman's shoulder turned to his left to focus on a grim-looking woman Kwazi instantly recognized. The sparkle of her emerald eyes, the defiant, upswept tips of her elfin ears—both bodymorph enhancements she'd carried forward from youth into middle age. She'd colored her hair silver, probably to hide the gray. Helena Telemachus, the eloquent mouthpiece of the Syndicate Corporation. She looked like a living avatar who'd just stepped from the fantasy landscape of a hologame for older adults who liked their porn soft.

"That's right, Merrick," she was saying. "This was an unprovoked attack with one purpose only: to take innocent lives."

"But it's caused a disruption for the Company too, right?" the commentator prompted. "I mean, a facility of this size—"

"Honestly, we haven't even given production a second thought," Helena said. Her expression suggested it was gauche of him to bring it up. "Our entire focus has been on rescuing those we can and—" Pause. "—comforting the loved ones of those we were unable to save." She turned to the camera and stared directly at Kwazi. "Our thoughts and prayers go out to their families. To all their loved ones."

The possibility of never seeing Amy again crept into Kwazi's consciousness. It layered damp, cold fear over his skin. His brain stopped thinking. His lungs stopped breathing. He felt a hole forming beneath where his heart beat loudly in his chest.

No, I saved her, he thought, pushing back against the fear. *If I made it, she made it. The others, I don't know, they were down the shaft. Beren said they were blocked by rock. But Amy—*

"Absolutely devastating," Merrick added, facing the camera as he said it. "What could the Ghosts be thinking? How does this help their cause?"

Helena offered a sigh. "How can you ascribe a rational intent to an irrational act? This is precisely why anyone identified as a member of the Resistance is classified as mentally ill by the Company. That's why we do all we can to reeducate them when we catch them. They deserve a life free of brainwashing."

Merrick turned to her, affecting the penetrating look of a hard-nosed reporter. "Helena, as the voice of the people, I have to tell you: it's said the Company kills them outright."

"Resistance propaganda," Helena said, shaking her head sadly. "Bald-faced lies. The Company does all it can to protect our society. *All* of its citizens." To the camera again: "Even the aberrant ones."

"Truly dreadful, this Resistance business. Thank you for your time, Ms. Telemachus." Merrick's eyes found Kwazi's again through the miracle of CorpNet. "We'll keep you updated as this situation develops."

"Monitor: off," Kwazi said. He couldn't look at the facility, with its outer dome ripped apart and gaping like that. He needed to find Amy. And then, together, they'd find Beren and Aika.

The door swept aside. Good. He planned to hold Dr. Stuart in his room by force, if need be, until he found out where Amy was. But it wasn't Stuart who passed through the door. It was a woman with two marshals as escorts. The marshals stood to either side of the door as it closed.

Kwazi stared, thinking absurdly that maybe he hadn't shut off the monitor properly.

"Hello, Mr. Jabari," said the woman, now much taller than she'd appeared just a few moments before. Her green eyes were more penetrating in person. "I'm Helena Telemachus."

Swallowing into an abruptly dry throat, Kwazi couldn't speak. *This can't be good. Whatever else this is, it can't be good.* The mouthpiece of the Syndicate Corporation offered him an understanding if sad smile.

"I'm afraid I have some bad news," she said in the same voice that had earlier promised thoughts and prayers.

8

STACKS FISCHER • EN ROUTE TO CALLISTO

I'd been aboard the *Cassini's Promise* for a couple of days before I decided to make a public appearance. It's six days from Earth to Callisto, and in another day or so, we'd be due to flip and start our decel burn. As good a time as any to mingle.

The *Promise* was an old-style bulk freighter, built just after the Company took over the United Nations a few decades back. Tony's strategy for cementing the hold of the Five Factions over the system had been pretty simple—spread out in all directions. Back then, the factions were often at odds with each other, but they could all agree on one thing: they might control the United Nations, Earth's de facto ruling body, but its member nations were still far too powerful.

So Tony stamped SynCorp's star logo wherever he could while Earth's governments recovered from Cassandra's War, named for the New Earth goddess who'd killed millions using tech intended to reverse climate change. Quick expansion required rapid construction of habitat domes, like on Mars, and converting over the UN-controlled LUNa City on the Moon to Company control. With a little creative spin from Helena Telemachus, Tony had even redubbed LUNa City as Darkside's End. Kind of a creepy name, if you ask me, but Helena insisted it was inspirational.

Okay, then.

Tony called his strategy the Great Expansion. Freighters like the *Promise* were fast-printed and assembled to move people and materiel first to Mars, then to the outer system. SynCorp granted adventurous types land grants along the most promising frontiers—Callisto around Jupiter and Titan around Saturn—full of natural resources for the taking. The ramp-up costs were huge, but once the assembly line of miners and freighters were in place, it'd be revenue ad infinitum for the Company while Earth rebuilt.

The real reason? Expansion and claim staking.

Enthusiasm to leave a broken world, while its governments reshaped themselves to survive under Company control, lasted for nearly a generation. When Elise Kisaan and the agro faction stratified Earth into growing zones that focused on animal or plant production, it limited career options. Staying on Earth became passé—what pussies who didn't have the courage to step off-world did instead of grabbing life by the balls. Moving out into the solar system became the thing manly men and womanly women did.

But the pendulum always swings back, and now, fewer and fewer folks were interested in leaving the creature comforts of the inner system for the frontiers beyond the Asteroid Belt, where a random asteroid strike could kill a colony. Still, a few hearty souls could be found to strike out now and then as miners and their families rotated back to Earth.

I was passing as one of those hearty souls. I'd made sure to dress in the standard dull gray shirt and suspender pants of the stereotypical miner—dressed in flat colors, aiming to mine wealth one cubic meter of gas at a time. I felt like an actor in costume. I'd shaved and everything.

I strolled into a communal cafeteria, angling straight for the black-root bitters the cooks onboard had the gall to call coffee. As for the food, you could eat it, but you wouldn't enjoy it. And there were no bars on the *Promise*, a cruel error in judgment I was still getting used to. Maybe they're preparing you for the frontier, I thought, where everything but the freedom to die in vacuum is in short supply.

"Anyone sitting here?"

A mixed-gender table of émigrés looked up, almost to a person.

"Well, ain't you the one with the nice manners asking?" one of the men said. He had a scar angling like a crescent from the corner of one eye down around his chin.

"I was raised by a nun."

A woman laughed around the bread in her mouth.

"Take a load off," another woman said.

One of the men moved to make space and pushed the bread in my direction. "Help yourself."

"Thanks."

"Callisto or Titan?" a man asked.

"Callisto. Gonna make my fortune mining deuterium."

The woman who'd laughed before laughed again.

"Yeah, us too," Scarman said. "We're all gonna be richer'n Adriana Rabh."

There was general enthusiasm around the table for the idea. The mention of Adriana gave me pause. It hadn't even registered, her being Callisto's regent, when Tony made my assignment. I'd worked for her once, a long time ago—a job I'd just as soon forget. She's a character, Adriana, the richest woman—person, actually—in the history of the solar system. Older than dirt now, and the moneybags behind most of the Erkennen Faction's research that developed cutting-edge tech, like MESH and the troubleshooters. That made sense, when I thought about it. Old people love to think they can cheat death. Nuzzling the low end of old age myself, I'm starting to see wisdom in the fantasy.

"Aren't you a little old for atmosphere mining?" the man who'd made room asked.

I looked him dead-on and smiled. "Haven't you heard? Fifty is the new thirty."

The woman with the sense of humor laughed again. "Maybe we ought to try out that notion."

Most of the table guffawed. Scarman didn't. "Watch yourself, Annie."

"Aw, hell, Allard, lighten up. She's just kiddin'," one of the other women said. Eyeballing Annie, I wasn't so sure. Neither was Allard.

"Name's Jaxson," said the man who'd made room. "And you are?"

"Sawyer," I said.

"Saw my what?" Annie asked. To say her voice was suggestive is to point out that stars twinkle.

"*Annie,*" Allard warned.

But he was looking at me when he said her name. I tried to keep the smartass out of my eyes. I was here for information, not a bar fight. And I'd left my artillery in my cabin. All I had was the spring blade under my right wrist. But if that had to come out, the jig was up. My cover would be blown.

"Haze and me," Jaxson said, nodding to the woman who wasn't Annie. "We're headed for Titan. The methane there makes up whole lakes. We figure the fusion thing is coming on, but there's still plenty of need for combustible fuels back on Earth."

"You're living in the past," Allard grumbled. "Callisto is where a man can make a fortune."

"Or a woman," Annie added, eyes glistening in my direction. Not that I noticed. The banter was starting to make my own eyes heavy. I don't do people well.

Somebody turned up the volume on one of the wallscreens. Set to the YourVoice Network, of course. As the sound came up, Helena Telemachus's voice filled the eatery. She was on Mars being interviewed about the sabotage of the QM extraction refinery. It'd been the only story worth streaming, apparently, since the explosions. I was constantly impressed how "breaking news" was, in fact, the same news I'd heard the previous hour. I mean, that's news with legs, you know? The leading questions from the SynCorp talking head set her up nicely. Turns out, the Resistance was behind the whole thing. Who knew?

Low-hanging fruit is SynCorp's journalistic specialty.

"Out there, you don't get that crap," Allard said, nodding at the wallscreen. "Rebels leave the outers alone."

"Oh yeah?" There was challenge in Haze's voice. Jaxson looked uncomfortable. "What about the pirates?"

Okay, that woke me up.

"Pirates?" I said with all the Boy Scout I could muster. Ignorance was an easy disguise for me.

Allard reared back on his bench. His scar seemed to lengthen and fill in with blood blushing into the crevice. I thought this must be what Annie saw every day: the hubs, impotent and full of hot air. There weren't any visible marks on her to indicate the contrary, though *visible* doesn't mean anything. No wonder she liked to tease him by flirting with anything swinging sausage.

"No pirates running out of Titan," Allard said, like he was reading it from a book. "That's just a bunch of stories."

Huh. I wonder where those stories came from. Tony said only the five faction leaders knew of the problem. Except the pirates knew, too, of course. The Company kept all three levels of CorpNet pretty well trolled and locked down, but sometimes things got out. And what's a sexier story than pirates stealing from the Company? Hell, maybe the Resistance had started the rumors just to destabilize the outer reaches. Why go in person when a rumor will do just as well?

Only, the pirates weren't just a rumor. They'd been siphoning off almost-undetectable levels of fusion fuel from the tankers sailing the Frater Lanes between the outer and inner planets.

"You know what they call the leader?" Haze asked.

"Do tell, honey," Annie said.

Did I mention pirates are sexy?

"The Dutchman."

"Oo, I like that!"

"Annie," Allard said, "there ain't no pirates. Keep your frillies on."

"You're no fun."

"How do you know that?" I asked Haze, ignoring the Bickering Bickersons. I tried to keep the enforcer out of my voice. I was just another rube heading outward to make his fortune. I was supposed to be afraid of the dark.

"You hear things," she said, like that gave me an answer. Jaxson was scooping the mediocre protein up faster out of his plate. Nervous, much? I decided not to press Haze for her source. Maybe later.

"I've heard that name too." A woman who'd been quiet up to now spoke from the other end of the table. She had the kind of voice that was soft in volume but loud in body. She could whisper in a loud room, I thought, and people would stop talking. Her dirty-blonde hair was tied back in a severe bun behind her head. She was young but her face was lined, a strange combination when you first see it. Then you chalk it up to a tough life and never notice it again. She looked like she'd already been to the frontier and back a few times. "And that he operates out of the Belt."

So, there was another half-fact confirmation of what Tony had passed along when he handed me this little assignment. For being ignorant hicks, these claimstakers seemed to know a lot. I'd thought Tony's sending me on the slow boat to Valhalla Station a fruitless venture, a fishing expedition in an empty lake. But as usual, Tony's instincts were pretty good.

"How do you know all this, friend?" I asked. "I ain't seen nothin' on the network about it. First I've heard of pirates outside Robert Louis Stevenson."

"Who?" Annie was interested in a new male name.

"Writer. Pirates. Never mind."

"Oh."

The woman at the end of the table held my gaze a bit longer than makes most people comfortable. "You hear things."

I returned her cool smile. "Well, *you* certainly do." I paused a beat. "And Haze hears things. Me? I'm downright deaf on the topic."

Her smile left her eyes first. I wasn't talking like an over-the-hill émigré looking to make an unlikely fortune. Her lips dipped at the corners, just the slightest bit. I was worried I'd have to blow my cover after all. Fortunately, for her, she kept her hands on top of the table.

Jaxson's fork scraped his metal plate.

Annie looked back and forth along the table, as if watching a tennis match.

Haze cleared her throat. "I heard it was Ceres."

Allard made a noise that said he'd had just about enough of pirate stories.

"That'd be the obvious choice," I said, holding the stranger's gaze. We'd both noticed the other's hands atop the table. She was no ordinary claimstaker either. "Which makes it an unlikely one."

"Why the Belt?" Annie asked, enjoying the tension between me and the woman at the other end of the table.

"The Asteroid Belt separating the inner planets from the outers is the dustbin of the solar system," the stranger said. "Refuse kicked into it from both sides."

"Lots of places to hide in there," I said, like we were co-teaching a course. "Lots of sensor interference."

"That's right," she said.

I wondered if Annie might be developing whiplash.

"You know a lot about the Belt," I said.

"I read a lot," she said.

"Funny you say that." I smiled. "Me too."

She smiled. "Something we have in common, then."

"Seems so. What's your name, friend?"

"Smith. Jane Smith."

Well, there you go. Nothing to worry about. Hail, fellow, and well met!

"Sawyer Finn," I said. "Can I call you Jane?"

"No," she said, doing the internal parsing of my name. "Only my friends call me Jane."

Touché, friend, I thought. I liked her. She reminded me of someone.

"I knew a marshal like you once," I said.

Her eyebrows arched. "Intelligent? Beautiful? Too much for you to handle?"

I winked. "She had more moxie than you'd think her slight build could manage."

"Small in stature only, then," she said.

"Something like that."

She nodded. "Sounds like me, all right."

I thought Annie might slide right off her seat.

But that was enough for today. We had another four days of close-quarters bonding ahead of us. No need to rush right for Jane's nethers on day one. I'd leave that to Annie, if she was so inclined.

"Going so soon, Mr. Finn?" Haze asked. Jaxson seemed to relax as I stood up from the table. Allard, too. Annie looked pouty.

"The pirate thing has me a little spooked," I said in a voice that even I didn't believe. I nodded to Miss Smith. "Plenty of time for conversation before we get to Callisto."

She didn't say anything, but her eyes looked wary. Had they blinked at all since we'd begun our verbal sparring?

I showed her my back and retired to my cabin.

9

EDITH BIRCH • VALHALLA STATION, CALLISTO

Edith focused on the patch of bruised skin around her right eye. The ruptured vessels formed a darkening ring beginning high along the supra-orbital ridge and extending around the maxilla to the zygomatic bone. But she could paint over that. The ache she could cover with pain meds till it subsided on its own. In a couple of days her skin would finish healing itself, be like new again.

The hum of the dermal regenerator sounded like the calming voice of a friend. Allowing for the backward image in the mirror, Edith drew over the darkened area carefully. An aberrant, morbid question came to mind: is this the way morticians make the dead presentable? Did it mean so much to the living to believe they could step into eternity with peaceful, perfect skin? Like it would matter in the cold dark of the grave. The corpse certainly wouldn't care.

Under the heat of the laser tip, the epidermal layer began to soften, to lighten. She knew how to use the regenerator and to use it well. As a tool, its function was to be used. It painted predictably, layering over the bruise like a bad stain, tanning the skin until it regained an approximation of its own healthy color.

He didn't like to be reminded.

Sometimes, as she made light brushstrokes with the laser tip, Edith felt like an artist. With satisfaction she watched the bruise disappear beneath the faux Caucasian hue. Each stroke of the laser was like a maestro conducting a symphony. The regenerator gave her control over the damaged skin. It bent the bruise to her will. Covering it up made Edith feel accomplished.

A snorting noise came from the bedroom behind her, breaking the spell she'd woven in the mirror. She snapped off the laser and pulled up the time on her retinal display. Luther wasn't due to be awake for another fifteen minutes. Plenty of time to finish here and get breakfast cooking. He liked to wake up to the smell of bacon and eggs—said it made him feel like a kid again. But if he woke too soon, his disappointment would set the tone for the rest of the day.

Edith fired up the laser again, pushing aside the artist fantasy in favor of an expert's pragmatism. Speed was her friend now. She widened the head of the beam to cover more skin with each stroke, making wide swaths over her eyelid. The warmth felt comforting, soothing. Only when she got close to the eyeball itself did she slow down again, narrow the beam. It wouldn't do to cut into the sclera. Breakfast would certainly be late then.

Unacceptable.

The snorting came again, but this time the covers shifted. It was something Edith had learned to listen for. Luther turned over onto his side, ensuring another few minutes of sleep. Another glance at the time: twelve minutes left. Just enough time to get breakfast going so that it was half cooked and filling their pod with the wondrous smells of powdered, rehydrated food. How they'd built the scent of frying bacon and scrambling eggs into the powder, Edith had no idea.

She turned her head first left, then right, checking her handiwork. Even close up it was hard to tell. Allowing herself a slim smile of victory, Edith unplugged the regenerator and placed it in a drawer beneath her tampons, where she knew he'd never go looking.

He didn't like to be reminded.

Knowing the secret of the tool's location—something Luther didn't know—made Edith feel powerful. Like there was a tiny island inside herself no one else could find.

In the kitchen, she was careful to lift a smaller pot off the skillet first before pulling the skillet itself from the cabinet. That minimized the noise. Placing it lightly on the small stovetop, she poured a spoonful of cooking oil in the skillet, then swirled it around with two fingers. Edith turned the knob, and heat flared up from the burner.

After wiping her hand dry, she pulled two sealed bags—one containing four slices' worth of bacon powder, the other two portions of egg powder—and inserted the water line into each in turn. The bacon expanded into four slices, fatty isles surrounded by thin rivers of pork. The eggs became four perfectly formed yolks, yellow irises surrounded by white.

Four minutes left.

Perfect timing, she thought.

Controlling the process, hitting her marks on the clock, doing everything just as it should be done. The ritual made Edith feel powerful, too.

She placed the bacon in the skillet. The reassuring sizzle began. It wasn't really necessary to cook the bacon. It came fully cooked out of its powdered state. You could even eat the powder without adding water, if you wanted to. But cooking it in a little oil not only released the heavenly aroma of reconstituted pork, it made Edith feel like a true pioneer.

People still talked of the Pioneers who'd fled Earth for life anew in another star system. No one knew what had become of them, but the myth of who they were and where they went inspired would-be colonists of the Sol System to set aside their fears of leaving Mother Earth for the other planets.

Everyone on Callisto fancied themselves pioneers, she thought as the warming slices popped oil from the skillet. Turning the bacon over, she reduced the heat before it could begin to burn.

Valhalla Station was hardly a decade old, a relatively new settlement learning how to civilize a moon that had been dead for four and a half billion years. The community was like a frontier town in America's Old West. The marshals maintained Company law and order, and the entire community toiled toward the same, individual end—amass a fortune in SynCorp bounties by scooping the precious helium-3 and deuterium from Jupiter's atmosphere and freighting it to the inner planets for sale as fusion reactor fuel. Or trading it in kind for the latest entertainments or exotic whatevers from Earth.

Edith pulled the bacon with tongs from the skillet and placed it aside to drain. Luther liked it greasy, but not too greasy.

Everyone might play the part of pioneer, Edith thought, but so many relied heavily on modern tech for their daily existence. She guessed she did too when she thought about it, glancing guiltily at the powdered food stores. But at least she *cooked* breakfast like a real pioneer. Didn't just irradiate it in the microwave.

Beating the eggs in a bowl, she poured them into the bacon grease. They made a satisfying crackle as the edges began to harden. Edith adjusted the heat upward again. Luther liked his eggs loose, but not too loose.

"Good morning, my love."

She jumped when she heard his voice. But she'd learned to cover, to make a game of it. To make *him* feel powerful.

"Oh lands, Luther!" Edith said, not looking at him. "You about scared me to death!"

A light chuckle came from her husband.

"Sorry, love," Luther said. "Breakfast smells heavenly."

"I'm glad."

Shorter answers were always better answers.

Safer.

Edith felt Luther's shadow before his chest pressed against her back. Focusing on the eggs, she reached to lower the burner. His large, calloused hand encircled hers. Not flinching took willpower, but she had that in abundance. Instead, a tension like steel cables strained between her shoulder blades. Her hand on the skillet's handle seemed part of a statue—stiff—the tendons and knuckles standing out against pale skin. A sculptor of pioneer statues could chime their door, ask so nicely to come in, ask her to stand in that perfect pose over the stove making breakfast before another hot day on the prairie, request to sculpt her as the perfect model of a pioneer wife. Or maybe he'd just pick Edith up and put her over his shoulder, still frozen in her morning cook's pose, the skillet still in her hand. Take her away and put her in a pioneer museum somewhere on permanent display making permanent eggs.

Oh, wouldn't that be lovely?

Luther's left arm encircled her from the other side.

Her body felt shackled, confined like in one of those heavy-duty vac-suits the miners wore outside the ring around Callisto. Only, the hydraulic-assisted limbs of the vac-suit weren't working, and so she couldn't move.

Luther squeezed.

"I'll overdo the eggs," she said.

"No, you won't," he said, bending to kiss her ear.

Was he close enough to hear the blood rushing like a river inside her head? Could he feel through the stretched skin of her back the hammer of her heartbeat?

Edith melted backward, into his chest, spooned back against the rising firmness pressing into her hip. Surrender was sometimes the quickest way to freedom.

"I wish we had more time this morning," Luther said, his tone pornographic. With a final squeeze, he released her. "But the weather's been bad lately. Gotta take advantage of a good day."

"Of course," she said remotely, darting her hand to the burner knob as soon as it was free. Edith resumed working the eggs, distressed at the barest hint of black in them. Perhaps with a little experienced artistry, she could camouflage it. As she had her eye.

The oppressive cloud of Luther's body lifted. He sat down at the small table behind her.

"Sprague might have the Company's sign-off, but sometimes I think he fell straight into a net from his momma's kooch," Luther said. "He don't know how to take a chance, even when it ain't really a chance."

Not knowing what to say, Edith said nothing. She concentrated on yellowing the eggs uniformly. She'd hidden the black as well as she could. Tumbling the skillet's contents onto a plate, careful not to scrape too much off the bottom of the skillet itself, she placed the four pieces of bacon next to it, each piece equidistant from the others like Luther liked, then brought the plate to the table.

Luther sat back as she placed it in front of him. "Now, don't that look like a fine breakfast for a heavy workday? Looks lovely, love."

"Thank you."

"Coffee?"

"Of course."

She returned to the stove and the automated coffeemaker sitting beside it. She'd set it, as always, for 6:30 a.m. *Some pioneer*, she thought to herself. *Can't even make coffee without a chrono.*

"But Sprague..." Luther's voice trailed off in disgust. "He wouldn't cross a street with traffic stopped for miles in all four directions. First sign of bad weather around the Eye, he thinks the whole damned planet is too dangerous to scoop."

Edith brought the coffee in a tin cup, a novelty she'd bought in the gift shop over Earth before they'd shipped out, shortly after they'd been married. She set it approximately three inches to the right of the plate. At two o'clock, a pilot might have said. Luther nodded and picked it up immediately. He blew the steam off the flat, black liquid and swigged the cooled layer.

"Perfect, my love. Just perfect."

"I'm glad," she said. "I guess it's both a blessing and a curse."

"What is?" he asked, spooning rehydrated eggs into his mouth.

"Constantly seeing Jupiter all the time in the sky," she said. "It's beautiful, but—"

Luther's grunt finished the thought for her. Callisto was tidally locked to its mother planet, making Jupiter a permanent fixture in the moon's sky. Watching the planet's Great Red Spot was one way the mining consortium decided whether or not to brave the planet's atmosphere to scoop up the precious deuterium and helium-3.

"Fucking Sprague, afraid of his own shadow," Luther said. Then, "Sit, love."

She sat.

"One day," Edith said, "there won't be a Bill Sprague, and then you'll run the crew."

Luther smiled around the piece of bacon he was chewing. A smattering of grease lined his lips, so the smile glistened.

"Right. In a place like this, a new frontier that's untried, you need a risk-taker. You need someone willing to step outside the safety zone. To show the Company something worth rewarding. As it is, we're barely making quota. Might even have to work a seven-day shift this week."

Edith kept her face neutral, but her hands under the table made fists of hope. If he were on the scoop an extra day, that was an extra day she'd have to herself. Maybe she'd go back to the station's market. See if there were any spices from the recent shipment from Earth left. She could make them an extravagant dinner for the extra workday. Luther would like that.

"How were the eggs?" Edith asked as he forked the last of them. She was feeling bold. Like a risk-taker.

"Perfect," he said around a mouthful. His face lit up again. His smile had less of a shine to it.

"I'm glad."

He picked up the coffee and downed the cup.

"And I'm almost late," Luther said, rising. He stuffed the last piece of bacon into his mouth and wiped his hands.

Almost is okay.

"I thought I might go back to the market today," Edith said. "Get some more spices for this week."

Luther's quick, almost-late movements stopped.

"Well, that's fine," he said, "but I'll go with you. Let's go after shift, if I'm not too tired."

Edith smiled brightly. "Oh, that would be lovely. I was just thinking—"

"After shift," he said again. She wondered if this was how he talked to Sprague. But probably not. Sprague was the boss.

"Okay, then," Edith said. After Market Day, whatever Luther wanted was what Luther should get. It was just easier all around. And required less need for an artist's touch. "We'll go when we can go together."

A smile and a nod from Luther.

A breath, quietly released, from Edith.

He came around the table, and it was clear he wanted her to stand. When she did, he wrapped her in his arms again.

"Thank you for the perfect breakfast," he said, looking down into her eyes. "You're the perfect wife."

She wrapped her arms around him. The morning's ritual was almost complete.

"You say the sweetest things, Luther."

"No time this morning for your reward," he said into her ear, his breath warm. It smelled of her morning labors. "But tonight, my love, I'll make sure you get it."

A moment's hesitation. *Off script*, she admonished herself. *Too long.*

"Can't wait," Edith said, her smile painted on.

10

RUBEN QINLAO • LANDER'S REACH, MARS

His sleep was restless. Ruben lingered in the semi-aware limb paralysis of waking twilight, half aware of being half awake. Half unaware of time's passing. He had the semiconscious thought that maybe this was how the dead slept—sensible of their own endless existence. The thought tickled something combative and coarse in his lizard brain. To be truly nonexistent after death—something he'd always feared—seemed not so bad after all.

Ruben's morbid thoughts dragged him back to consciousness. Truth be told, he should be sleeping like a baby. The sex had been that good. Then again, when you haven't had sex for a while, any sex is good.

No, Ruben thought, *objectively speaking, that was really good sex.*

His fingers traced the short distance over the thin silk sheets to the woman sleeping next to him. She was turned away on her side, and he rested his hand on the warm curve of her right hip. He liked feeling her there, having the usually empty side of his bed filled with another breathing human being.

Lying in the cool, still-drying silk sheets of his bed, Ruben stared up into darkness. A mental image formed of the air processor above him, its constant, mechanical hum the white noise beneath his dreams for as long as he could remember. Ever since Ming had stepped out of the transport that day and renamed Taulke's Mars Station to Lander's Reach for an old comrade in arms. Ruben, who'd been a boy then, had spent most of his life on Mars. Remembering Ming stepping off that ship, looking out over Valles Mariners, and claiming the Red Planet as her own seemed more than a lifetime ago. When he thought of her in those days, his memory had a soft veneer of love and awe over it. It was like a dream from someone else's life, told to him in simple terms of right and wrong and black and white.

Growing up here with her, Ruben had become so comfortable on Mars that whenever he visited Earth now, it seemed like a luscious, luxurious planet. To Ruben, a Martian, Earth was a world overwhelming and overly lavish in its colors, claustrophobic in its population density. Despite the climate catastrophes of a few decades earlier, Earth was still the rich kid of the solar system, her people blissfully ignorant of their own privilege. Humans had abused her bounty for so long and in so many ways that they'd almost signed the bottom line on their own extinction. Then, SynCorp had stepped in. In the last generation, the Company had accomplished miraculous repairs to a world ravaged by the Weather War.

Mars, on the other hand—now here was a planet for the prudent. Mars gave you nothing for free. Anything you ate had to be grown, nurtured, and reaped with human hands. There were no trees to wander by and pick fruit from. No wildlife roaming lush, green forests to stand patiently by till you shot, skinned, and cooked them. No oceans teeming with fish easily fooled by rubber worms.

But Mars was home. He'd visited the outlying colonies on Callisto and Titan. Sampled the loud extravagance of Earth's Vegas-in-the-Clouds. Even climbed the petrified cliffs of California's Redwood District on Earth. Anywhere else was a nice place to visit, but living there? No, thanks. Mars was home, and it made Ruben feel stronger knowing that. An easy existence wasn't something he needed or wanted. Luxury in life was something to be earned. The universe was justice, an equilibrium of give and take that equated to a zero sum.

That was true of the species, too. Humans, he'd learned long ago, were themselves a balance of contrasts. Deceit and honor could reside in the same person. Ming had taught him that. Hardness and softness, emotional brutality and delicate kindness, intellectual curiosity and knee-jerk anger. As much as he liked to think of himself as independent—a true Martian with a need only for the basics of survival—Ruben knew it was both true and false at the same time. Like all humans, he craved companionship. The willing ear of understanding. Someone to surrender to, safely.

He considered slipping his hand under the silk to touch the skin of her hip, then thought that maybe that was an intimacy he hadn't yet earned. Despite the fact that thirty minutes earlier they'd been making love, his body inside hers, their eyes sharing souls. Hesitating to slide his skin beneath the sheet seemed almost a silly exercise in schoolboy embarrassment. But she was sleeping, so the idea of touching her seemed to violate a code he hadn't known existed before this moment. He settled instead for lightly squeezing the rise beneath the sheet.

Mai Pang didn't stir. The even rhythm of her breathing spoke of a deep, untroubled slumber on a sea of exhausted endorphins. It had been their second night together. Ruben, usually shy and reticent when it came to trusting others, had surprised himself at how quickly he'd opened up to her. Even knowing she was Tony Taulke's personal assistant and here on Mars to support Helena, Tony's agent, hadn't stopped that. He wondered if that was Mai's secret superpower—getting unwitting faction heirs to open up to her. The thought unnerved him a little, but his hand continued to cup her hip.

Mai made a noise in her sleep. The un-word stirred something in him. She reached down, a dream gesture, and took his hand in hers, drawing it around her and holding it against her chest, pulling Ruben closer. They'd been able to shed the self-consciousness of that first night, displacing it with a raw, delightful sharing in the discovery of one another. A human male and a human female, with tens of thousands of years of instinct speaking through their fingertips, guided by a knowledge from inside their bones. Sharing, one with the other, a unique experience that was unreproducible with anyone else at any other time under any other circumstance in time and space.

Curled against her back, Ruben felt her heart beating through his hand held against her chest. He felt himself growing hard again, not self-consciously, and knew it was a sensual not sexual response to their togetherness. He smiled, wondering if he could fall asleep feeling the warmth of

Mai's back against his chest and stay here for the rest of the night. Or maybe forever.

His sceye flashed, startling him, making him jerk against her back. Mai groaned, mumble-cursing something unpleasant in a dream. Ruben slowly disengaged from her, pulling away to his side of the bed.

Tony's calling?

Ruben had the sudden, uncomfortable feeling of a father catching him in bed with his daughter. But Tony Taulke wasn't Mai's father. As far as Ruben knew...

He lifted the sheet and pulled on a pair of shorts. The red light on the lens of his eye flashed again. Even Tony's sceye notifications seemed irritated. Carefully but quickly, Ruben slipped from the bed and pulled the pagoda doors together behind him with a *snick*.

"Mr. Taulke," he said, engaging the call. "What a pleasant surprise."

Tony's angular temple and iron jawline tilted slightly. He hadn't been trying to sleep. Of course he hadn't. It should be the middle of the afternoon over Earth.

"Ruben," Tony said, seemingly amused. "Don't blow smoke up my ass. It's not my thing."

"Okay."

"My apologies for the lateness of the call. Or earliness, depending on how you look at it."

"It's all right," Ruben said by reflex. But—Tony Taulke apologizing? That was just plain disconcerting.

"I'll keep this short. You'll need your sleep after we finish talking."

Yeah, well—

"I'm going to call her once I've finished talking to you. And here's the point of it: I want you to take over as chief executive officer of Qinlao Manufacturing."

Ruben's focus blurred for a moment. He thought he might still be half asleep, his mind playing twilight tricks on him.

"I'm sorry?" he said. Tony's suggestion felt divorced from a reality Ruben could anchor to. The ruler of the solar system gave him a moment to adjust. "You want me to ... but Ming is ... she's been regent—"

"As long as her health holds out, Ming will continue to represent the

Company and your faction at public events," Tony said. "But you'll be making operational decisions on Mars. And for the Qinlao Faction."

"A figurehead," Ruben said, his voice edged with contempt. "You're turning her into a figurehead?"

"I'm allowing her an honorable exit."

The words sounded to Ruben like the most truthful ones he'd ever heard Tony Taulke utter. And that made them all the more foreign. Tony Taulke helping Ming Qinlao save face?

"Why?" he found himself asking.

Tony appeared thoughtful. It was a strange look on him. Ruben thought it made him look weak.

"Ming and I have had our differences over the years," Tony began, choosing his words carefully. "But she has been a good steward for the Company. I have no reason to publicly embarrass her."

"But privately?" The bitterness had returned. Jumping to Ming's defense was instinctive. And Tony Taulke never did anything that didn't benefit Tony Taulke.

The image jumped. Subspace interference. Tony let it settle before continuing.

"The other factions have to be aware. We'll keep it off CorpNet. Like I said, from the public's perspective, nothing will have changed. You'll even sign official documents with Ming's seal."

"It's the Qinlao Faction's seal. It doesn't belong to one person."

"Precisely."

Ruben cocked his head, feeling like he'd just been maneuvered right where Tony wanted him. "What's this really about, Tony? Are you making a play to take over Mars—"

"Stop talking," Tony interrupted. "Listen to me, Ruben. If I wanted Mars, I would never have given it to Ming in the first place. I need the Qinlao Faction there, running resource extraction and product manufacturing. That, in fact, is why I'm doing this."

"I don't understand." This felt wrong. Tony was sweeping Ming, his old frenemy, aside and elevating Ruben to power in her place. Most of Ruben wanted to curse Tony Taulke for even suggesting such a thing. But a small part—the part that didn't feel shame at the spark of ambition in his belly—

was suddenly eager. To take over operational control. To run the Qinlao Faction in a way that wouldn't keep him up at night.

"The attack on the refinery was just a piece of the puzzle. Other cracks are forming across the Company. I need someone I can rely on there. A steady hand. Not an aging, mentally degraded—"

"Shut your fucking mouth!"

It exploded from him before Ruben could stop it. An instinctive shield he'd raised in defense of his big sister. The woman who'd saved him on the Moon a lifetime ago. His mentor and teacher. The most venerated person he'd ever known in his life.

Ruben started to open his mouth.

"If you apologize for that, I'll reverse my decision," Tony said. "I'll find another Qinlao to take the helm."

Ruben remained silent.

"I know you love her," Tony said. "I've seen it when you intervene on her behalf in meetings."

A fist began to clench in Ruben's chest. A hard knowledge that the day had finally come when Tony Taulke was empathizing with him. He hadn't known, hadn't even suspected, that Tony had it in him. What had Ming taught Ruben? How two seemingly incompatible halves—intellectual yet superstitious, forward thinking yet reactionary, loving yet spiteful—existed in every human being?

Respectful yet ambitious.

"You've protected her," Tony continued, sounding every bit the elder statesman. "You've acted honorably."

What the fuck would you know of honor?

"And now, for the sake of your faction—and Ming's sake—I need you to step up."

The fist in Ruben's chest changed, oozing like a thick, sticky liquid into his gut. This is what Tony Taulke did. This is how he made the deals he made to keep the Company even keeled. He took an immoral idea and wrapped it in a bow of necessity. He sold snake oil in a bottle labeled *miracle cure.*

"Are you in or out?"

The understanding father figure had left Tony's voice. The syndicate boss had returned.

"I have complete control," Ruben said. "I run the faction."

"Nothing changes but who's in charge," Tony said. "You have my word."

Your word.

But Tony's word was what Ruben had. And knowing Tony, if Ruben didn't agree, he'd make good on his promise and find someone else in the Qinlao clan to put in power. At least this way, Ruben could protect Ming. And direct the way his family faction helped shape the future of SynCorp.

"All right, then," Ruben said. "I'm in."

11

KWAZI JABARI • SYNCORP HEADQUARTERS, LOW
EARTH ORBIT

"I'm afraid I have some bad news."

Those seven words, spoken by Helena Telemachus, had changed his life forever. Seven simple words. Existence became something foreign after hearing them. Like a sorceress had cast a spell pulling Kwazi into an alternate reality. Like his life before had been a dream he hadn't known he'd been in. More than a dream, a fantasy. Now he was in a real world that could be bent and shaped by seven simple words. It was like he'd been bound to Prometheus's rock by Helena Telemachus, his memories of Amy eating away at his heart.

Maybe we could try Polynesian?

That sounds wonderful.

And beyond that, on a quantum level at the core of his being, a cavern deeper and broader than any mining shaft on Mars, than all that planet's mining shafts put together. A growing emptiness, a blackness, red rimmed and raw, where Kwazi's happiness and hopes for the future used to live.

Now he was the Hollow Man. A ghost in his own life, haunting this reality with his own memories.

"Dr. Stuart shared with me your concerns for Amanda Topulos. I'm afraid Ms. Topulos died," the woman who'd stepped out of the newscast told him. "Your whole crew—with so many others. I'm so sorry, Mr. Jabari."

Vacant. Deserted.

Alone.

He'd wanted to leap out of his hospital bed, force the words back down her throat. When Telemachus sat beside him on the bed and placed her hand on his arm to console him, it'd felt like a violation. The dry cold of her palm on his skin. He remembered every detail. Helena's green eyes, unblinking, her mouth somber and sympathetic. The way the hospital air recyclers hummed. The sterile chill of the hospital air. Milani Stuart, lurking behind her in the doorway, as if afraid her patient might explode and kill them all.

"I'm sorry to break it to you this way," Telemachus said. He listened with ears flooded with the white noise of his blood rushing in them. "But sometimes ripping off the bandage is best."

Yes, best, he'd thought without thinking. That was the back-channel of his mind, the one that monitored the world around him for threats, like atmo pressure in the mine or whether or not the guy staring at him from across the bar looked likely to roll him for cash in the alley. Now his brain's back-channel noticed Helena's eyes, her mouth, her we-must-go-on demeanor, and painted them on a protected, incorruptible sector of his memory. The front channel of his mind began its own part of the process—assigning meaning to her words and recognizing the future that lay before him.

A future without Amy. Without any of his crew-family. It stretched out in front of him. Decades living alone as the Hollow Man. Decades chained to reality's rock, the happiness of his own memories eating away at him, bit by bit. Bite by bite.

The door to the green room opened, waking Kwazi from his stupor. A blast of media and rented enthusiasm for Tony Taulke's speech invaded the room. Helena stepped through, her face painted with the same look she'd worn for their entire three-day trip to Earth. Patient and pained. Empathetic. Dr. Stuart stepped in behind her, crowding into the doorway. The image gave him a sickening sense of déjà vu.

"How are you doing, Kwazi?" Telemachus asked, the spotlights flashing behind her. "How are you feeling?"

Vacant. Deserted.

"Fine. Just fine, thanks."

"That's good," Helena said, sitting beside him on the divan. "Would you like a drink?"

"Yes, please."

Dr. Stuart stepped inside and the door swished shut. The room felt sealed, like an enlarged coffin. Stuart seemed uneasy, nervous. She took a seat and looked on.

Without fanfare, without public acknowledgment of any kind, the Company had sequestered him aboard the space station that served as the Syndicate Corporation's Headquarters. There was something happening. A ceremony of some kind. That's why Helena was here, to collect him for the ceremony. Kwazi wasn't quite sure he understood what it was, what it meant, though Helena had explained it to him several times. He wasn't sure he gave a fuck what it was, or what it meant. The details seemed never to stick in the front-channel of his brain.

"Here. A glass of Tony's best bourbon. It'll help settle you," Telemachus said.

When she'd explained it all before, he'd nodded, acquiesced, agreed to it. He'd moved when she told him to move, checked out of Wallace Med and joined her aboard her ship bound for Earth. Milani Stuart had been commandeered as well, his personal doctor to see him through ... whatever this was. With the help of Dr. Stuart's sedatives, he'd slept on board when Helena told him to sleep. The outside world was just a stage he walked across. It was like Kwazi could see the ropes hauling the backdrops up and down around him, the people around him like Helena saying their lines. Facial expressions appeared exaggerated, overly large and caricatured so the people in the back of the theater would know the emotion on the actors' faces. It all felt distant, something he wasn't physically a part of.

"So this is how it will go," Telemachus said as he downed the dark liquor. When it burned his throat, it felt like penance. "Mr. Taulke is making a speech about the terrible loss on Mars—your friends, and so many others—"

"Amy died," Kwazi said. "And Max and Mikel and Aika and Beren."

Telemachus released a breath. She glanced briefly at Stuart, then addressed Kwazi with slow speech. "Yes. And many others. The Resistance murdered them, Kwazi."

"Murdered," he said, tasting the word.

"But you and the others who survived—you're heroes of the Company. You helped guide the rescue teams. You helped save lives."

That didn't sound right. If he'd been a hero, why was Amy dead? Hadn't she barely even been injured? His back-channel offered up her twitching hand as evidence. Why were any of them dead?

"Did I?" Kwazi wondered. He didn't remember saving anyone. In fact, he remembered *not* saving *everyone*.

"Yes," Telemachus said, her voice lined with impatience. "We've been over this many times."

Dr. Stuart cleared her throat, and Helena forced a smile as Kwazi looked at her. Her expression made him want to fade into the wall away from her. Every time he gazed into Helena's piercing green eyes, he heard the seven words again, felt Helena's cool hand on his arm, guiding him through the chilly room. Saw Amy dead, her body blue against the cold metal of the bed in Wallace Med's morgue. It had made him sad and angry to see her there, naked under the examiner's thin sheet. She hated the cold.

Sometimes ripping off the bandage is best.

"And now you can help them all again," Telemachus said.

"I'd like to help them," Kwazi said, "but it's too late." What he thought was: *I want Amy back.*

"It's time to move forward now," she pressed. "We can ... we can honor their memory today."

I don't want to move forward. I want to go backward.

"Okay," he said.

Telemachus blinked acknowledgment to her sceye. "We're on our way." Turning to Kwazi, she laid a hand on his bare arm.

So cold. Like Amy now.

"It's time to go, Kwazi."

"Okay," he said.

Rising, Telemachus pushed Kwazi forward, and the door slid aside. Tony Taulke's baritone was winding up his speech with words like "Resistance" and "will not negotiate" and "terrible loss." Helena led Kwazi up a short staircase just off stage. From behind a podium emblazoned with the five-pointed SynCorp star, Taulke gestured to an audience of handpicked citizen-workers. Camerabots shot him from various angles, spreading his speech across the solar system. Kwazi swallowed into a dry throat.

"But, ladies and gentlemen, this story isn't all sad," Taulke was saying. "Amid the tragedy of that day on Mars, amid the blood and bedlam of wanton destruction, the true nature of the human spirit shone through. Heroes were forged. Heroes who helped others, who saved the lives of their fellow human beings. Those heroes represent the shining spirit that ensures our triumph over those who intend our Company harm."

Taulke turned, a broad, proud smile stretching the otherwise angular features of his face.

"Helena, would you please?"

Telemachus ascended the steps to the podium. Kwazi followed, hand in hand. When they reached the top, she led him forward.

"Ladies and gentlemen, this man is one such hero," Taulke said. The lights from above forced Kwazi to squint. His legs felt made of rubber, but they held him up. "Kwazi Jabari selflessly put his own life in jeopardy to save others."

Did I?

The back-channel of Kwazi's brain moved his legs. He knew to stop next to Tony Taulke. This is what he'd rehearsed with Helena on the trip from Mars. How this would go, over and over again. He didn't have to think about it, which was good. His muscles seemed to think for him.

"Come closer to the podium, Mr. Jabari," Taulke said, smiling. "See, folks? Even now he shuns the spotlight."

The lights were too bright, but Kwazi complied. His eyes had begun to adjust. When Taulke extended his right hand, Kwazi took it. More back-channel programming. More muscle memory.

"Mr. Jabari, I want to thank you for your heroism. You embody the very spirit we encourage in our citizen-workers. You embody bravery. You embody initiative. You're someone our children can look up to and admire as they enter the workforce."

A smile formed on Kwazi's face. It felt odd, but it wasn't something he could control. The lights, Taulke's own smile, the firm grip holding Kwazi's hand hard. It all seemed to demand that he smile in response. His cheeks trembled with the effort.

"I say this as the man blessed enough to lead the Syndicate Corporation: without people like you, humanity would've succumbed to the consequences of its own avarice more than a generation ago. Thank you, Mr. Jabari. Thank you for showing us that the human spirit endures—no matter the circumstances. No matter the cost."

The crowd erupted with clapping, their voices raised in accolades for a man none of them had ever seen before. The smile slowly slid from Kwazi's face.

The cost.

Taulke released his hand and looked past him. "Helena, can you join us?"

Her face beaming, Helena Telemachus approached center stage with a small, square velvet case. She opened it.

"Today, I'm bestowing upon Mr. Jabari the Order of the First Citizen. As I'm sure you know, this is SynCorp's highest civilian award." Taulke regarded him with a solemn expression and clapped a hand on Kwazi's shoulder. "And more than well deserved. Helena?"

She took up position opposite her boss, flanking Kwazi. Despite the open air of the auditorium and the vast crowd on the deck below, Kwazi suddenly felt hemmed in. The unreality around him thickened, crystallized. In the front-channel of his mind he felt he was about to be sealed into this new reality as the Hollow Man forever.

Right here. Right now.

That's what this ceremony was for. Kwazi finally understood. And was terrified.

Taulke removed the ribbon and medal from the box and held it up briefly for the people watching, those below and around the system. The air swelled with approval. The Syndicate Corporation's CEO fastened the ribbon around Kwazi's neck, then withdrew. Taulke swept his arm toward Kwazi, as if the Martian miner were newly minted, fresh off the assembly line to be admired.

Kwazi looked down at his chest as Helena turned him gently to face the crowd. The embossed, generic, angular profile of a man looked back at him, upside down, from inside the Company's five-pointed star. It might have been Caesar's profile, but it more than resembled Tony Taulke. It made Kwazi feel small.

"Every single one of you here," Taulke was saying, "can look up to this man. You could do much worse than to emulate him. Good corporate citizens make for a strong corporation. And the Company will always take care of its own."

More applause. More shouts of corporate unity.

"And one other thing," Taulke said, quieting the crowd with his hands. "We'll catch those who murdered your loved ones, Mr. Jabari." He said it without looking at Kwazi. His eyes swept the crowd below and across the solar system via CorpNet. "We'll bring them to justice. Your sacrifice—and their deaths—will not have been in vain."

A calmness descended over Kwazi with those words, coalescing around him like a second skin. Taulke stepped back from the podium and extended his hand again. When Kwazi took it automatically, Taulke pulled him in close.

"You're now my number-one ambassador to the Sol system. Don't fuck it up."

12

STACKS FISCHER • VALHALLA STATION, CALLISTO

Stepping off the *Cassini's Promise* was like being released from prison. The ship had started to smell funky with the uncomfortable closeness of people you don't know well enough to know them that well.

The artificial gravity, like everything else aboard, had been reliably half assed. My feet dragged coming down the ramp as I adjusted to Callisto's state-of-the-art gravity generators. Another of Erkennen's miracles, the rods that produced the g's were built right into the deck and foundation alongside the rebar. Callisto pulled a natural third-of-a-g, and Erkennen's gravimetric enhancers—the semi-technical name for them—supplemented that. Like a thermostat, it could be dialed up and down. Lower gravity to make the heavy lifting lighter, normal gravity in the hospital to make sure blood clots. Variant Gravity Syndrome was a problem for some, and if you couldn't get over VGS, space wasn't for you. The Community Dome pulled a steady one-g, which kept Earth-evolved muscles from getting lazy and cut down on the Company's medical and fitness budget. Low-g can cause all kinds of health problems, mental and physical.

Above, Callisto's orbital ring—where miners and materiel were transferred between shuttles and gashaulers—shone with the amber-orange light of Jupiter. A shuttle was docking, likely bringing in an off-cycle work crew from a gas platform in low orbit of the big planet. Mining happened 'round-the-clock. There was a scoopship right behind the shuttle, waiting to dump its cargo of Jupiter's gassy gold, where they'd separate out the helium-3 and deuterium before they were hypercompacted into a gashauler and launched into the Frater Lanes for transport to the inner planets.

It'd been a long time since I'd been to Callisto. A long time since I'd seen the Company's arteries pumping like this. I'd gotten too used to shiny walls and aged scotch at The Slate. The last time I was here, maybe ten years before, SynCorp had still been recruiting pioneers for its second colonization attempt since the first one hadn't gone so well twenty years earlier. See the Stars, Build a Future—part of Tony's effort to brand the system for the Company. Valhalla Station had been much smaller then, cruder, and that was part of its charm for the roughhousers Tony recruited to homestead here. Now the community had three huge domes—residences, agroresources, the utility center—and looked like a truly civilized attempt at one giant leap for mankind.

But the *Promise* was the only ship docked in the half a dozen slips, and she sure looked lonely. Only a handful of customs personnel were present. A big man with a beard drove a loader to the freighter's slip, ready to pull seed and medical supplies and Earth luxuries for sale in the local market. I stepped out of the way. Other passengers streamed off the ramp, including my dinner companions from a few nights before. Jaxson and Haze. Allard and Annie, who made sure to wink my way as she passed. Jane Smith? Nowhere to be seen.

I'd been trying to guess who she worked for since we'd had our verbal tennis match. If I was here on Tony's orders, maybe another faction had sent its own fixer to solve the pirate problem. I'd be more surprised if they hadn't. Or maybe she worked for the Bosswoman of Callisto, Adriana Rabh. In any case, I figured I'd be seeing Jane again soon enough.

I joined the small crowd of claimstakers in the customs line. I flashed Sawyer Finn's faked bona fides to the Company man and entered the station proper. Unlike dockside, the interior of the Community Dome was vital, alive. Citizens milled among the shops strategically placed along the boardwalk leading away from the port. They were cordial to one another, much more refined in their manners than a decade earlier. Valhalla Station had gone from selling furs on the edge of the tundra to a Western town with a promising future. It was like the mirror image of Earth's own Moon, twenty years behind. Man's first step there had started out this way, too. Shiny and new with the dreams of what mankind could accomplish. Now the Moon and its main city—now just called Darkside—were the backwater of the system, where the Company collected its refuse in the squalor of squandered potential. Made me wonder what Callisto would look like in another generation or two.

A short member of one of those generations ran past me, followed by a girl in pigtails playing some game I'd forgotten about long before either of them was born. Neither of them seemed too worried about the future. Which is how it oughta be, I guess.

"Real leather, handcrafted from our own livestock!"

I turned to find a man advancing from a stall along the boardwalk. He was snapping the neck of a boot between his hands, twisting and stretching it.

"Sturdier than the stuff they synthesize on Earth! Much tougher, like everything else out here, friend. Let me fit you a pair."

If I weren't trying to stay low key, I would've questioned the man's assumption that we were chums. With earnest, if not extreme, prejudice. But the over-the-hill miner I was supposed to be just held up my travel bag. "Nice boots. But I got all I need right here ... friend."

"Oh, you'll be back," he said, sure of himself. "That inner planet shit falls apart out here. Made for walking the dog back home, not standing on rocks shaped by the gods. Mark my words."

I gave him half a grin. "Consider them marked. Now, can you direct me to the best bar on Callisto? I'm parched." Six days of sobriety was five and a half too many.

Boots seemed to hesitate. No one likes giving anything away for free on the frontier. I'd just remembered that old lesson. Different customs, different people out here. But he seemed to weigh the value of being friendly. Favors are like any other commodity. Tradeable.

"Keep walking toward the center. This is the Market District. The Entertainment District is about halfway between here and Justice Hall," he said, gesturing at the spire in the middle of the dome. It was five or six kilometers distant. "You'll find everything you need to divert yourself there. You'll just have step off the main drag once you cross into it. If you know what I mean."

I knew what he meant. I'd find the bars and whorehouses in the alleys behind the prettier facades of more family-oriented vid-centers and restaurants. If I wanted to find out about the seedier side of life on Callisto, I wouldn't discover it over aperitifs in one of the upscale establishments. I'd find it across the alleys, where the drunks slept off their vice. Cards on the table, I'm way more comfortable stepping over drunks than dancing with socialites.

"Thanks. I appreciate it."

"Come back for the boots!" he said to my back.

The *Promise* had arrived at the end of a Jovian day. Jupiter hung as a permanent fixture in Callisto's sky with its yellow-golden bands and its one angry, red eye. Plastisteel panels in the dome's roof began to shade to true transparency, allowing the natural light from the big planet to shine through as if humans had never set foot here. The panels were programmed to signal the time of day via color manipulation, the Company's attempt at regulating Callistans' circadian rhythms with a tolerable approximation of Earth's light cycle. Earth's night has a silver sheen from her Moon, but here, it's the planet that shines on the moon. Sunlight reflected from Father Jupiter, bathing Callisto in the warm browns of a bourbon sky. Night was coming on.

More kids ran by me. One bumped into me, then bounced off again.

"Sorry, Mister."

Shouldn't they be getting home soon?

"Forget it, kid."

He raced after his compadres.

Tony wanted me to sniff around, not bull my way in, so I took my time strolling as the dome grew darker. Everything in a colony dome is designed for utility. Luxury is something you pay a vendor for. Translation: the corridors are cramped, with minimal width along the narrow streets. The Company encourages personal mobility, part of its Health First initiative. Healthy, happy workers are productive workers. No need for physical fitness centers when you have to walk everywhere to get anything.

The streets slowly cleared out. Callistans wound down their day, retreating into apartments to cook family dinner. Shops began to shut down, but I was surprised to see no security gates descending over the storefronts. Then I reminded myself that stealing was always a rarity on Callisto. Valhalla Station had a fairly black-and-white code: do unto others all you want, but be prepared for the consequences. Communal judgment was swift, fierce, and non-negotiable.

Everything on the frontier has a certain life-preserving urgency about it, even the most trivial things—like local-made boots. This wasn't Earth, where everyone's born with a silver planet in their mouth. This was one small moon revolving around a huge outer planet on the edge of nowhere. A wayward asteroid might punch through a hydroponic dome. The gravity generators might fail. The air processors might break down. The underground water supply might become contaminated by an alien virus. The people who made a life on Callisto weren't scared by any of that, or if they were, they got over it quick or picked up their ball and glove and ran home to Earth. But that kind of life made for a pretty simple moral code, and most abided by it without complaint. Respecting and enforcing it are part of what held them together as a community. Callistans are a hardy stock.

The Market District streets were nearly deserted by the time I crossed the border into the Entertainment District. I slipped past the more refined restaurants and diversion centers where families gathered and followed the singles to the more practical establishments off the main drag. The boot-maker's advice was spot on. One of my rules in life: any place with a sign showing a bare-breasted, winged woman swinging a sword out front is worth a closer look.

From the alley I heard a gasp. Aha! I'd found the business side of town, all right. I sneaked a peek and was surprised to find a young woman sitting alone in the alley muck. I'd expected to find a John nearby, or maybe she was the Jane paying for the pleasure from local talent. But nope, she was flying solo. She was young, with a thousand-yard stare. A lazy smile and lazier eyes. I took a closer look, but she didn't notice. No drug parapher-nalia I could see. Then I remembered Mickey's short course on the latest escape: the hack you could buy for the SCI, the one that floated you away on your own endorphins to La-La Land. This girl was certainly enjoying her own imagination. She started to move her fingers in the direction of her fun bits, so I decided it was time for that drink.

"Welcome to Valkyrie's Perch," a waitress said as I walked through the faux log door. She could've been the model for the sign out front. She certainly looked the part. "I'm Lagertha. What—or who—can I get you?"

I inhaled deeply through my nose. Sweat, beer, and the underscent of too much beer, recycled. This was my kind of place. After nearly a week on a ship with the gall to have *Promise* in its name, I was finally beginning to feel fulfilled.

"Scotch and a beer," I said. Passwords to happiness.

"Brands?"

"Surprise me." I smiled up at her eyes.

"Maybe later," she answered with a sideways grin. "Pick a seat. I'll find you."

I had no doubt. The whole place was skinned with holo-tech in the style of a Viking mead hall. Long tables with benches took up the floor space. Faux antler chandeliers full of fake candles twittered above. Somewhere, digital musicians rendered an ancient drinking song with pre-battle enthusiasm. Actually, it was coming from everywhere. The wonders of modern technology bringing to life such a historically realistic fantasy tickled me.

People are funny. As humanity stepped out into space, they reshaped it with their own myths. Makes it more comfortable, maybe. Callisto was home to modern-day Vikings. Mickey had his Western saloon. Lander's Reach on Mars had a thing for Europe, which was ironic since the Qinlao Faction ruled there. My favorite bordello in Darkside was a throwback to Ancient Greece called the Arms of Artemis. Even SCHQ had started out as Olympus Station before Helena Telemachus convinced Tony to rebrand it as Company headquarters. People are just funny.

"Hey, Fischer!"

My good humor evaporated. And I almost fell for it. The hail had come from a smaller table on the far side of the drinking hall. With the loud music and the crowd beginning to settle into their cups, it was easy to pretend I hadn't heard my own name called out across a busy, public place.

"Hey, Finn!"

Slowly, I turned. A raised stein was pointed at me like a gun. The short arm holding it belonged to Jane Smith.

"First round's on me!" she called.

I walked toward the offer, the envious mumblings of miners fresh off shift nibbling at me along the way.

"Surprised to see you here," I said.

"No, you're not," she answered, gesturing at the empty bench next to her. "Have a seat."

Why not?

"You following me?" I asked easily.

I felt a body behind me, and instinct made me glance over my shoulder. It was Lagertha with her two best girlfriends on ample display. She set my beer and scotch down on the table, graciously taking her time, just in case the fake gravity suddenly gave way or something.

"Anything else?" she asked in a way that sounded like she might be besties with Pioneer Annie.

"Maybe later."

"I get off at midnight." She leaned over again and said into my ear, "Or, y'know, shortly thereafter."

Yeah, this was my kinda place.

"I'll keep that in mind."

Lagertha moved on to another potential paying customer. I returned my attention and faculties to Jane Smith: "I asked you a question."

"Did you? Sorry, I was distracted by the carnal display of pioneer mating rituals."

"Funny. I like women with a sense of humor."

"I'd think, for spending time with you, it'd be a requirement."

I shot the scotch.

"No, Fischer, I'm not following you," she said before swigging her beer. "Not exactly."

"Not exactly." I didn't demand to know how she'd recognized me. That'd be tied to who she was and who she worked for. I'd have answers to both those questions presently. One way or the other.

"I'm here for the same reason you are," she said.

"You like buxom waitresses too?"

"Pirates," she said.

"Buxom pirates, then," I said, sampling my own beer. Not bad. Hoppy.

"Damn it, Fischer—"

I set my mug down on the wooden table and leaned in. "Call me that again where others can hear, and I'll stove in your head with this stein."

Smith began to draw herself up—defense mechanism. The fingers of her right hand got nervous, but they stayed above the table. Lucky for her. I was packing. The baggy miner shirt was good for something after all. She settled down.

"Fair enough," Smith said.

"Now, let's level the playing field," I said. "What's your real name, Jane Smith? I want to know who I'm dealing with. Whisper it."

The lights in the Perch went from ambient amber to severe red. The lusty drinking song cut out, replaced by a twenty-first-century Klaxon. Mugs hung, halfway to mouths. Time slipped into slow motion. Smith was up and moving. I was slower but got it in gear.

"Impact event. Orbital ring compromised. All station personnel, alert."

The calm of the automated voice overrode the quick confusion erupting around us.

Smith had elbowed her small frame to the Perch's doors and pushed through to the street. I stood beside her and followed her gaze upward.

Remember the shuttles I'd seen docking earlier above Callisto? One of them had crashed into the orbital ring. The debris was still spreading outward. The sound of massive hydraulics flooded my ears. A heavy asteroid deflector shield began to segment its way up from the ground, covering the clear plastisteel of the overhead dome. It was a race between the slow-moving shield and the debris raining down from the ring. Both horses seemed determined to win.

"That was unexpected," Smith said. Then, looking at me: "Bosswoman's not gonna like it."

Well ... now, at least, I knew who employed her.

13

EDITH BIRCH • VALHALLA STATION, CALLISTO

"Are you sure? The box says twenty bottles."

Sighing, Krystin Drake put the handful of potassium iodate boxes back in the crate and started again. Edith watched, counting along silently as Krystin inventoried out loud.

"Okay, you're right," Krystin said. "I must've skipped one before."

Edith made a never-mind motion. "It's easy to lose count."

In the infirmary's outer office, a man laughed at something Edith hadn't heard. The arrival of a new batch of medical supplies always energized the staff with newfound purpose. An entire palette of pills and stims and anti-inflammatory steroids had just been delivered from the *Cassini's Promise*, and every item needed to be counted, scanned, and stocked in the infirmary's stores. Once the crates had been unpacked and the supplies stacked in perfect rows, the medical staff would go back to their daily routine of treating unsexy conditions like diarrhea and skinned knees and the occasional bout of VGS. New arrivals—whose romantic self-image of being a Viking outstripped their ability to adapt to a multi-g environment—tended to suffer from Variant Gravity Syndrome, and a transdermal dimenhydrinate anti-nausea patch usually fixed that. Since there were fewer and fewer immigrants to Callisto these days, even that diversion from routine had become rare.

Krystin patted the last box of pills and closed up the crate. "This ought to last us a few—"

"—years?" Edith said, and both women laughed.

This far out from Jupiter and its closer moons, radiation exposure wasn't much of an issue. Occasionally, a miner would come back pinging the red end of the rad detector and need a ration of pills, but most of the medicine was backstocked should catastrophe strike. The same was true of most of the station's supplies. Tetraglycine hydroperiodide–laced iodine pills for treating contaminated water, hardly needed once the community's water treatment facility had come online eight years earlier. The more standard stuff, like saline solution for hydration, antibiotics for bacterial infections, antivirals for the other kind, vitamin shots heavy on antioxidants like A and C to help protect against radiation sickness, Vitamin D to supplement what the dome's panels filtered out along with ultraviolet light... And yet the routineness of it all—the daily mundanity of keeping people healthy and alive in a hostile environment that, without human ingenuity, would have killed them outright—was special in its own way to Edith. The fact that everyone on Valhalla Station could take their health for granted was a tribute not only to the pioneering spirit of the colony's inhabitants, but also to the professional dedication and competence of their onsite protectors.

Edith was good at numbers, and the infirmary employed her to keep its medical supplies organized. Luther seemed not to mind her working there, something that had surprised her at first. When he pressed her to pilfer the odd medication now and then, she did so sparingly and on the sly. She hated stealing, but she considered it the price for freedom during the day and for helping others. Working in the infirmary gave her a place to go not full of her own memories. And, more than that, it felt like she was contributing something to the colony, something that mattered.

"You know, what we do here is important," Edith said, watching Krystin open another crate. "Maybe next to the hydroponic teams, we're the most important people on the station."

"Ha." Krystin wasn't convinced. "If a miner heard you say that, he'd..." Her voice hit a hard stop. An uncomfortable calm stretched between them. "I'm sorry, Edith," she said. "I wasn't thinking."

Edith tapped her personal access data device, checking off the crate of anti-radiation pills. She double-checked the entry on the PADD, then triple-checked it. Krystin made a tiny sound that might have been frustration or regret or self-flagellation.

"Don't worry about it," Edith said, feeling bad that her friend appeared to feel guilty. What in the world had Krystin done to feel guilty?

In the outer office the laughter returned. Edith seized on it, saying, "Sounds like someone's inventorying the good stuff. How'd they get so lucky?"

Krystin's quiet humor broke the tension. "You know, sometimes I want to—"

A harsh, grating Klaxon made them both jump.

"Impact event. Orbital ring compromised. All station personnel, alert."

The alarm was so loud it hurt Edith's ears. She stared at Krystin for several seconds, her own fear playing out in Krystin's eyes—a sudden, shared reminder that life here was stolen from death in an airless, heatless vacuum.

A man appeared in the doorway. His dark, graying, close-cropped beard was an arrowhead pointing down from his chin. *Estevez* was stitched on his white coveralls.

"Emergency vac-suits," he said. "Follow protocol. Do it now."

Krystin moved past her. "Come on, Edith."

"Impact event. Orbital ring compromised. All station personnel, alert."

Edith followed. *This is a drill*, she thought. They hadn't had one in forever. This was how they kept on their toes. That was all this was.

"Edith!"

She took the heavy vac-suit Krystin held out to her and tried to remember how to put it on.

"Hurry up! Bring me that foamer!" Dr. Estevez shouted, his voice muffled inside the vac-suit. Comms were flooded with frenzied, sometimes conflicting orders over the common channel as the wounded from the shuttle and ring were brought in. Out of his head, the miner on the table was moaning, fighting them. "Strap him down, for godsake!"

Edith stood against the wall, out of the way, watching Krystin attempt to restrain the man. An accountant couldn't help here. Hot and bulky, the vac-suit made her body feel small and frail inside it. The sound of her own breathing, short and coarse, filled her helmet. Her breath fogged a circle of condensate on the plastic shield.

"Help me, Edith!" Krystin said. "Hold him down so I can get these straps secured."

Edith hardly heard her over frantic demands for bandages and tourniquets. Old-fashioned tools for a completely modern accident. She moved forward without having to think about it.

"Hold his arm."

The miner thrashed. Estevez held down one side, Edith the other. Krystin worked the straps quickly. The more she bound him, the more the man fought them. He tried to sit up, his elbow jabbing Edith high in the ribs. The vac-suit deflected most of it, but a sharp pain jutted inward. Ignoring it was easy to do. Krystin strapped the offending arm down. The midazolam the triage staff had pumped into the miner was finally taking effect. His struggles had faded to rambling, mumbled curses.

"Now where the hell is that foamer?"

"Here, Doctor," Krystin said, handing Estevez the sealant. He began applying it to a large gash across the left side of the man's head, fighting to hold it still as the patient raved lazily under sedation. He was one of two dozen survivors they'd pulled from the shuttle and the orbital ring. Twice that many had perished, mostly ring personnel vented into space by the shuttle's impact.

That was the current estimate, anyway. There would likely be more.

Edith stepped back again. Maybe the midazolam had kicked in harder, or maybe Estevez's ministrations with the healing foam were having an effect. It was like the miner on the table had become human again instead of a wounded animal desperate to escape a trap. Her eyes fell to his nametag. The name *Brandt* was stitched beneath the capital R with two vertical bars running through it, the Rabh Faction's logo. That was good. He should have a name, now that he was human again.

Estevez seemed happy with his work, told Krystin something lost to Edith in the comms traffic, and moved to the next table. On it lay a woman in blood-soaked coveralls. She'd suffered heavy trauma to her abdomen and chest.

Edith probed the ache in her own side and felt no break. Then she became self-conscious at worrying about her small hurt while others were bleeding their lives out on the floor.

"Mrs. Birch, we could use your help again," Estevez grunted.

"Of course, Doctor."

"Krys, get her prepped," Estevez said, nodding at the IV line in the woman's arm. "I need to get in there. Mrs. Birch—"

"Edith, please."

"Edith, do whatever Krys tells you."

"Sure."

A single, long note calling them all to attention blanked out the comms traffic.

"*Testudo secured,*" said a very human voice, full of relief. "*The dome's structural integrity is intact.*"

The message repeated, but no one heard it. A collective shout erupted as everyone in the infirmary celebrated. After a moment of wondering if she should, Edith joined in. The segmented shield intended to protect the colony from asteroids had been secured over the transparent dome that usually filtered the sky.

"Thank the snaky-staff for that," Estevez said, pulling at the heavy suit's gloves. "I had no idea how I was gonna work on this woman in this goddamned monkey suit." Over the common channel: "Keep your headsets on, but mute the mics! We need to hear the big picture out there."

The infirmary was soon strewn with the heavy vac-suits. Orderlies began to drag and stack them out of the way.

"Ever assisted in surgery, Edith?" Estevez asked.

"Um. No."

Krystin smiled warmly. "Don't worry. Miguel and I will do the heavy lifting. You just hand me stuff when I ask for it. Okay?"

"Okay." Edith glanced around. They were short on beds, so the less serious patients lay on the floor. They were short on medical staff, too. But everyone, now relieved of the fear of being sucked into space, had turned back to their chosen profession of saving lives. "Whatever you need me to do."

"That's the spirit," Estevez said. "Now, let's start with a mobile sterile field generator."

Edith looked around.

"There," Krystin said. "The box with the tiny tent on the side."

Edith picked it up and handed it to her. As long as there were pictures, she'd be fine. How hard could it be?

Unmoving, Edith sat on the infirmary floor. Her eyes were dry. Her legs hurt. Her brain throbbed inside her skull.

"You did good work." Krystin's voice sounded depressed, but she was just tired—make that exhausted—like everyone else on staff.

"Thanks," Edith said. "How many?"

"Patients?" Krystin asked.

"Hours."

Krystin Drake made a sound like a corpse exhaling its last breath. Or maybe a cow farting.

"Too many."

Where patients weren't occupying beds or floor space, medical staff had collapsed where they'd stood. Estevez was snoring lightly in a chair, his head resting ungracefully on a diagnostic console.

"You were right, you know," Krystin said.

"About?"

"We saved lives today," Krystin clarified with a lazy, lingering smile. "*You* saved lives today."

Edith grunted. "See? Only the hydroponic crews—"

"*Fuck* the farmers!" Krystin said. Her voice had gotten its second wind. "We just took the fucking crown, lady."

Edith somehow found the energy to laugh. It was a little anemic, but it felt good. Except for the twinge in her side from that miner's elbow. *Brandt*, she reminded herself.

Something in the back of Edith's brain stirred. She'd heard that name before.

Yeah, me and Brandt, we worked that scoop like a...

Luther's voice. Brandt had been one of the men in his mining crew.

"What was the number of the crew in here today?" Edith whispered.

"What?" Krystin said from a half doze.

"The crew number!" Edith rose and leaned against the wall. The woman they'd operated on for hours lay on the table beside her. Stable, her chest rose and fell inside a heavily sedated sleep. Edith kneeled to where the woman's ragged coveralls, cut off for surgery, were piled in a bloody heap beneath the table. Edith rifled through until she found the upper arm patch. Crew 34.

Luther's crew.

"Oh no," Edith said.

She moved from table to table. Her movements were jerky, uncoordinated, like she'd just reentered standard-g after a month in the weightlessness of space. The grunts of disturbed, exhausted colleagues babbled up as she stumbled over them. When she didn't find him on one of the tables, Edith dropped to her knees and crawled from patient to patient over the floor.

No Luther.

Had he been blown into space on impact? Was he still alive, unhurt? Or maybe in one of the tertiary facilities converted to triage work when the infirmary filled up...

She should call him. Find out if he was okay. Edith engaged her sceye and inhaled a breath to execute a search query. The cursor on the query screen pulsed, awaiting her command.

The words seemed reluctant to come.

Was he alive or dead? And which would she rather be true? He hadn't attempted contact to let her know he was all right. Maybe he *was* dead. His body frozen in space, spinning to infinity.

Edith knew what she *should* want to be true. Luther was her husband. Bound together by God and law, he was the man she'd chosen for herself. Without him, she'd be—

Free.

The lightness in her heart rode the back of that thought easily, then quickly crumbled into shame. It must be the fatigue. Her thoughts weren't her own. Desiring Luther dead, well, that was—

Justice?

Stop it! Just, stop!

Edith leaned against a cabinet. She was just tired. That was all. She wasn't thinking straight. She'd be free, yes, but not like that. Edith had a plan. She just needed to be patient, work the plan. Luther was fine—he had to be fine. If she found out he was dead now, the superstitious part of her would wonder if she'd somehow willed the dark fantasy into reality.

She stared at the flashing cursor, mustering the courage to—what?

"Contamination event. Possible pathogen released. All station personnel, alert."

The Klaxon erupted. The alert repeated. Medical personnel began to stir, cursing their interrupted sleep.

Krystin moaned on the floor, starting to rise. "What the fuck else can go wrong today?"

Edith blinked, closing the query screen.

"Come on," Estevez said, eyelids struggling to open. There was a plastic imprint on his left cheek from the console. "We're not done yet."

14

STACKS FISCHER • EN ROUTE TO RABH REGENCY STATION

"Does it always take this long?" I asked.

"A man your age must ask that a lot."

I gave Smith an *eat-shit* look and returned to gazing over Callisto as we ascended. The space elevator moved slowly as hell. Another example of low-grade tech in the boonies. The elevator connecting Earth to SynCorp HQ was specially outfitted with inertial compensators, it rose so fast.

Smith cleared her throat. "Extra safety protocols," she said, deciding to be helpful after all. "Something like that happens out here..." She gestured toward the ring. It was elegant, a state-of-the-art work of art, a tribute to man's technical achievement: an orbiting, habitable football circling Callisto, complete with a maglev train for quick access, one side to the other. Badmouthing the boonies aside, the ring was an impressive sight.

"It's beyond rare," Smith said, her eyes locked on the part of the ring no longer pristine. There were work crews still separating ring metal from shuttle hull.

"The orbital ring?" I said. "The one over Earth is—"

"Accidents," she corrected me. "We're so far away from any real help—our maintenance schedules are aggressive. We have three spare parts in storage for anything that might need fixing. Training is matrixed, so if the chief engineer gets pneumonia, the next guy in line can take up the slack. Our redundancies have redundancies."

"So, security is in *oh-shit* mode," I said.

"Something like that." Her tone was reflective, almost vulnerable. We were becoming buds.

"Sounds like a well-oiled machine."

"*The corporate machine is all*," she mumbled, translating the usual Latin of the Syndicate Corporation motto. Smith sounded more like a pragmatist than a true believer. That was interesting enough to file away.

The elevator slowed, if that was possible, and I decided the sluggish speed of ascent had been an optical illusion. The dull-brown pockmarks of Callisto's surface spread out below. In the vastness of space, it's hard to focus on things very far away because distance is so great and most bodies so small. But Callisto was impressive through the window, one inch of life-preserving plastisteel. That particular Erkennen invention was as much responsible for mankind being out here as the Frater Drive or gravity generators. Seeing the vastness of space every day? Well, there's something that'll make you dream of bigger things.

The elevator paused. Hydraulics worked to stabilize the lift. Seals sealed. I imagined—given Smith's description of the extra precautions after the accident—a computer program running a double and triple check before opening the door.

"Home sweet home," Smith said.

When it did open, the relative quiet of the lift vanished. Personnel bustled about Regent Adriana Rabh's castle-in-the-sky. Smaller than SCHQ (of course), it was the Texas-sized belt buckle of Callisto's orbital ring. I suspected on a normal day station natives would be a bit less hurried, though Regent Rabh's appreciation for efficiency would never have embraced a leisurely work pace. The staff and upper crust of Regency Station got to look down on the rest of Callisto and its squatters—literally. Only an idiot would take that for granted.

"Come on," Smith said, "this way."

I followed her into the bustle. Despite their own hurry, people made way. When you're the lead enforcer for the richest faction leader in the solar system, folks tend to give you a wide berth. I know because I enjoy the same respect aboard SCHQ. But out here, I doubted anyone recognized me, especially done up like a grunt from a scooper ship.

A few lift switches inside the station to get us to the tippy-top, and we were walking through Adriana Rabh's outer office. Adriana's bulldog at the front desk glanced up, saw it was Smith, and went back to whatever he'd been doing at his terminal. I almost stumbled when we walked into the Queen Bee's office—we'd entered a rainforest, complete with the ambient sounds of animals and reptiles and chirp-chirp-chirping insects. Adriana had her office walls skinned like an Amazonian jungle.

The Bosswoman looked up.

"Well, as I live and breathe," she said.

"Still doing both, I see," I replied. Adriana Rabh had been ancient when I still had hair on the top of my head. And that was a while ago.

"Eugene Fischer, you sonofabitch," she continued. She smiled, and it seemed genuine. "Daisy claimed it was you, but I had to see it with my own eyes."

"Daisy?" I took a seat across from Adriana. For a regent, she kept a plain office, if you didn't count the expensive tech wetting the walls with fake rain. I'd always assumed Adriana's affinity for Spartan accommodations was a pretension of the rich who claim they got that way by being frugal.

Adriana nodded briefly at Smith, who'd kept her feet and settled herself with her back to a wall full of 3D human-sized ferns. Like a good guard dog should. The one-hundred-eighty degrees of her forward view were filled with Adriana and me. She had her hands behind her back, close to her weapons. She'd checked off all the boxes you do when your boss might be in danger.

"Your name's Daisy?" I asked. "You gotta be kidding."

"Glass houses, *Eugene*," Daisy said.

Touché.

"Daisy Smith?"

"Daisy Brace."

"Okay."

"Want to whip it out and see whose is bigger?" Adriana asked, impatience in her eyes. "Because I'm pretty sure it's Daisy's."

I winked at Daisy. "I'm pretty sure you're right."

Any one-hundred-ten-pound woman who killed for hire for Adriana Rabh and had the guts to go by Daisy—well, I wasn't sure I'd ever want to tangle with that, pants on *or* off. Caution is a virtue I've tried to perfect.

"Good, then we can get down to business," Adriana said, leaning forward. "Tony sent you here. Why?"

"Why, Adriana, whatsoever do you mean? I just came to visit. Take in the Callistan nightlife. Maybe fly a glider on Titan—"

"Dressed as an atmo-miner?" Daisy said. "You should do a dress rehearsal for lying. You don't ad-lib well."

I gave her broad smile. "Maybe I'm not trying."

Adriana held up a hand. "Stacks, it's been a long time. But I recall your service to me fondly."

"I'm touched," I said, "considering I failed."

It wasn't as smarmy as it probably sounds. I have a fond place in my heart for Adriana Rabh. Our previous association *had* been a failure, but it set my life on a certain course, gave me a certain code to live by. And kill by. Meanwhile, she'd built a financial empire that fuels the Company's economic engine. And she'd been fiercely loyal to Tony and the SynCorp power structure for three decades. Dependable. Hard as nails. A no-nonsense kind of gal.

Adriana stood and walked round the desk. I kept my seat. Daisy stood up off the wall, more ready to move if she had to. Another checkbox in the *good* category. When Adriana sat on the edge of her desk in front of me, her silk dress settling around her still-alluring curves, I considered falling in love with her again. Power is a perfect enhancement to beauty.

"I don't expect you to betray Tony's confidence," she said. "I wouldn't insult you by tempting you to do that."

Too late.

"Appreciate that," I said.

"But that shuttle crashing into the ring on the same day you arrive on Callisto..." She swept a fold of her gown from one leg to the other, revealing a long calf. Adriana was in her eighties, but her calf seemed to have missed the memo by forty years or so. Maybe the new troubleshooter implants really could give the middle finger to growing old. "I don't believe in coincidences," she said.

No wonder you and Tony get along so well.

"Neither do I."

"Tony didn't tell me you were coming, which means he didn't want me to know. You're dressed like an atmo-miner, which means you're undercover."

An amused grunt sounded from the rainforest. Adriana held up her hand again, and Daisy resumed her adopted profession of observant gargoyle.

"I doubt Tony is moving against me," she said, searching my face to see if kicking over that particular rock revealed a nugget of anything. Apparently satisfied it hadn't, she continued, "But that wouldn't make much sense. He knows the Company's profit margin is maxed when the rudder is steady."

I nodded. That was Tony's unwritten rule, and all the faction heads knew it. An even keel is good for business.

"I can tell you that I'm not here to assassinate you," I said. Daisy tensed behind me. I might even have a stunner pointed at the back of my head by now. Instant electric chair. "I said, I'm *not* here to assassinate your boss."

"I heard what you said," Daisy said. Now I was sure there was a stunner pointed at my head.

Again Adriana raised a placating hand. "Put it away, Daisy. This man can't kill me."

"Don't be so sure," warned the woman being paid to keep Adriana alive.

"I don't kill women," I said, turning to stare at the business end of Daisy's stunner.

It's true. Whatever you're thinking, it's not some throwback chivalry or some contemporary inverse misogyny. I'd killed a woman once, a long time ago. It was a mistake, a terrible mistake. Things like that stick in your craw, even when you do what I do for a living. I'd made it a rule now, not killing women, so I'd never make that particular mistake again. Now, paying someone *else* to kill them ... well, there's principle and then there's business.

"Well," said Daisy, sounding unconvinced but more relaxed, "you could've led with that."

"Stacks," Adriana said, leaning toward me. Her face, elegant in its lines, her silver-gray hair full and flowing like the mane of a lioness, the old-fashioned cameo hanging in the air over her still-distracting cleavage. The cameo was embossed with the profile of an ancient woman who looked Egyptian. I remembered Adriana had a thing for Isis, the sky goddess. "Tell me why you're here."

"First," I said, tracing the profile of Isis with my eyes, "why was Daisy on the *Promise* if you didn't know I was coming? What was so important that you sent your personal bodyguard to Earth?"

Adriana sat back. Isis rested, content, against her breastbone again. "There's a new drug problem," she said. "It's starting to impact production here. New drugs always come from Earth. *Always.* I sent Daisy to try and discover its origin."

"It's not a drug," I said. "It's an algorithm."

"I know that now, thanks to Daisy," Adriana said, rising and returning to her seat behind her smartdesk. She swiped left and up to project a schematic of the SCI. Next to the implant scrolled some tech gobbledygook that was complex enough to solve the secret of the universe. "On the market it's called Dreamscape."

"Okay."

Marketing!

Daisy decided to join the conversation. "Programmers sell it. Once installed, it drowns the user in a sea of their own endorphins."

"Hackheads," I said.

"What?" Adriana said.

"Users are called hackheads. Maybe someone was high on hack when that shuttle crashed."

The room was quiet for a moment while three brains turned over that idea.

"Maybe," Adriana allowed. "But back to my question, Stacks. Why are *you* here?"

"The pirates operating out of the Belt."

Adriana's eyes narrowed. Even the troubleshooter couldn't cure crow's feet, I guess.

"Pirates?" she said.

You know those moments when you have a split second to make a decision before appearing to do it? In one word, Adriana had claimed ignorance of the topic. But something in the way she'd said that word *pirates* sounded off. Nervous. Like she hadn't run through one of Daisy's suggested dress rehearsals for lying. I filed that away.

"Small, almost immeasurable amounts of fusion fuel are being leeched off the tankers before they reach the inner system," I said, deciding transparency was my best strategy. "I'm here to shut them down."

"Why didn't Tony inform me of this?" Adriana demanded.

I shrugged.

"He thinks I'm involved?"

I shrugged again. Daisy was back on alert.

"To my knowledge? No," I said.

Adriana seemed to make a quick decision. "I have a request."

I opened my hands.

"Maybe there's a link between the pirates and the 'accident' over Callisto, too. You and Daisy work together. Start with the pirates."

"I work alone," I said.

My voice had a slightly higher register shadowing it. That's because Daisy had said the same thing at the same time. We were twins from different eras.

"Now you work together," Adriana said. Her eyes held her fixer's. "I'll inform Tony."

Thinking about it, Adriana Rabh was probably the only faction leader that could *inform* Tony about anything. Okay, maybe Ming Qinlao too. I decided: let's see how this plays out. Having Daisy next to me instead of behind me would at least keep her where I could see her.

"Okay," I said. "But I'll need to report progress on the pirates to Tony. Soon."

"No sense wasting time, then," Daisy said. Her tone was downright unfriendly. She clearly didn't like the idea of having a partner. Join the club, sister. I'm president.

"Agreed," I said, rising, and with a proper nod of respect to Adriana. I needed to retrieve my hand artillery and get out of these farmer duds. I turned and looked above Daisy's set jaw to find her eyes hard as stone. "But shove the attitude up your ass. We're either working *together*, or we're working apart. I'm not gonna spend time worrying about you or about myself with you. Understood?"

Daisy cocked a hip out. Her chin dipped.

"Daisy," Adriana said. There was a warning in her voice.

"Fine," Daisy Brace said. "Just don't slow me down."

I flipped her the bird and led her out of the regent's suite. I wondered if I was escorting her, or she me. Which one of us was keeping tabs on the other? And was Adriana more involved with Tony's pirate problem than she'd let on? Then I suddenly didn't give a damn about any of that when the PA system started screeching again.

"Contamination event. Possible pathogen released. All station personnel, alert."

15

RUBEN QINLAO • LANDER'S REACH, MARS

Ruben's finger hovered over the door chime. Ming's summons had come unexpectedly, in the middle of the night. They'd barely spoken since Tony Taulke had maneuvered her from power and put Ruben in her place.

A part of him had always been intimidated by Ming, ever since he'd met her when he was only fourteen. They shared a father in Jie Qinlao, but she'd been Jie's first child. Lovely and distant. Smart and accomplished. And then Ming had become more than an older sister. She'd raised him after Sying, his mother, committed suicide.

Even in his mid-forties, it was hard for Ruben to see past his boyhood awe of her, despite her worsening health. Ming was barely a shell of the woman who'd been so ruthlessness, so heartless over the years as she murdered and manipulated to ensure the Qinlao Faction's survival. Yes, *intimidated* seemed the right word. Maybe there was just a little fear, too. Maybe more than a little.

The meeting of SynCorp's full board would happen two days hence. It would be Ruben's first time representing the Qinlao Faction to the other four. His coming-out party, Ming had called it. For some reason, she'd insisted they talk in the middle of the night, far in advance of the meeting.

He pressed the chime.

"Come in," she said formally. Her voice sounded different somehow. Surprisingly strong, in fact. Ruben entered. "Thank you for coming."

To ease her mobility, Ming kept her quarters set to half Mars's natural gravity, twenty percent that of Earth. Sometimes she turned the gravity off altogether here, giving her true freedom from the maglev-chair she'd been confined to for so long. Ruben had to consciously underpower his movements to avoid inadvertently leaping across the room.

The door sealed shut, and his eyes adjusted to the dim lighting. For a regent with such immense power, Ming kept her quarters simple: a bed, a small table with a carafe of Jameson's whiskey, a bathroom specially fashioned to meet her low-g needs. A shower, not a tub, which Ruben had always found strange for a woman with limited mobility in a variable gravity environment. The walls were skinned with her favorite projection, the countryside a few hours outside Shanghai. The family retreat on Earth when she'd been a girl. Moonlight shimmered silver on an oval lake.

"That was a thousand years ago," she said as he looked around. Again he heard the strength in her voice, raised above the patter of light rain falling on the vibrant flora of the Yangtze River Delta. "When I was a young woman with an infinite future ahead of me."

"And I was a young boy," he answered, his smile wistful. "Sometimes I wonder how that kid ever survived. He used to be afraid of his own shadow."

A songbird chirped in the hologram. Its mate answered.

Distinguishing the different calls of the delta's native birds was something else Ming had taught him when he was young, a game to help him learn the native flora and wildlife of the Yangtze. Laughing with her, even when he'd guessed wrong, was one of his fondest memories of childhood.

"That's a white-eye," Ruben said.

"Very good," Ming said. Her maglev-chair purred in the shadows of the room. "Never lose that, Ruben—that ability to see the trees for the forest. Life is too dangerous to lose that. Details matter."

Ruben was shocked to realize what was different about her voice. It was *her* voice. Not the modulated, enhanced electronica he'd become accustomed to. Ming's voice was deeper than he remembered, more world weary. But it was hers.

"Lights: fifty percent," Ming said. Her chair glided forward. Ruben gasped as the brightness grew in the room. She was still gray, yes, still brittle. Her skin was the color of old candle wax. But her eyes shone with a fire he hadn't seen in years. And she was sitting almost erect.

Ming stopped the chair in front of him and carefully stood up. She was smiling. When had he last seen her stand? When had it last even been possible?

"Ming," he said, his voice like the Shanghai wind whispering in the walls. "How?"

"Gregor Erkennen," Ming answered. "You know how close we've been to that faction."

Ruben nodded. Gregor's father, Viktor, had been like a friendly old uncle to both of them until he died. Viktor had always blamed himself for the radiation poisoning Ming suffered from, caused by tech he'd designed. They'd thought her cured of its effects a long time ago, but over the years, mutations in her DNA had turned Ming's own body against her. Not even the new SynCorp medical implant could mitigate the rate at which she was failing.

Or *had been* failing.

"Are you..." Ruben couldn't quite bring himself to say it out loud. "Did Gregor...?"

With a sigh, Ming returned to her chair. Her body seemed to cave in on itself. Atrophied tendons and muscles contorted her frame. Squinting hard with effort, Ming managed a kind of prideful slump.

"Cure me?" she said. "No. He was able to augment my SCI. My body is pumping itself full of synthetic hormones. 'Jet fuel,' Gregor calls it."

Ruben approached her. The white-eyes called to one another, professing love or lust or both, trying to be heard over the light China rain. He kneeled next to her chair.

"So, it's true then," he said. "The rumors are true."

"What's true?"

As she looked down at him, for a moment Ruben saw past the teary sclera of her milky eyes. Underneath the crust of old age he found the bright, energetic woman Ming had been when he'd first met her—brilliant, with a passion for life. It was like seeing past layers of old varnish on a canvas to find the original, hidden masterpiece beneath.

"About the implants," he said. "They can reverse cellular damage, rebuild DNA to counter the aging process." Ruben stared up at her. "They really are a Fountain of Youth."

Ming smiled sadly. "I'm afraid not, little brother. That's the thing about fuel. Eventually it burns up."

"I don't understand."

Reaching down, Ming cupped his face. Her own seemed fuller, healthier. But the skin of her hand felt dry.

"I needed my mind back for a short while," she said. "The body came as a bonus."

"I still don't—"

"I'm glad you're taking over the faction, Ruben," she said, her thumb stroking his cheek. "I'm glad you're taking over the family. It should have happened a long time ago."

He understood then. The rumors were fat fictions riding on thin facts, myths fueled by hope and fear as rumors always were. There was no Fountain of Youth, no technological marvel to slam the door on death. Not all the genius in the entire Erkennen Faction could accomplish that. Ming's return from mental and physical oblivion was only temporary.

"How long do you have?" Ruben asked.

"Long enough." Ming smiled, trying to draw him out of his sudden funk. "We need to prepare you for your coming-out party."

"Prepare me? What do you mean?"

She backed her maglev-chair away. It hummed across the floor of her quarters.

"I promised your mother Sying a long time ago that I would teach you to be more like your father," Ming said. She turned her chair around to face him again. "*Our* father."

Ruben stood. The rains of Shanghai dimpled lotus leaves on the quiet lake behind Ming. "You have. You've kept your promise to her."

Ming looked away. The chair's antigrav hummed, like a monk in meditation.

"I made decisions in my youth that I've come to regret," she said. "Taking you as my ward isn't one of them."

Ruben remained silent. Hearing Ming speak again in a voice that was authoritative—a voice that was present and aware of the world around her —grounded him.

"You're in the prime of your life, Ruben. And like our father, you're a moral man. Your better instincts guide your decision-making. Which is as it should be."

He wanted to return the compliment. He wanted to tell Ming that she too was a moral person. But there had been so many times Ruben had questioned her harsh exercise of power: denying workers in the mines improved safety because it was too expensive. The backroom deals with other factions to assassinate key labor leaders. He wanted to return the compliment, but his own sense of decency, his regard for objective truth, kept him from doing so.

"I know what you're thinking, little brother," she said, startling him. "You're thinking, who is my sister to speak of morality—the Red Widow of Mars. Ming the Murderer."

"What other people call you—"

"—is well earned," Ming finished for him. She guided her chair toward Ruben again. "Though that makes them sound like compliments. Titles of honor. They aren't either of those things. Let's just call them accurate and leave it at that."

Ruben answered with silence.

"I carved out our place in Tony Taulke's corporate empire by being cold, Ruben. By not allowing emotion to guide my actions. Many times you disagreed with me," she said, stopping in front of him. She stared into Ruben's eyes, her own awake and bright. "You were wrong."

He started to reply. Years of frustration standing by her side, watching her earn her reputation for coldness and cruelty, coalesced in the pit of his stomach.

Her raised hand cut him off.

"You were wrong *then*," she continued. "But now—now yours is the hand the Qinlao Faction needs guiding it to survive. Empires are built with cruelty. They're preserved with caring." She backed her chair away and settled it on the floor of her quarters. Slowly, with effort, Ming rose to her feet again.

So she can look me in the eye, Ruben thought. *As an equal. Not an invalid.*

"Some queens are builders," Ming said. "Others are preservers. Building an empire, particularly in the wake of all that craziness on Earth —the mass migrations, governments failing worldwide, Molotovs in the streets—required hard decisions. Like who should live and who should die —for the greater good."

"And the financial fortunes of our family?" Ruben asked, unable to temper his disgust. It was something old and almost forgotten in the day-to-day reality of life under SynCorp. How quickly it returned, hot and vibrant, surprised him.

"And that," she acknowledged. Ming's face grew increasingly flushed as she spoke. "The fortunes of Mars—and all the people who live here—are tied to our faction's fortunes. The fortunes of all of Sol are tied to ours, and the other factions'. Each has its place, its role to play in maintaining the delicate balance Taulke created. That's why what's happening now is such a threat." She began to shake. Ruben reached a hand out, helping Ming lower herself into the chair.

"I was cold blooded in helping to build this empire, it's true," Ming said, her voice weaker but still her own. "But now, to preserve what we've built, it must be nurtured. A steady hand, yes, but a compassionate one. *Your* hand, Ruben."

He regarded her a moment. "What are we talking about, Ming? Why am I really here?"

When she stared again from below, her eyelids seemed too heavy, even in the minimal gravity.

"I will not be alive much longer," she said. "And you must be ready for what's coming."

Ming held his eyes. Ruben wanted to protest, to say what was expected. *What are you talking about? You're healthier than I've seen you in years. You have many years ahead of you.* But in her steady, resigned gaze he could see the truth: that Gregor Erkennen's hormone therapy had bought her a last rally before the end. To help him get ready to truly rule the Qinlao Faction.

Somewhere inside him, a little boy began to cry. His voice trembling, Ruben began, "Ming, I—"

"Grieve later, little brother," Ming said. "Now, we must prepare you."

He swallowed. "Prepare me for what, exactly?"

"There's a conspiracy against the Taulke Faction. It's growing like a cancer."

"A conspiracy?" Ruben's mind focused. "What do you mean?"

"I was approached virtually, through a third party, untraceable. A circle-and-sniff to assess interest and willingness to join the others."

"The others? You mean the other three factions are part of it?"

Ming affected her version of a shrug, bent and one shouldered. Erkennen's therapy was flagging already. "The contact made it sound that way. But he might have been selling a lie to gain a first recruit."

Ruben's eyes narrowed. How many of these discussions had he had as Ming's *consiglieri* over the years, advising her from behind the Martian throne? The first rule you learned in that role is to never take anything at face value, especially when it concerned Tony Taulke.

"Maybe it was Tony himself," he suggested, remembering his recent late-night conversation with Taulke. Nothing was beyond SynCorp's CEO. "Testing loyalty. Seeing if he could suck you into a fake scheme, then out you as a traitor."

Ming's slanted half smile appeared. "That would be something Tony Taulke would do, all right. But this felt real."

"How long ago did this occur?"

"Six weeks," Ming answered.

"Six weeks?" Ruben tried and failed to keep the concern from his voice. Six weeks ago Ming had been in and out of lucidity, a prisoner in her own broken body. A conspiracy against the head of the Syndicate Corporation sounded suspiciously like the product of a waning mind. "Why am I just now hearing about this?"

"Because until now, little brother, you didn't need to know."

Her answer infuriated him. "Goddammit, Ming! Had I known, we might have prevented the sabotage in the refinery! We could've saved those workers, we could've—"

"That," she said in her quiet, steely way that always undercut his anger, "*that* is what the Qinlao Faction needs now. And I'll show you the communiqué. It self-erased, but I made a recording of it. It should put to rest the concern you've been too Ruben to voice out loud, little brother. My warped mind didn't dream this up. The threat is very real."

Ruben took a deep breath. "Even if it's true," he said, "worst case scenario: the other three factions are moving against Taulke. What can we do about it?"

"Not we, little brother. *You.*" She was getting worked up. "Everything we've built—not just the Qinlao Faction, but all across this solar system —*everything* is put at risk by this ... this coup attempt. Clearly, some are willing to risk what they have in hopes of taking over the entire Company. I'm not one of them. *You*, Ruben. *You* have to save Tony Taulke. Find a way. *Preserve* what we've fought so hard to build."

The fire in Ming's eyes had faded. Her body sagged against one arm of the chair. Ruben reached out and touched her hand.

"What is that?" she said. Her voice was thinner. Frailer.

"What?" he asked quietly. The only sound above the China rain was the frantic chirping of a bird. It seemed lonely for companionship.

"*That.*"

"That's a white-eye," Ruben said.

"Oh," Ming said, nodding. "I haven't heard a..."

"White-eye."

"...a white-eye in forever. Isn't it pretty?"

Yes, Ruben thought. *It's beautiful.*

"What were we talking about?" she asked. "I asked you to come here, didn't I?"

"You did," he said. "We were just ... reminiscing. But I think it's time you get some rest, big sister."

"I think you're right," she said with a little of the old Ming's humor. She smiled pleasantly at him. "I need to rest."

16

EDITH BIRCH • VALHALLA STATION, CALLISTO

"Is it true?" the miner asked. She couldn't seem to keep still on the medical bed. *Parker*, her name patch read. "Some kind of plague or something?"

"Not so far," Krys said, swabbing the crook of the miner's elbow. She stroked Parker's skin once, twice to find a vein.

Edith watched Krystin Drake work. She couldn't shake the feeling something bad was heading their way. The impact shield now extending over the plastisteel dome kept out the ambient, coppery sunlight reflected from Valhalla Station's solar mirrors. Residents now relied on the silver illumination of manmade rods imported from Earth, even in the common areas like the marketplace. After so long beneath the warm, amber glow of Jupiter, the artificial, sterile lighting made Edith's eyes queasy. It was adding to the tension inside her, a nervousness shared among everyone in the infirmary.

"Can't you just scan my SCI or something?" Parker asked. "Isn't it supposed to make medical stuff easier?"

"The implants are still new," Krys said. "When there's fear of a new virus, we still rely on tried-and-true methods as a double check."

"Makes sense, I guess."

"You're gonna feel a little prick."

Parker relaxed a little. "Not the first time that's happened."

"Don't make me laugh," Krys said, a smile teasing the corners of her mouth. "I don't want this to hurt."

"That was his excuse, too." Parker winced as the needle went in.

Marshals with the Rabh Faction's double-bar-R on their right shoulders and the five-pointed star of the Marshals Service on their left stood guard around the infirmary, ensuring compliance with the required blood screenings. The pathogen alert had thrown Callistans into another frenzy close on the heels of the impact incident and shutting the testudo shield. Mobilizing the marshals and Regent Rabh's personal security force had restored a semblance of order in the colony. Everyone seemed to believe that safety could be assured as long as a uniform was present. The marshals observed as the infirmary's staff did its work. The badgers were seemingly more at ease than the staff they watched over. Edith found that ironic.

Krys popped the tube of blood into a scanner and peered closely at the data.

"Well?" Parker asked after a moment. "Am I Patient Zero?"

Krys tilted her head. "Only for anemia. You haven't been listening to your implant. You need iron supplements. Edith, can you seal up Ms. Parker's arm while I get the hypo?"

"Sure," Edith said, picking up the flesh sealant. "This might be a little chilly."

Parker shivered as Edith applied the foam sealant over the tiny hole in her arm. "Thanks," the miner said.

"Sure."

A *phish* of air against her shoulder made Parker jump.

"Sorry," said Krys, withdrawing the hypo. "But at least it's air this time instead of a needle."

"Copy that," Parker said.

"That should fix you up for a month or so. But you need to start regular iron supplements as part of your regular diet. Twenty milligrams a day. Come back and see us at the end of the production quarter."

"Okay." Parker rubbed her shoulder. "Can I go now?"

"Yep," Krys said. "Thanks for coming in."

The miner grunted. "Like I had a choice." She nodded at the nearest marshal and slipped off the table and past the line of others waiting for blood screenings. "Thanks," she said as an afterthought.

"Next!" Krys called.

"We haven't found a single thing," Edith said. "No sign of any bug. What set off the alarm in the first place?"

A man with a few days' growth of beard took Parker's place on the bed. He looked tired and pale. He looked worried.

"Who knows?" Krys said. "But this is protocol. So we follow it. What was that you were saying before about being more important than the farmers here?"

"*You* said that," Edith said. "But I get your point."

Her sceye flashed. It was Luther. A fist closed around the top of her spine. The old response. Pavlov's dog salivated when a bell rang. Her back clenched when Luther called.

"It's Luther," she said. "I haven't talked to him since this whole thing started. Can I take a break?"

Krys nodded, already assessing the miner on the table. "Just leave the sealant. I'll cover for a bit."

"Thanks."

Edith retreated to a corner of the infirmary. There was no real privacy. The room was packed with patients and personnel. A marshal watched her closely, then returned his attention to the room.

"Hi, Luther," Edith said, working to present a warm smile on her tired face. But she wanted the exhaustion to show too. Exhaustion was her excuse. "I'm so glad to see you're all right."

"Where the hell have you been? I've been home for hours!"

Her expression faltered. "Home? I thought—"

"The Company released us after the shuttle hit," Luther said. His face, puffy from lack of sleep, was still shaded by the grime of work. "With the ring compromised, they're having to figure out a workaround for the schedule. So I'm taking the day off. You haven't answered my question."

"I'm at work," she answered. "There were a lot of—"

"Work?" he said. "Why does the infirmary need an accountant? You counting pill bottles again?"

"No. They kind of—well, pressed me into service to help with the wounded."

"Uh-huh," Luther said, his tone that of a detective judging a suspect's story.

"You should be here, Luther." Edith injected as much concern into her voice as she could fake. "They think the pilot was carrying some virus or something. They're screening everyone in case there's danger of an outbreak."

"Fuck that," he said. "I feel fine. It's a day off. I'm not gonna spend it in a line."

Across the room, a commotion drew her attention. The miner with the scruff on his face was refusing Krys's attempts to take his blood. Dr. Estevez was already intervening.

"But, Luther, if you don't come in..." She glanced at a nearby marshal. Whispering, she said, "The marshals are rounding up everyone who might've been—"

"Fuck the badgers." Luther liked to bluster about the marshals, about the money-bitch Adriana Rabh, about anyone he figured thought they were better than him. He liked to do it in private, anyway. "A day off is a day off."

"Okay," she said. The miner on the bed was sweating. She could see it from here. Estevez was trying to calm him down.

"I want you home," Luther said. "Tell them you need to go home."

"I—"

"You're only a volunteer," Luther said. "No one will give a shit."

"I..." Edith pulled her eyes from the scene across the infirmary so she could think. Whispering again, she said, "If I leave, the marshals will get suspicious." Invoking Luther's fear of the marshals was an old strategy.

"Maybe." Luther grimaced, debate playing across his features. "Fucking badgers."

"I'll get home as soon as I can, okay? I promise." Edith pulled her lips into a tired smile again. "I just want to help out." Then, for good measure: "And I don't want to get you in trouble, love."

"You could help me out by having dinner done when it's supposed to be," he said, though his voice had lost most of its fire. "Fuck it. I'm going out. And you better be home when I get back."

Edith nodded. Did the relief show on her face? A little more time on furlough. A little more time feeling relevant. She'd never complain about so-far-unnecessary health alerts again.

"Okay. And I'll make some of that—"

Luther broke the connection.

"I heard it's everywhere!" the man on the table yelled.

The marshals stood up a little straighter. Recalling the fight earlier with the miner Brandt, Edith crossed the room. The man's voice became covert, like it was hiding a secret.

"It's the Soldiers of the Solar Revolution," he said. "They're behind it. They're gonna kill us all!"

"So far we've discovered nothing, sir," Estevez was saying. "The alert was merely a precaution. And I don't know anything about any soldiers."

"They're behind it!" the miner exclaimed. His eyes were wild, his color blanched. "The virus!"

"If you'll just let us test your blood, we can have you up and out of here in a few minutes," Krys said. She nodded to Edith at the foot of the bed. Krys wanted her to get ready to hold the man's feet. "Conspiracy theories won't help anyone, okay?"

"I don't want you to stick me," he said, trying to rise off the bed. "And it's no theory!"

Two of the marshals began to move toward them.

"Sir, you can't leave yet," Estevez said, his hand on the man's chest. "We have to examine you."

"Go to hell! I..."

Phish.

The man looked at Krys as she withdrew the hypo from his neck.

"What the hell was that?"

"Consider it a cocktail," Krys said as the man began to lie back. "Free of charge."

"You bitch, I'll—"

"Why don't you tone it down," said one of the marshals, a big man with a broad chest and a narrow waist. His smile was reassuring, his hand resting lightly on his sidearm. "Don't abuse the medical staff, buddy. They're just trying to help."

But the man, sedated, had already closed his eyes. His fingers wiggled, and then he was quiet.

"I think I can handle this now, Krys," Estevez said. "Thanks, Marshal."

The big man nodded and stepped away, one eye still on the miner.

"Sure you don't want me to deal with it?" Krys asked.

"There's something wrong with him," Estevez said. "Just look at his coloring. More likely radiation exposure than some killer alien bacteria. I've got him."

"Right," Krys said. "Next!"

Edith followed her to the empty bed where Estevez had been seeing patients.

"That's the second one in less than twenty-four hours," Krys said. "Panicking, I mean. I thought pioneers, especially this far out, were supposed to be tough."

"Everyone fears something," Edith said. "Like being one crack away from death by vacuum."

"I guess. We do tend to take things for granted around here. Hey! I said, next!"

An older man dressed in a long coat and holding an old-fashioned hat in his hand approached. He had a grizzled look like the miner they'd just put under, though his unshaven face was gray, not brown. A salt-and-pepper jawline. There was a smaller, younger woman behind him, though she didn't seem to be in line. Her face looked like it'd been sculpted from sarcasm. She held up her hands.

"Doc already got me. All clean."

Nodding, Krys gestured to the man. "Up here, please. You don't look like a miner."

"Not anymore," he said. He shared a look with the short woman standing apart from them. "Private joke."

"Okay," Krys said. "Edith, hand me a sticker."

Edith had to dig through the nearby cabinet to find the blood-draw kit. They'd need more of those in the next supply run.

"In fact," Krys said while she waited, "you look like you crawled out of a twentieth-century paperback."

"Thanks." The man peered at her shrewdly. "I work hard on my image."

"I wouldn't have guessed," Krys said wryly.

The woman leaning against the wall laughed out loud.

"Do all the women in this colony come fully equipped with smartass?" the patient asked. He looked to Edith like he could reach out and touch sixty years old. And those years had been hard won.

"Yes," Krys answered, taking the kit from Edith. "I need your name."

"Why?"

"Because this screening is Company ordered, and we have to know who we've screened," Krys answered.

"Whom."

"What?"

"The pronoun you're looking for," the man said, "is whom."

"Okay. To *whom* am I speaking, then?"

"Finn," he said. "Sawyer Finn."

"You were aboard the *Cassini's Promise*?"

"I was."

Nodding, Krys turned to Edith. "Check the passenger manifest." Turning back to her patient, she said, "If you're lying, we'll know. Patient ID by DNA is automatic with the test I'm gonna run."

Finn cocked his head. "What makes you think I'm lying?"

"You have that face," Krys said.

Before he could offer his opinion on that, Edith said, "I've got him here. Sawyer Finn. Migrant miner. Coming from Mars via Earth."

Krys looked him up and down. "Miner, huh?"

"I changed my mind," Finn said, gesturing around the room. "It's too dangerous."

"Uh-huh. Forearm, please."

He rolled up the coat sleeve of his left arm.

"What happened here?" Krys asked, running her forefinger lightly over his scars.

"Mining accident," he said shrewdly.

"I see you took your own smartass pill today," Krys said.

"I try. By all means, keep doing that," Finn said, glancing down as she stroked his arm. "It's the most action I've had in weeks."

Edith watched the red creep up the back of Krystin Drake's neck. She couldn't remember the last time she'd seen her friend embarrassed. Krys was usually the one doing the embarrassing.

"Just searching for a vein," Krys said, her color deepening. She began to tap the skin at the crook of Finn's elbow. Edith suppressed a smile.

"I can show you a thicker one than that."

Krys stared at the old man, who smiled wickedly, eyebrows dancing. Then, without caution, she pressed the needle into his arm.

"Ow!"

Dark blood began to flow through the narrow tube and into her reader. "Imagine that in the thicker one," Krys purred.

"I'll pass, thanks."

The woman leaning on the wall was enjoying every minute of their exchange. And, if she was honest with herself, so was Edith. A welcome moment of levity in a long, stressful day from hell.

"Well?" The woman on the wall sounded almost hopeful. "Is he dying?"

"Not today," Krys said, curiosity belying the good news. "He's all clean."

Edith pointed at the red light on Krys's reader. "What's that mean?"

"It means..." Krys began, then looked up at Finn. "It means you don't have an implant."

"I don't," he confirmed.

"That's not possible," Edith said. "Everyone has one. SCIs are mandatory."

"Not me. I'm a special case. Look me up."

Krys's gaze lingered a moment longer, then she nodded to Edith. "Seal him up while I check."

Edith moved to the bedside as Krys stepped away.

"This might be a little chilly," she said.

"At my age, everything's a little chilly," Finn replied. But he didn't flinch as the flesh seal layered over the hole in his arm. Tougher than he let on, she supposed. "Thank you," he said. The playfulness he'd shown toward Krys had been replaced with a softer expression, an open look of gratitude.

"You're welcome," Edith said, suddenly nervous under his gray eyes.

"Okay, you're all clear," Krys said. "I see in your record: 'SCI exempt.' I've never seen that for anyone before."

"Well, we can't all be as special as me," Finn said, rolling down the sleeve of his longcoat. "I'm free to go?"

"Sure," Krys said, still distracted by the anomaly of a patient with no implant.

"Thanks again," he said, with a glance at Edith. "Ready, Ms. Smith?"

The short woman levered herself off the wall. Finn muttered something Edith barely heard. She thought maybe she'd misheard, in fact. Now, who in God's name would name their ship the Hearse?

"Next!" Krys called.

17

KWAZI JABARI • ABOARD THE PAX CORPORATUM

Kwazi gazed out at the stars. He'd turned down the lights of the private observation lounge so he could see them better. Since he was the sole occupant of the lounge, no one had protested.

The stars seemed not to move, though his back-channel told him that wasn't really true. Human eyes, and the brain that processed what they saw, were hardwired to see things close up, not far away. Faraway tigers aren't a threat to the camp.

Standing here, feeling small and insignificant among the thousands of stars he could see with his naked eye, made him somehow feel real again. *Significant*, ironically. A substantial speck of dust dwarfed by the majesty of the universe.

Feeling inconsequential was, at least, feeling.

"This is your new mission," Helena Telemachus had told him, "holding the Company together. Help us keep another Facility Twelve from happening."

Try as he might, Kwazi couldn't keep her out of his head. Helena was a constant, like the starlight outside the thick plastisteel of the ship's viewport. Whenever he thought he'd found a moment away from missing Amy, from remembering her body on that cold, metal slab, from feeling like he would fold in on himself and disappear into the hole at the center of his being, Helena would take her place. Either in person or in thought, reminding Kwazi how important he was. What a hero he was. How vital he was to the Company.

That explained, he supposed, why Tony Taulke had dispatched them on his personal starship to the Jovian system. The *Pax Corporatum*, the largest civilian vessel in the solar system, the soaring symbol of Taulke's power as CEO of SynCorp. When the *Corporatum* sailed to a planet, whether bearing Tony Taulke or not, the message was loud and clear.

SynCorp is watching. SynCorp is here.

"When we get to Callisto, I need you engaged, Kwazi," Telemachus had said once they'd settled aboard. "The cancer of sabotage is metastasizing in the corporate body. I don't mean to minimize your loss, but—"

"—sometimes ripping off the bandage is best," Kwazi explained to the stars.

Reluctantly, he closed his eyes. Orange speckles, tiny suns, twinkled on the canvas of his eyelids. The starship's engines massaged the soles of his feet through the deck. He pretended it was the harmony of the cosmos reaching to touch him through the hull of the ship. It was a mental exercise Milani had taught him. A way of centering himself by connecting to the world around him. A speck linked to the universe through the dark ether between the stars. Connection through nothingness.

Meaning from meaninglessness.

Opening his eyes, Kwazi stared at the middle star in Orion's Belt, the brightest point of light he could see. He squinted, trying to focus harder to make it brighter. He concentrated on the slight tremor in the deck. He imagined more than felt it traveling through his bones to his fingertips. He imagined the softness of Amy's fingertips touching his. One of the accidental connections that happens among miners working in close quarters.

Innocent and pure. Electrifying.

"Can I join you?"

The voice, intruding again. Helena, reasserting control.

"Not now," he whispered, holding onto the stars with his eyes. "Please, not now."

"Kwazi?"

Amy's soft fingertips withdrew.

Kwazi had had enough. Enough of Helena's lectures about moving on and his duty to the Company. Enough of Helena telling him how he should feel, what he should do. He turned quickly to confront her, once and for all.

Milani Stuart stepped back, surprise on her face. Her hand, extended in concern, withdrew.

"Dr. Stuart?"

"I'm sorry," she said. "I didn't mean to disturb you. I—I couldn't sleep. I didn't think there'd be anyone up here, honestly."

His anger liquefied, draining quickly out of him. When he allowed himself to feel, Milani Stuart was the one bright spot in his life now. A confidant, a nurse, a friend, a counselor. The antidote to Helena's subtle, constant influence.

At first, Kwazi had resisted talking to Stuart about losing Amy and the others. Helena insisted. Kwazi considered it the one right thing she'd done for him. He was far from better. Better was a faraway planet circling one of the stars outside the window. But Milani Stuart and her kindness, her patient willingness to sit in silence with him—to be alone together with him—had allowed him to gently, painfully begin to process his loss. Silence had become tears, and tears had become words. About Amy and his feeling guilty for surviving. Words had only recently become the first new skin of healing.

"I'm sorry, Dr. Stuart. I thought ... I thought I was the only one here."

"I can leave if you like," she said, her voice tentative but warm. "This ship is so big ... I'll find another—"

Kwazi reached out and took her hand before she could turn away. "No, please," he said. "Please stay."

Milani hesitated, holding his hand for a moment and allowing hers to be held.

"All right. Do you need a new prescription? If you're still having trouble sleeping—"

"No. I just wanted to ... enjoy the calm."

She smiled kindly. Her smile reflected his own, he realized. It felt odd and out of place on him. He squeezed her hand once, then let it go and returned to the window to center himself again.

"It's funny," Milani said, drawing near him. "I was practically raised in space, but I never get tired of losing myself in the view. My parents were early settlers on Mars. My father was an ice-miner. My mother was a botanist."

"Your father was a miner?" Kwazi said.

"Yes."

"You never told me that before."

She shrugged. "It never came up."

He let himself feel the power of the ship's engines in his feet again. *The resonance of the universe*, he told himself. But no, that moment had passed. It was just the engines thrumming in the deck.

"Besides," he said, "therapists aren't supposed to reveal themselves, right?"

Milani grunted. "Don't call me that," she said playfully. "I'm not licensed by the Company for therapy."

Kwazi focused on the brightest star he could see, a different one from before, one of the middle stars of Taurus the Bull. "Maybe not officially," he said, "but that's how I see you." Then, turning to her: "And as a friend."

"That makes it official," she said.

"What do you mean?"

"It's unethical for therapists to counsel friends." She offered him a playful expression. "So I can't be a counselor, see?"

"I see," he said.

She cleared her throat. "I was kidding, Kwazi."

"I know."

Milani looked up at him, her smile returning. "I'm glad you see me that way. As a friend."

He nodded, as if agreeing on the existence of a universal constant. They stared into space, appreciating a view so full of stars there seemed more points of light than darkness between.

"What about your parents?" she asked. "You've never spoken of them, either."

"My mother was a cultural anthropologist," Kwazi said. "She's the one who named me."

"You're Kenyan, yes?"

"Yes, on my father's side," he answered. His earliest memory of pulling water from a well on Earth resurfaced. Kwazi could hear his mother calling his name. "My mother was English. My father fled Kenya during the Drought Wars. He finally stopped running in Ghana, where my mother was part of a university expedition. He was injured, and she became his nurse. Then I came along, and they got married."

His speech accelerated as he spoke. It was the most he'd said outside his informal counseling sessions with Milani since...

Speaking of his mother made him realize how much he missed her.

"I've read about that time on Earth," Milani said. "Populations moving in herds from flooded coastlines. Constant conflict. Borders closing."

Kwazi said nothing.

"But we survived," Milani said. "Thank goodness for the Company."

"Yes. Thank goodness for the Company," he echoed.

"Have you spoken with her lately?" Milani asked.

"Who?"

"Your mother," she said. "You sound like you miss her. I try to see my parents on Mars at least once a week. But now—I guess I should call them, actually."

"I used to talk to her all the time." His voice sounded distant even to him, like he was thinking about something other than what he was saying. "But ... it's been a while."

"I'll bet Helena the All Powerful could arrange it. Maybe talking with her would—"

"She died when I was eight," Kwazi said.

The silence of the dim lounge swelled around them. Had the Bull moved at all? Kwazi thought his focus star had, but it was so far away and hard to tell.

"I'm sorry, Kwazi," Milani said. "I didn't mean to bring up a painful subject."

He nodded an acknowledgment. "I know. My father took it pretty hard. Disconnected from everything. My grandfather raised me until I hopped a shuttle off-planet." A sudden restlessness came over him. He'd been standing so still for so long. "I think I'll take a walk."

Milani nodded. He saw it reflected in the ship's window. "I'm sorry if I—"

"No, it's not you, Milani," he said turning to face her. Was that the first time he'd called her by her first name? Placing one hand on her shoulder, Kwazi said, "I enjoyed talking with you. I always enjoy talking with you."

Her faint smile returned. "Do you want me to come with you?"

Kwazi shook his head, but it was a half gesture. He didn't want her to think he was angry with her.

"I'm enjoying the alone time," he said. "I seem to get so little of it now."

"I understand," she said. "Now—when you need it most."

"Yes."

"All right, then. See you tomorrow?"

"Sure."

———

"You're not allowed in this section."

Two armed guards stood in the doorway connecting the mid and aft sections of the *Corporatum*. Kwazi's onboard walkabout had taken him toward Engineering, where he hoped being closer to the starship's engines would help calm him again. A corner near the converters turning fusion power into thrust, maybe, where he could sit down, maybe lean against the ship's hull. Get a poor man's massage.

"Did you hear me?" the guard asked. His partner laid a loose hand on his sidearm.

"I did," Kwazi said. He really wanted to sit next to those converters.

"Hey—you're the guy," the first guard said. He elbowed the partner. "You're the hero."

Inside, Kwazi winced. He tried to keep it off his face. He drew up, trying to be what they wanted him to be.

"I was just one guy," he said, quoting a line from one of Helena's interview scripts. Then another. "I was one of the lucky ones."

His skin grew hot when he said it. Did he really need the alone time this badly?

"You're that guy?" asked the partner. His hand came off the weapon, extended forward. Kwazi took it, an involuntary response. "I heard you were on board, but ... wow, my kid's gonna be psyched. Can I get a snap?"

Kwazi's cheek trembled. "Sure."

The guard sidled up next to him, put his arm around him. "Snap it, Matt." The other guard, the one who'd stopped Kwazi, stared straight at them and blinked.

"Done," he said, "and sent to you. Now, do me."

The guards traded positions. Kwazi felt like a prop in a two-man show. The first guard repeated the process.

"So psyched," the one not named Matt said.

Kwazi offered a pale smile. "Is it okay if I—"

"Oh, sure, sure," Matt the guard said, opening the door. "Just don't touch anything, yeah?"

"Wait, are you sure we should—"

"Hey, this guy? He's the most famous man in the Company, next to Tony Two-point-oh. And he's a hero."

Not-Matt still seemed dubious, but shrugged.

"Thanks," Kwazi said, passing between them. He touched the panel on the other side.

"Thank *you*," Matt said. "It's men like you who—"

The door slid shut.

Kwazi walked. The *Pax Corporatum* seemed endless, and he started to wonder if he was walking in circles. The movement, at least, was doing him good. The hull droned with the engines, and while it wasn't magical like earlier, it was something he could focus on.

ENGINEERING
MAIN CONVERTERS
AUTHORIZED PERSONNEL ONLY

Finally. He touched the door controls, half-expecting rejection. The doors separated.

Maybe he'd get his poor man's massage after all.

As soon as the door closed behind him, he saw the feet. They extended beyond a console. Kwazi moved into the control room to find three people, the faction's corporate logo emblazoned in black upon their blue jumpsuits. Taulke personnel but not ship's complement. All three—two men and a woman—looked alive but ... out of it. They lay on the floor, their bodies slack, their eyes staring. Gravity hung open their mouths.

They looked drugged.

"Hey," Kwazi said, not sure he wanted any of them to answer. The last thing he'd wanted to find was more people to deal with. This was his spot. He'd claimed it already. "*Hey.*"

One of the men dragged his gaze to Kwazi. "Don't," he said. His nametag read *Abrams*. "It's just ending for me. We're taking it in shifts." Something about that was funny to him because he laughed.

"You guys need to go," Kwazi said. He was tired of being patient. He had only a few hours left before he became Helena's puppet again. "I need some alone time."

"No, you need to join us," Abrams said. "We're all having alone time."

Kwazi knelt next to them. Their eyes were dilated. "You're on drugs," he said.

Abrams shook his head. "Not drugs, friend." His awareness seemed to stir, and he stared at Kwazi hard. "Hey, you're *him*. You're the hero, man."

You mean the Hollow Man.

"Yeah, that's me. I'm the hero," he said. Whatever it took to get them to vacate. Or wait, what the hell—he could just find another spot, right?

"If anyone deserves a little nirvana, it's you, man." Abrams reached out, but Kwazi withdrew.

"I don't do drugs," he said. When you worked the mines of Mars, drugs could get you and your whole crew-family killed.

No danger of that now.

Fuck off.

"No, not drugs," Abrams said. "Better than drugs. No physical nothing. It's all in your head, man. It's all in your head."

The woman next to Abrams made a sound like a baby. Her hand flexed.

"You've never felt better in your whole life," Abrams said. "Know why?"

Kwazi stared as the woman relaxed into her personal heaven.

"No. Why?"

"Because you can't feel anything out here at all." Abrams motioned lazily at the room, at the world around them, then thumbed his chest. "And in here? It's whatever you want to feel, man. Whatever you want to feel."

Turning his eyes to Abrams, Kwazi said, "Tell me more."

18

STACKS FISCHER • APPROACHING THE ASTEROID BELT

Daisy was beginning to smell. Or maybe it was me.

Two days in the tight quarters of the Hearse, and even the best of friends would be grating on one another. That meant Daisy and I were ready to kill each other. And if anyone was an expert on how to do that, it was Daisy and I.

"I guess you knew the Bosswoman back in the day," Daisy said. She seemed to feel the need to fill up the quiet. Me? I'd rather be reading a book. I'd just woken up to take the duty. In theory, she'd be asleep soon. I'd stretched my social skills and made nice during our little bug-in-a-rug surveillance operation. No need to go and undo all that effort now, I guess.

"Yeah," I said. "Tony loaned me out to her for a job once. It didn't go well."

"Ah." She shifted a little, stretching. "My legs are starting to cramp."

Unlike bigger ships, the Hearse didn't have much in the way of making long trips pleasant. It was meant for hopping back and forth from the Earth to the Moon, not days-long journeys like this one. Drugs helped counter that, but you were stuck in your seat for long periods.

"Hey, don't feel the need to keep me company. You're probably tired. Pop a relaxer, take a nap."

We'd shadowed the gashauler *Starwind* after its departure from Callisto.

I figure a twelve-year-old who likes fart humor named her. An automated juice tanker full of deuterium and helium-3, the *Starwind* tracked a predetermined course along the Company's Frater Lanes, headed for the dockyards over the Moon. From there its cargo would head to wherever there was a fusion reactor that needed gassing up.

"Not really," Daisy said. "I'm wide awake."

Great.

I stared through the clear canopy of the Hearse, taking in the stars. It helped me feel less cramped. I loved my ship, but I loved it more when it was just me and her. Three's a crowd.

"You ever worry about dying, Fischer?"

I turned to her and saw she was looking up at space too. Staring into that void has a way of making you feel small and large at the same time. Small because, well, compared to that you *are*. Large because, at the same time, it can make you feel like a part of Mother Universe.

"What's to worry?" I said. "When Mother Universe decides to take me into her arms, I doubt I'll have much to say about it." Daisy looked at me then, and I saw a seriousness in her eyes. I'd been a little flippant with my answer, so I tried to give her a better one. Her expression had earned it. "I focus on the job. Which usually means worrying about someone else dying."

It's not that I like taking a life. Sometimes it's just a necessary thing. It's what I get paid to do, and business is business. But no one I ever killed didn't deserve it for one reason or another. That's a lie, actually. I've made a few mistakes. I live with those every day. I wouldn't say I have a conscience, mind you. That'd be a liability. But I do have a code. I don't kill women. I don't kill children. Not after—

"Proximity alert."

The Hearse's feminine voice brought us both back to reality. There was a new blip on the LiDAR screen. I'd set the ship's navigation sensors to long range to pick up anything unusual while it was still plenty far out. A bunch of new blips were on the screen now. I tightened the sensors to focus on the immediate area of the *Starwind*. Most of the blips disappeared.

"We're on the edge of the Belt," Daisy said.

"Thanks for that. I thought it might be hail or something."

She ignored me and reviewed the navigation plot. Frater Lane flight paths were auto-fed into ship navigation by the subspace satellite network connecting the breadth and depth of the SynCorp empire. Using those faster-than-light frequencies, it was easy to account in real time for the movement of foreign bodies like asteroids. Daisy was making sure the sensors were talking nice-nice to the nav computer. She needn't have bothered. The Hearse always takes care of me.

We knew we were in the Asteroid Belt because the nav computer told us we were. Those blips on the LiDAR screen, for instance. The myth of the Belt is that asteroids are flying this way and that like bugs in a jungle—if you're not careful, you'll get squashed. The reality is there's lots of space in space. Asteroids are easily maneuvered around.

"Sure you don't want to catch some shut-eye? Me and the Hearse, we got this."

I tried not to sound too anxious for it. I was looking forward to diving into a Dashiell Hammett novel. Maybe *The Thin Man* or *The Maltese Falcon*. I was bored. The appearance of a few big space rocks isn't all it's cracked up to be.

See what I did there?

"What's that?" Daisy said.

Well, I guess that was a no. I followed her finger. We were close enough to have visual on the *Starwind*.

"In the business, we call that an asteroid."

"I don't think so."

"No, I'm sure that's what we call it in the business."

"Fischer, shut up and *look*."

I did. For some reason my eyes always work better when my mouth is closed.

I saw what Daisy saw. One of the asteroids seemed to be moving toward the *Starwind*. That wasn't what was odd. It's not like all the billions of asteroids in the Belt swirl around in a circle like you see in the vids. The hauler's nav system should pick up on it and adjust the course within the defined boundaries of the Frater Lanes as a matter of routine. But the tanker wasn't doing that. It proceeded upon its predetermined course.

Meanwhile, the asteroid seemed to be accelerating.

"There's another one," Daisy said.

"I see it. Make that two more."

"Huh," she said.

Huh is right. Those weren't asteroids.

"Canopy: opaque," I said. "Engage stealth mode, darling."

"What?" Daisy said.

"I wasn't talking to you."

The starfield above us dimmed. I'd engaged the Hearse's darkglass. We could still see out, though we relied more now on our sensors. But the canopy above us was now as black to external observers as the rest of the Hearse. The engines cut off, and Newton's First Law became our fuel.

"Now that's fucking genius," Daisy said. There was an air of wonder in her voice. You don't much hear that from an assassin. We're rarely surprised.

"Thanks," I said. "The Hearse—"

"No, idiot. Look at *that*."

The rock-ships had hooked up to the hauler. They were siphoning gas off without the *Starwind* ever slowing down. But they weren't getting much. I remembered what Tony said, that the amount of gas taken was so slight, only a paranoid bean counter would notice it. The first of the rock-ships had already detached and was moving off. Another was maneuvering to take its place. They were like mosquitos drawing blood from a body in motion.

Who *were* these pirates, anyway?

"Why go to all that trouble camouflaging tankers," Daisy mused.

I grunted. It really was an ingenious operation. Tony would've been impressed. Right after he had me execute the perps for stealing from him.

"Remember how they showed up," I said, nodding at the sensor screen. "They look just like asteroids. Maybe the pirates outfitted the hulls with real rock, or maybe it's just rock-shaped hull. In any case, unless you're looking at them, you wouldn't know they weren't asteroids."

"Where the hell is the fleet?"

That was a goddamned good question. Fleet Admiral Matthias Galatz was supposed to be out here tracking down these guys. You'd think he'd be staking out the Frater Lanes or tracking the *Starwind* like we were. He didn't have the reputation of a slacker. I had to wonder if he'd ever played pirate as a kid, though.

"Proximity alert."

The Hearse, warning us again. I glanced at the sensors, expecting to see an asteroid, real or fake, getting a little too close for comfort. If only we'd been so lucky.

"Uh-oh."

"Uh-oh?"

I indicated the display. On the edge of the screen, the faint shape of a ship's hull appeared, outlined by the pings from our sensors. It was moving fast. Toward us.

"Uh-oh," Daisy said.

"It's okay," I said, tapping a few controls. I made Newton work for his supper, and we glided on momentum. I didn't want our thrusters kicking in to correct our course and showing the new guy where we were. The Hearse was a blackhull, a stealth ship. The new guy's sensors should slide right over us and move on.

"Keep quiet," I whispered. "So they don't hear us."

Daisy gave me a look. The sensors had filled in more of the ship's outline. It was big. Frigate-sized big.

"I'm kidding," I said. "Sound doesn't travel in—"

"Stealth ship, heave to and prepare to be tractored," said a voice over comms. Somehow they'd hacked and slaved our system. That was some impressive tech. The Hearse had the best anti-hack software around. *"Any attempt to escape, and we'll fire."*

"I thought this was a stealth ship," Daisy said.

"It is."

And that truth was a trifle disconcerting. Either the vessel closing on us had new tech that could sniff out blackhulls, or someone had told the pirates we were coming. I laid equal money on both possibilities. Make that sixty-forty, we were ratted out.

I started working my girl's controls.

"What are you doing?"

"I don't like being told what to do," I said.

"You're gonna run? Fischer, that's nuts! Power down!"

"What'd I just say?"

I fired up the engines. Newton threw up his hands and said, Whatever, man.

"*Weapons lock.*"

I know it was just my ears assigning my own human fear to the warning, but the Hearse seemed to agree with Daisy. Running was a bad idea.

Daisy reached forward to the nav controls. She stopped. With my right hand, I was fast-plotting an evasive course. With my left, I held my stunner to her temple.

"Hands off," I said.

She obeyed.

"You should've taken those relaxers," I said. "This is gonna hurt." To my reluctant ship, I said, "Engage engines at full—"

Tracer fire arced over the canopy. The angry red slugs zipped past, several hundred suggestions that I really should learn to listen to the females in my life. Those were military-grade tracers shot from a respectable distance. Seriously, who were these so-called pirates?

"*This is your last warning,*" my comms said. "*Heave to or be destroyed.*"

The order echoed in the small cabin. I was ready to make a run for it anyway. My mouth hovered over the command to punch it. I had no weapons to fight back. The Hearse was made for quick-hauling and doing it quietly, not fighting. And even if I'd had weapons...

"Fischer, this is our chance," Daisy said. "This is what we came here for, right?"

She had a point. We'd followed the *Starwind* to find the pirates. Looks like we'd found them.

I powered down the engines. The Hearse shuddered. They'd grabbed her in a sensitive spot.

"This isn't how this was supposed to go," Daisy said, relaxing. She sounded more annoyed than intimidated. I had to remind myself that, despite her small frame, she was a killer like me. And, like me, she was probably already cooking up a plan to get out of this.

"Look at it this way," I said, sitting back while the vessel hauled us aboard. "We'll get a chance to stretch our legs."

I switched off the canopy's shading as the underside of our captor appeared overhead. Two bay doors were opening. The lines of the ship were hard and angular, ugly. Like the Hearse, it was built for stealth, not military parades. It was somewhere between a corvette and a frigate, size-wise, though I'd never seen this particular ship's profile before. That meant it was new, probably developed off-grid.

These "pirates" were looking more and more organized. New ship design. Top-of-the-line military weaponry and stealth. Tony had a bigger problem on his hands than he knew.

The Hearse settled on the hangar deck. The pull of generated gravity made my blood feel heavy. The older you get, the longer it takes to get used to that.

One at a time, Daisy and I exited the Hearse. We were both wobbly. I wondered if her leg cramps were better or worse under the burden of one-g.

Six armed soldiers approached. Their uniforms were Kelly green with black lines. I'd never seen their like before. Definitely military. Not an eyepatch or peg leg on the lot. They carried ranks on their shoulders like fleet guys. Over the right breast of the uniforms was a symbol: the letter S formed the right half, with its mirror image on the left. The S and its back-ward self were connected at the bottom like two serpents joined at the tail. SS?

Nazis?

Not Nazis. Couldn't be Nazis. I have a standing rule never to be taken prisoner by a cliché.

The guy with the most stripes on his shoulder came forward. "You are now prisoners of the Soldiers of the Solar Revolution. Hand over any and all weapons." His eyes hardened. "*Now.*"

Officer Friendly certainly had the manners of a Nazi.

Daisy stepped forward, handing over her stunner.

"I'm here as a formal representative of Adriana Rabh, head of the Rabh Faction and Regent of Jupiter," she said to the officer. I thought that was nice of her to step up, let them think she was in charge. Good tactical thinking on her part. "Regent Rabh wishes to open formal negotiations with the Dutchman."

Wait, what?

My smile evaporated as Daisy moved to the officer's side and turned to look at me.

"He's holding three weapons," she said. "A stunner, a .38 revolver, and a spring blade under his right wrist. Be sure you get all three."

I took half a heartbeat to catch up.

"You fucking..."

One of the grunts moved forward, hands out. The other grunts pointed their weapons at me. Daisy extended her hand to Officer Friendly, who shook it warily.

"This is how they knew how to track us," I said, handing over my stunner. I knelt and pulled the .38 from my ankle holster. Last came the knife. "They waited till we were in the Belt and then—"

"You're getting old, Fischer," Daisy said. "You should have smelled this coming a solar system away."

"Fuck you," I said. I'd let my affection for Adriana Rabh dull my instincts. Or maybe Daisy was right, and my dullness came from age. Either way, she was free and I wasn't. Well, I guess that answers the question of whose side Adriana Rabh is on. Not Tony Taulke's.

Daisy smiled in victory. "Hate to break it to you, but I'm not the one bent over here."

Yep, she was right about that too.

Fuck me.

19

RUBEN QINLAO • LANDER'S REACH, MARS

"Our first order of business it to express condolences to Ruben Qinlao," Tony Taulke stated formally. "Ruben, your sister Ming and I didn't always agree. In fact, we often disagreed."

Politic laughter passed around the virtual meeting table.

"But I respected her immensely." Tony paused, then: "And I can say, honestly, there would have been no Syndicate Corporation without her leadership."

"That's stating it mildly," Gregor Erkennen muttered.

Tony offered Erkennen's holo-image a tight smile.

"Thank you, Tony," Ruben said. He still felt a little outside himself. Ming's passing, while expected, had nevertheless opened a hole inside him. "I know she held you in ... similar regard."

Elise Kisaan, the striking and deadly Regent of Earth, cleared her throat. She seemed bored, and the meeting had hardly begun.

"One of the few positive parts of this meeting," Tony continued, "is to welcome you to the council as the Regent of Mars. When I spoke with Ming before her death, she was overjoyed that you would succeed her."

"I'm humbled by her faith in me," Ruben said. "And yours."

"I don't wish to minimize Ruben's loss," Elise Kisaan said, "but can we take up new business? Specifically, just what the hell is happening in the system?"

Ruben regarded her quietly. He'd decided before the meeting that he'd rather watch and listen than speak—follow the old wisdom of having two ears and two eyes, but only one mouth. Kisaan, he knew, was the canniest of all the faction leaders, next to Tony. She'd eliminated famine on Earth in the last quarter century, turning the planet into a massive agricultural supply center for the Company. She'd segmented its land masses into longitudinal belts of farming communities offering localized cultivation and intersystem distribution nodes not unlike the mining-refinery hybrid model the Qinlaos had implemented on Mars—refinement paired with resource gathering at the source, cutting costs and maximizing efficiency. After Kisaan had won Earth's hearts and minds by ensuring its dominant species stayed atop the food chain in the wake of global climate catastrophe, she'd gone on to achieve the same kind of dependent respect from the rest of the system.

Controlling the food supply made her dangerous, the most powerful regent in the system. Add to that Kisaan's history, and she seemed the most likely suspect behind the conspiracy Ming had warned Ruben about.

"Agreed," Adriana Rabh chimed in. Then, as an afterthought, "Welcome, Ruben."

"All right, then," Tony said. He seemed calmer than Ruben would have expected, given all that was happening. Tony wasn't known for his even temper. "Let's start with you, Adriana. Update us."

"We're still repairing the orbital ring," Rabh said. "There was a report the shuttle pilot might have picked up some kind of alien virus that would threaten the colony. Medical screenings of everyone on or off Callisto in the last week revealed nothing, however. Between the incident and the rumor, the station nearly rioted with panic."

"Sounds like textbook Resistance work," Kisaan said. "Throwing shoes into the works, then spreading stories to destabilize us."

"They'll do anything to disrupt the Company," Erkennen agreed.

"Maybe," Tony said. Ruben heard something in his voice that wasn't quite disbelief. Musing, maybe. "It's been a long time since Graves's Rebellion."

"My father said that Graves died with his rebellion," Erkennen said.

Kisaan presented a wicked smile. "Maybe Graves isn't in his grave after all."

"Maybe," Tony said again.

"The C-4B."

"Gregor?" Tony prompted.

"It's the C-4B used to blow up the Martian refinery," Gregor Erkennen said. "Old-fashioned, military-grade explosives not manufactured in a quarter century." That, Gregor seemed to be saying in his typically obscure Russian fashion, should tell them everything they needed to know.

"And also the weapon of choice for the Resistance," Adriana Rabh said. "In the old days."

Tony looked thoughtful. "Maybe. First, the refinery on Mars. Then, the ring over Callisto. From one end of the system—of the Company—to the other."

"Not quite," Erkennen said, finger raised.

"That's true," Tony allowed. "Titan has remained untouched. As has Earth." When he said it, he turned his eyes on Kisaan.

"And let's hope it stays that way," she said, holding his gaze. She'd dropped the cleverness from her mood. "The Company can sustain a hit in manufacturing capacity. Even a short-term loss of Callisto's raw gases for fusion reactors since we have reserves on the Moon. But a drop in the food supply? Want a panic systemwide? Cut a few grain and fresh vegetable shipments to the outlying colonies."

"Mars has significant hydroponic capability," Ruben said, feeling a strange need to defend his planet. *When you defend Mars, you defend our faction*, Ming had told him once. Even dead, she continued to advise him.

"Mars grows what amounts to the parsley for the plate," Kisaan said. "Earth still supplies the meat and potatoes—and vegetables and fruits and spices and, beyond all that, luxuries—to the system." Her eye roamed over the projections of Adriana Rabh and Gregor Erkennen. "That goes for Callisto and Titan, too."

Kisaan had outlined just how dependent they were on her matter-of-factly, without malice, but with her familiar imperious self-importance. *Always watch your back around Elise Kisaan*, Ming said in his mind. *If you're not careful, you're likely to feel a knife in it.* Kisaan had risen to power on the blood of millions. In context, the Red Widow of Mars didn't seem so bad.

"Ruben," Tony said, waking him from his thoughts, "what's the word from Mars? We've been playing the headline on CorpNet for weeks. We need evidence. We need those responsible for the refinery bombing in custody."

"Before she ... passed ... Ming had our faction troops and the local marshals scouring Lander's Reach and beyond—the outer colonies, the extraction facilities. They still are, of course. But short of our initial findings —the precise, measured nature of the bombing, the use of C-4B explosives —there's nothing new to report."

"Nothing new to report?" Kisaan said, incredulous. "You've had weeks to round up whatever rebels are still on Mars. All the resources of the Qinlao Faction, and you don't have a single bomber in custody?"

"We don't call them Ghosts for nothing," Erkennen said.

"Regent Kisaan, as Chairman Taulke indicated, it has been a long time since Graves's Rebellion." Ruben presented his argument in a measured way, logically. He used formal titles to help him slow his speech, to give himself time to think before speaking. *One mouth.* "I fear we've all become complacent, assuming the Resistance was crushed once and for all. We have Qinlao operatives infiltrating the factories and refineries on Mars, insinuating themselves into work groups, getting to know workers person- ally. But trust takes time. If there are covert pockets of Resistance on Mars, we'll find them. In time."

"If? In time?" Elise Kisaan's venom lost none of its potency over the hundreds of thousands of kilometers separating them. "These sound like the excuses of a weak regent to me. Ming would never have—"

"Please don't do that," Ruben said before he could stop himself. *One mouth.* But now he was committed. "I bury my sister tomorrow. Please don't wield her name like a political weapon."

Kisaan's eyes widened, but her mouth closed.

See? Even she gets it, Ruben admonished himself.

"It was not my intention to dishonor your sister's memory," Kisaan allowed. It was a gracious, even gushing statement—for her. Turning to a fresh target, she continued, "And what are you doing, Tony, to counter this threat? Sending public relations reps to the outer planets? What is that accomplishing?"

The virtual call became still, save for the flickering of the 3D images of the five principals. Of all of them, only Elise Kisaan—secure on Earth as keeper of the Company's food supply—had ever dared challenge Tony Taulke, high in his aerie above the planet, in an open meeting. No, that wasn't quite true, Ruben corrected. In years past, when she still had her strength, Ming hadn't been shy either. But she was gone now. And Ruben ... well, Ruben was determined to be a different kind of leader. A wiser one who picked his battles prudently.

"Having Jabari here has been reassuring to Callistans," Adriana explained. "Their Viking ethos respects his sacrifice for the Company."

"Glad to hear it," Tony said. "And Fischer? I assume you know he's on Callisto by now."

Adriana raised her head. Ruben had the distinct impression she was looking down her nose at SynCorp's CEO.

"He *was* here, yes," she said. "Next time, I'd appreciate a heads-up when you send your personal enforcer to my regency."

"Now where would be the fun in that?" Tony shot back. "And what do you mean *was*?"

"He and one of my operatives are investigating the intercepts of our tankers," she said.

"You mean the pirates," Erkennen said.

Adriana sighed. "I hesitate to call them that. We have enough frayed nerves here already."

"But that's what we're talking about here," Tony said. Then, "I haven't heard from him in a while. Have you?"

"No," Adriana answered, "but is that unusual?"

"Not really, I suppose," he allowed. "Depends on the job."

"Can we get back to the problems at hand?" Kisaan said. "Rebels, pirates, and bombings, oh my! And you send your Helena Telemachus and a glassy-eyed worker bee to the far reaches of the system."

"Messaging is everything," Tony answered. "Control the message, control the masses: Politics 101. Meanwhile, we root out the problem through back channels."

"Which brings us back to the Resistance," Kisaan said.

"Maybe," Tony said again. "Maybe not."

"You keep saying that—maybe, maybe," Erkennen said. He was a scientist, an empirical thinker. Unknowns bothered him. They were variables that begged discovery. "What does that mean?"

"It means these attacks are not random," Tony said calmly. "They might seem random, but they appear designed to stretch our resources thin."

"What do you mean, Tony?" Ruben asked.

"An explosion on Mars," Tony said. "A damaged ring over Callisto." His voice was unusually patient. A lawyer's voice, carefully laying out evidence. "The pirates operating out of the Belt, siphoning reactor fuel in such small quantities, we were lucky to even notice. And now I'm hearing of a black market that hacks directly into the SCIs."

"The medical implants?" Ruben asked. "Hacks how?"

Gregor Erkennen shifted uncomfortably. "It is a sophisticated, self-replicating algorithm that adapts to patches as quickly as we distribute them." It was clear the Company's head of tech development didn't like admitting a weakness in his faction's latest miracle invention. "The worm emulates source code so closely, we're having a hard time stopping it. It mutates once it realizes it's been found. But once we crack its encryption—"

"That almost sounds like artificial-intelligence level sophistication," Elise Kisaan said.

"Well, you would know, wouldn't you?" Adriana Rabh had never liked Earth's regent. And she'd never trusted Kisaan, either.

"That was a long time ago," Kisaan said. "I've done nothing but support the Company since we established the Five Factions."

"People get bored," Adriana suggested.

The two women fenced over subspace with their eyes. Tony watched their exchange. Ruben watched Tony.

"How does it work?" Ruben asked finally.

"Users—hackheads—purchase the hack," Rabh explained. "Once installed, it slaves the SCI to produce a timed release of endorphins, a euphoric state enticed from the user's own pleasure centers in the brain. They're calling it Dreamscape."

"We could outlaw it," Ruben said. "Make its use illegal, have the marshals enforce—"

Gregor Erkennen grunted. "I'd rather have it out in the open until we find a fix. As long as it's legal, we can more readily study its effects."

"Which are significant," Tony said. "Under the influence of this Dreamscape, workers are useless. Productivity is zero. It's why we banned recreational drugs years ago."

"Only you can't ban a person's own brain chemistry," Rabh said.

"I am working on the hack," Erkennen offered, quick to defend his area of expertise. "Give me time—"

"See, that's the most precious commodity now, isn't it?" Tony said. "Everyone needs more time. Ruben needs time to infiltrate whoever blew up his refinery. Adriana needs time to repair the ring over Callisto. And you, Gregor, need time to counter this Dreamscape. Time, it seems, is more precious than platinum these days."

"Callisto was an accident," Kisaan insisted. "From time to time, the Resistance pops its head up like a gopher, conducts some sabotage, then disappears again. These kinds of problems are nothing new, Tony."

"The coordination of them, though," said Tony, staring hard at Kisaan's holo. "That's *very* new."

"You think they're coordinated?" Ruben asked.

"Well," Tony said, leaning forward and staring at each of them in turn, "I don't believe in coincidence. And they all share one thing in common."

"Which is?" prompted Erkennen.

"They all strike at our bottom line," Tony noted. "Refining capacity on Mars. Gas mining on Jupiter. And productivity itself, as more workers become addicted to Dreamscape."

"But the attacks are so small—" Adriana began.

"And so are the amounts of gases pulled out of those tankers in the Belt," Tony said. "So small, and yet over time..."

The five of them sat quietly, considering the implications. Erkennen, the scientist, was the first to solve the equation.

"They're trying to subvert the corporate economy," he said. "But at this rate, it would take many years to—"

"Would it?" Adriana Rabh asked. "Factor in citizen morale, Gregor. It's not just about a balance sheet. We can make those numbers look however we want. But, at the end of the day—"

"It's about the billions of workers who keep the economy moving," Ruben said. He turned to Elise Kisaan. "And Earth still has the most indentured workers of any colony in the system, working all those factory farms and traditional industrial centers."

"Paranoia," Kisaan said. "You see conspiracies in the shadows."

"A refinery here. A docking ring there," Tony said. "Seemingly small incidents in the grand scheme but with high public profiles, stretching us across the system to deal with them. And now, our workers indulge themselves in Dreamscape, which is more than our paid vacations and free pleasure palaces ever did for them. They're becoming addicted to their own endorphins."

Elise Kisaan jerked forward suddenly. In the 3D world of holograms, Ruben couldn't see what it was that had demanded her attention. When she began cursing, a sinking feeling spawned in his stomach.

"What is it, Elise?" Tony asked.

"The Midwestern Collective, North America," she answered, though her attention was on the problem. "Our monitors are reporting ... a blight? How is that even possible? From the moment a seed is planted, we monitor—"

"Are you a believer now, Elise?" Adriana asked.

In answer, the Regent of Earth killed her connection. The four remaining faction leaders sat looking at one another.

"Gregor," Tony said quietly. There was rage beneath the façade. Ruben had seen it before. Someone near at hand would bear the brunt of Tony's wrath later. "So far, you are the only faction unaffected by this ... effort. I suggest you increase security around your most sensitive tech projects."

"Of course," Erkennen said. "I'll attend to it immediately."

As his image disappeared, Adriana sighed.

"Hold it together, old lady," Tony said. "And strengthen the firewalls around our corporate accounts."

"Yes, Tony." For the first time since Ruben had known Adriana Rabh, the normally unflappable empress of finance sounded frightened. "I'll get right on it."

Her image too faded.

"That leaves just the two of us, Ruben."

"Actually," Ruben said, "we should talk."

"Yeah?"

"Yeah."

20

EDITH BIRCH • VALHALLA STATION, CALLISTO

Seventeen hundred.

Luther slept soundly.

He should after all that bourbon, Edith thought. She'd been liberal with it as she'd made his drinks that evening. She needed him docile before she left the bed and logged in.

The close quiet of night lay over the Community Dome. Luther's arm draped over her, his body spooning her from behind. She wondered how that intimacy would feel with a different man, a better man. Luther's embrace felt like captivity, shackling her to the bed. One of his thick hands cupped her left breast, an earlier attempt at foreplay by a drunkard. Edith's skin was too warm where their bodies touched. Luther's sweaty bulk had quickly absorbed the alcohol in his bloodstream, carrying it to his brain where it targeted his GABA-A receptors and worked with his own brain chemistry to sedate him into sleep. Volunteering in the infirmary had taught Edith a few things.

Seventeen twenty-two.

She'd lain here, in this position for almost half an hour. Once Luther's clumsy pawing had stopped, Edith had begun counting the seconds. It should be safe to move again soon. Sometimes it was hard to hold back rushing the count. To take her leave a little early.

Seventeen thirty-eight.

But hurrying risked waking Luther. So Edith was patient and ignored the sweat forming along the skin of her naked back and buttocks and legs. She ignored the sour breath pulsing at the back of her neck. She counted calmly, precisely, in a way that gave her the confidence of control.

Seventeen fifty.

She'd played along with the progressive stages of Luther's intoxication: from demanding Don Juan to slurring Lothario to fever-dreamed Rip Van Winkle. She'd acquiesced to his grunting, sloppy demand for sex, as always, while the alcohol did its work. And, as always, she'd checked out while he moved on top of her. When his brain had at last sunk beneath an ocher sea of bourbon, she'd turned away, drawing his arm around her and cuddling him close to her to hasten his sleep. When Luther had at last reached the Van Winkle stage, the countdown had begun.

Eighteen hundred.

Now was the most dangerous moment, the moment just before freedom. Edith could almost taste its sweetness. This was the time to be the most disciplined, to fight against grabbing that moment too quickly and too hard. The anticipation of being away from Luther could be just as intoxicating as the bourbon she'd plied him with.

She lifted his arm. Luther shifted, mumbling annoyance. Slowly, carefully, Edith slipped out of bed. She'd practiced the maneuver so many times, she was able to rise and replace her body with a pillow in one smooth motion. Luther blew out his opinion with a wet breath before settling back into amber dreams.

Edith pulled on a nightshirt, stepped lightly from the bedroom and pulled the door behind her to keep the computer's light from waking him. Drunk and disturbed could be far worse than sober and focused. But she left the door open a crack. She needed to be able to hear him.

Sitting down at the small desk, Edith sighed and accessed CorpNet via the computer terminal they shared. She logged in and was surprised when a new verification requirement popped up.

This must be what they were talking about today, she thought, remembering conversations she'd overheard in the marketplace. *Enhanced security*.

In the days since the shuttle crashed into the orbital ring, she'd seen marshals and Regent Rabh's private security personnel on practically every street corner inside the Community Dome. CorpNet's talking heads insisted the incident—like the refinery mishap on Mars—had been the work of the Resistance, stirring unease and whispered conversations among Callistans.

The Resistance—that fifth column of self-proclaimed freedom fighters doing their best to overthrow SynCorp and achieve self-rule for all mankind, or so they claimed. Edith had never been quite sure what all the fuss was about. The Company took care of everyone. Without SynCorp, the governments of Earth would have strangled humanity with the red tape of bureaucracy until the planet itself flogged them into extinction with hurricanes and dust storms and wildfires. It was SynCorp that had taken control, and mankind had survived. Edith supposed she could admire the principles the Resistance stood for, but she was perfectly happy to live the life SynCorp offered.

With one exception. She was determined to get away from Luther. But to make that happen—and to live safely beyond his reach—she needed money. The Company didn't like change. Oh, she could take her black eyes and bruised forearms to the Marshals Service, and they'd dutifully arrest Luther. But likely as not, they'd garnish his wages for bail and put him back in orbit over Jupiter, mining its gases. Edith knew that, of the two of them, she was less essential, less a part of the Company's bottom line. And that made her less valuable. SynCorp would enforce the letter of the law but without any real motivation to protect her. And then Luther would be out of jail, out the money she'd cost him from every future paycheck until his bail was paid, and pissed off.

Maybe the rebels aren't so crazy after all, Edith mused.

She answered the security question and logged into her data trader account. Using fake credentials, she routed the link to CorpNet through multiple IP hubs both on-world and off. Anyone trying to track her transactions would have a difficult time finding their source.

From the bedroom, Luther's snoring became animated. Edith's fingers froze over the keys. The only light in the small room came from the terminal. It shouldn't be visible through the crack in the doorway. She could hear the shuffling of covers and Luther mumbling. Then he calmed again, and the silence of their quarters broadened. He was still sleeping, if restless. Luther was a lummox when it came to online tech, but he had the devil's own luck finding her out if he suspected something. Even when there was nothing to find, like with his jealousy over Reyansh. She couldn't be too careful.

After forcing herself to count to thirty, she began working again. Three messages greeted her onscreen, all from someone she'd only ever known as Crow. She scanned them, determined what she could and couldn't provide in trade, then logged in to the black-market site linked from Crow's data requests. The promised amount of SynCorp Dollars for each à la carte data request was significant. She accessed Luther's work schedule on the terminal, located the necessary information, and filled four of Crow's five data requests.

Edith waited as the data transferred, when time always seemed to move slowest. This part of the process never failed to make her nervous. If she were going to get caught, this would be when. A Company worm would tag and backtrack her encrypted transaction. Marshals would pound on the door, demanding entry. And she'd be taken away—away from her life, away from Luther.

Would that be so bad after all? she wondered.

No, there was another way. Edith focused on that future. Another one or two transactions and she'd have enough SCDs to leave covertly, no questions asked. She'd planned it all out and run through the list of steps a hundred times, a thousand. She'd wait until Luther was on one of his extended shifts over Jupiter to make her move, near the end of the month when he'd work extra to earn overtime. She'd book passage on a ship returning to the inner planets and pay well enough for privacy, traveling under fake credentials bought from the same black marketeer who'd given her the fake log-in and routing protection algorithm. Since Luther inevitably took his overtime pay and hit the casino with his buddies, she'd be nearly a day out, a day closer to home, before he realized she was gone. With the rest of the SCDs Crow paid her, she'd purchase a new life as matron of a farming community on Earth. Matrons were revered by their workers—the good ones were, anyway—and Edith was determined to be one of the good ones.

To see green, growing fields again—and blue skies! To feel the rain on her face. To breathe air without the tint of machine oil beneath it.

Iowa. She'd always dreamed of living on a farm in Iowa. Now, with enough cash, she could.

Edith sent a silent thank-you prayer Crow's way. As if in answer, four individual payment receipts appeared onscreen. Edith's face lit up. She was suddenly aware of an emotion deep inside her, spreading outward along her limbs. It felt alien. When she finally recognized the feeling for what it was, her eyes began to blur. For the first time in a very long time, she had *hope*. Edith was close to freedom. She allowed herself a moment to know that, to record it in her memory. To imagine feeling the cool Iowa wind on her face.

The covers shifted again in the bedroom. Edith pushed away her dream and sat quietly until Luther had settled again. He took longer this time. The haze of alcohol was lifting.

That's okay. I've done what I needed to do.

Her smile returned. Just a few more payments from Crow. That's all she needed.

Emboldened, Edith logged out of the fake account and into her legitimate personal one, just to see if there might be a message from home. Like many young girls, she'd been anxious to leave her family and begin living life with a new husband. After reality had displaced her little-girl fantasy of what that married life would be, she'd experienced a keen sense of homesickness, a kind of longing for the simplicity of being cared for by others. That was years ago, though, and over time the acute desire to return to Mississippi had become a dull ache of nostalgia. Hearing from home took the edge off that.

Her inbox popped up. Nothing new from home, unfortunately. But there was a message from Krys. That was weird. And it'd been sent at 2 a.m. Why hadn't Krys just pinged her sceye? Edith opened it.

HI, EDITH. COULD YOU COME TO THE INFIRMARY TODAY? ALL THE STUFF THAT'S HAPPENED LATELY—WE NEED TO DO ANOTHER INVENTORY. PING ME WHEN YOU GET THIS AND LET ME KNOW, OKAY?

KRYS

Edith read it again. Nothing unusual in the content, though the message itself still felt odd. Maybe Krys had been worried about waking her up, so she'd sent a message instead of calling.

Maybe she's worried about Luther. About making him angry if she woke us both up.

That was probably it.

"Shyeedith." A rumble from the bedroom. "Where are you?"

Startled, Edith quickly logged out and pressed the two-fingered shortcut key for the session erase protocol.

"Shyeedith?"

"Couldn't sleep," she called back. "Didn't want to wake you."

"Get back in 'ere," Luther said, his words trailing off.

Edith returned to the bedroom and crawled into bed. The heat of his body pressed against her back. She pulled his heavy arm around her chest.

"Do'n like it when're gone," Luther drawled. "Do'n like it..."

"I know, dear," she said. "But I'm here now."

For now.

He grunted and began to snore.

But Edith was too excited to sleep. Partly because the horizon of freedom was so near. Partly because she always experienced a thrill when holding secrets close from Luther. No matter how small, they felt like a victory worth celebrating inside.

And there was a third reason sleep wouldn't find her. Edith couldn't shake the tumor of foreboding that had settled in the back of her skull. Something was off about Krys's message. Something bad.

Edith waited as Krys finished with a patient. The infirmary was reassuming its natural state of mediocrity. One of the Beven kids had an earache. Someone in that household was always getting sick, part of the process of acclimating to life on Callisto.

Sometimes you don't know how good you've got it, Edith thought.

Krys had nodded to her with what seemed like a forced smile when

Edith entered the clinic. Still nervous from last night's restless wakefulness, Edith had tried to make polite conversation.

"I'd have been here earlier, but Luther had a hangover," she explained. Krys had merely nodded with a kind smile and a quick flick of the eyes that let Edith know she needed to care for the Bevens first. Now, fifteen minutes later, an excited kind of anticipation resurrected Edith's fear from the previous night.

"The gravity can sometimes play havoc with a growing boy's inner ear," Krys told Maya Beven. "The prescription should stabilize him. Once he's not dizzy anymore, the steroid will help flush him out."

"Thanks, Dr. Krys," Darinn Beven said with the twinkle of a crush in his eyes.

"Yes, thank you." His mother's smile was one of relief.

"I'm not a doctor," Krys said to the boy, "but you're welcome all the same."

Maya Beven gathered up her son, nodding to Edith as they left.

"Must be nice just having a little earache to treat after everything that happened," Edith said, forcing herself to be patient.

"You've got that right," Krys sighed. She looked beyond Edith to find an empty waiting room. Something in her eyes said she'd almost rather it be full.

"What is it, Krys? You've got me in knots! Please, whatever it is, just tell me."

Krys closed the door to the private examination room. She seemed to be steeling herself to a task she was loath to do.

Jesus Christ, what the hell? Is Luther having an affair and she saw him with his mistress at a bar? Actually, that wasn't as threatening a thought as it should have been. Edith was surprised to realize that.

"You know the blood test we all had to take," Krys said. "When we thought there was a virus or something that might've caused the pilot to crash into the ring."

"Yeah, of course. Oh, Jesus." Edith's eyes grew wide. "I've got it. What-ever it is, I've got it. Luther passed it on to me or—"

"No," Krys said, "no. Edith, have a seat." She motioned to the exam table. Edith sat down, releasing a long breath. "Your SCI will confirm this in a few days. But I thought you'd want to know as soon as possible."

"Krys, what is it?"

Krystin Drake blinked once, then put a hand on Edith's shoulder and squeezed.

"Edith ... you're pregnant."

21

STACKS FISCHER • IMPRISONED IN THE BELT

I have to admit, the accommodations weren't bad. I had a bed almost long enough for my feet. The space paste they fed me tasted like oranges. The water was wet enough. The toilet flushed down. As prisons go —not bad.

Daisy had betrayed me, which suggested Adriana Rabh was throwing in her lot with the Dutchman. But I'd had two days in resort-like comfort to think about that—up, down, and sideways—and it didn't make sense. The pirates were skimming gas off haulers like the *Starwind* in flight, in the relative, camouflaged comfort of the Belt, hoping no one would notice. Now, Adriana Rabh's the bloody Regent of Jupiter. If she wanted to skim a little Jovian treasure for herself, she could just hook up a hose when the scooper ships docked at Valhalla Station's orbital ring, before the gases are transferred to the tankers. Extraction records would be easy enough to fake on the front end. No one would be the wiser.

Maybe Daisy was working for herself. She'd announced herself as Adriana's envoy, but maybe that was just for my ears. And that doesn't square with her job description. Assassins always work for someone else, someone who can afford to pay them for the wet work. Skimming gas for pennies isn't our style.

I was turning over the situation in my mind for the thousandth time when the door to my cell slipped aside. The guard motioned for me to stand and exit. Time to meet the landlord.

"Right, then," I said.

The hallways were crude, carved out of the regolith of an asteroid. The facility maintained an Earth-standard atmosphere, though, so someone had stopped up all the right holes. Gravity generators kept the little-girl enthusiasm in my step from bumping my head against the rock overhead. This wasn't a penny-ante operation. You think of pirates, you think catch-as-catch-can. Not these people. The infrastructure was colony quality.

A few rights here, a couple lefts there, and we entered a large room with —I shit you not—what looked like a throne raised on a dais facing half a dozen screens lining the wall. Okay, maybe more a control chair than a throne. The screens monitored the Belt outside the facility.

Daisy Brace stood next to the seat of power. She turned as the guards escorted me in, then leaned over and whispered in the ear of whoever was in the chair. The Dutchman, I assumed.

The chair turned around.

"You're the Dutchman?" I said, surprised.

A strikingly beautiful woman in her mid-twenties stood up. Her face was a deep brown, though it almost glowed with a golden undertone. Her skin could have been manufactured on Callisto. Indian, I thought, if I had to guess its origin. Hers was a face I knew I should recognize but couldn't quite place. Her short-cropped hair made her look military.

"Some call me that, yes," she said. Her accent was pure Earth common, no hint of the Indus at all.

"Someone forgot to look under the hood before they hung a name on you, huh?"

The Dutchman stepped down from the platform with a gait that was graceful, athletic even. She approached slowly, a catlike smile spreading her dark lips. It was like she was pouring syrup on pancakes. And I was the pancakes.

"So you're Stacks Fischer, Tony Taulke's assassin to the stars." She stopped in front me and reached to cup the silver scrabble of my jawline. Her lips put on a pout. "I thought you'd be taller."

"That's okay," I said, determined not to notice how soft the skin of her palm was, or the mischief behind her almond-colored eyes. "I thought you'd be male."

Her lips turned up again at the corners. "I'm glad you have a sense of humor. Assassins can be so dour, so serious." Her thumb stroked my cheek. I did my best to think of baseball and why the fields have to be so much bigger in low gravity. "It's a shame I have to kill you."

Yeah, that *was* a shame. She turned away and walked back to her throne, pulling at the air with an index finger for me to follow. I followed. Wouldn't want to be rude.

Who *was* this woman? Damn it, her face was on the tip of my tongue!

It's basic physics, you see, the need for a bigger field. The balls fly farther in low-g.

No, I'm still talking about baseball.

I stood in front of her tech-throne and gazed up at her. That's why thrones are always set up high. So the common folk have to look up.

"Your friend here's been telling me all about you," she said, nodding Daisy's way. "And, of course, there are the stories everyone hears."

"She's no friend of mine," I growled. If I'd had my way, Daisy's corpse would be stinking up the place by now. I'm sure I could find an exception to my rule about killing women somewhere if I looked hard enough.

"Don't be too hard on Ms. Brace," Queen Buzzcut said. "Business is business, right?"

"Speaking of that," I said, "what's with the Nazi brand on the armed faithful over there." I jerked my head at the two guards by the door.

"Nazi brand? What are you talking about?"

"The mirrored-S logo. Reminds me of the lighting-S emblem Uncle Adolf used to brand terror during his Thousand-Year Reich that lasted twelve years."

Her expression showed she didn't like the comparison. "We are the Soldiers of the Solar Revolution."

"Ah, there *is* a military component, then."

"Only as a means to an end. And that end is to return the solar system to a state where mankind and the universe exist as one—a mutual existence of giving and receiving. Right now, mankind takes and gives nothing back."

Now my déjà vu really was firing on all cylinders.

"You sound like the New Earthers on steroids," I said. The Neos were a religious cult that, thirty years before, had wiped out millions on Earth in pursuit of their goddess, Cassandra's, goal to return a planet suffering climate-change convulsions to a simpler age. When humans weren't so wasteful. Or plentiful. Tony's pop, Anthony, had made a deal with their leader, Elise Kisaan, that brought her into the Company and stopped the mass destruction on Earth. Cassandra—an artificial intelligence, not a goddess, it turned out—had been unplugged by way of explosion.

"We have embraced Cassandra's teachings and taken them to their natural next stage," she said. Her words were reverent and tonal, like a priest's chant. When she invoked Cassandra's name, something clicked. I mean, like, universal-tumbler-snapping-into-place clicked.

"Which one are you?" I wondered aloud. It was the skin color, the eyes, the canary-fed smile. But I can't fault my recall, for once. I'd been trying to reconcile the woman's face in front of me with thirty-year-old memories without even knowing it. That's what had caused the short circuit. I was looking at a young, smooth version of Elise Kisaan, the current Regent of Earth's factory farms and former New Earther high priestess. Only, Elise Kisaan was in her fifties now.

Buzzcut's eyebrow arched. She knew I knew. A quick glance at Traitor Daisy confirmed it.

"I'm Elaena," she answered.

"A Kisaan clone," I nodded. "One of 'em, anyway."

Her face hardened. "We prefer to be called daughters. You make me sound inhuman."

I shrugged. "If you dropped out of Elise Kisaan's DNA, I'd say that's a given. How many of you are there, *really*? I know three's the rumor, but really..."

Elaena took a breath before answering. Cats don't like it when the rat snaps back. "I'm the oldest, the First among Three."

The first created in a test tube, she meant. Company gossip had it that, decades earlier, Elise Kisaan—paranoid that one or another of the factions would assassinate her, a fair bet by the way—had cloned herself. There were three so-called daughters, trained as assassins in their mother's killer image, whose first duty was to protect their human progenitor's life.

"First among Three, huh?" I said. "Well, I guess that makes you executrix of the will." I do my best thinking on my feet, so I began to walk. "So, let me see if I can put this pirate puzzle together. Elise is *finally* making a move to take over SynCorp from Tony. She sent you out here to play Pirate Queen, to steal resources to fuel the coup. But what do you need all that fusion fuel for?"

"You don't know half what you think—" Elaena began.

"To take out Tony, you'll first have to defeat Galatz and the corporate fleet," I interrupted. "That explains the need for the fuel. For the fleet you're building."

Elaena's silence told me I was on the right track.

"Where is the corporate fleet, by the way? How have you managed to avoid Admiral Galatz? The rock-ships are clever, I'll give you that. But he should have sniffed you out by now."

Elaena tilted her head, deciding if it mattered to give away secrets to a dead man.

"We randomize our intercepts," she said. "If we're pulling gas near Jupiter, we seed chatter on the Undernet days ahead of time that something's up near Mars. It's just encrypted enough that the navy boys have to work to break the code. While we're siphoning here, they're looking there."

In other words, they kept the fleet running all over the Belt by shining a light on the wall across the room and watching the cat chase it. It was so stupidly simple it was brilliant.

"Which leads us to Daisy, here," I continued. "Adriana Rabh saw an opportunity. Maybe Elise reached out to her to cook some corporate books, provide a little financing for the venture. You'd need massive 3D printing centers to prefab hulls and weapon systems. Not to mention dockyards to assemble the ships. No wonder you based yourself in the Belt. So many places to hide. And Daisy, well, she was the ambassador between traitor factions. Which begs the question—why am I still alive?"

"Because I wanted to tell you personally, before you die, that your patron is already dead," Elaena answered. "For what you did—for what you *tried* to do so long ago—justice is finally being served."

That was unexpected. The Kisaan Faction and I have a history going way back. Before there was a Syndicate Corporation, back when Tony Taulke was still a young man and so was I, I'd been tasked with murdering Elise Kisaan's child, Cassandra. Don't judge. The child was the cyborg incarnation of the Neos' same-named AI goddess. The kid had golden eyes, unnatural eyes—freakish. No one wanted a second act after millions died on Earth at the hands of the Neos. Better to nip the threat in the bud. But I missed the kid, killed a woman instead; a woman who didn't deserve to die. I'm not sure that'll weigh much better in my favor when Mother Universe calls me to account.

"So Elise is behind this," I said. She'd bided her time for thirty years, growing her clones and making the entire system dependent on her factory farms. And now she was making her move.

"Did you hear what I said?" Irritated, Elaena had risen from her tech-throne. "Tony Taulke is dead. And you're about to chase him into the Long Dark, you murdering sonofabitch."

When another assassin calls you a murdering sonofabitch, you know you've arrived.

"I don't believe you," I said. When I get serious, I get serious. I was justice-come-to-town serious now. I enjoyed taking her power away. "I don't believe Tony Taulke is dead."

Elaena was apparently unpracticed in the art of being disagreed with. She didn't know how to react.

"It doesn't matter what you believe," she said. "Because you're next." A stunner appeared in her hand.

"Let me," Daisy said. Her tongue wrapped itself around the words. From the look on her face, they must have tasted good.

I turned my eyes on Adriana Rabh's lead assassin. It was odd that Elaena Kisaan was striking a deal with Rabh. It was Adriana who'd sent me on the mission to murder the hardwired baby Cassandra. If Kisaan was settling accounts with the gunman who'd tried to kill the kid, why was she making chummy with the woman who'd sent me to do the deed? Maybe the Cause just needed money that badly.

"Why?" Elaena said. "It's my family he wronged."

"Because I had to spend two days in a cramped ship listening to the old

bastard rattle on about how great he is at his job. About how the new generation of enforcers like me can't even kill time right. I want to show him how
wrong he is."

"Fine," Elaena said. "Consider it a sweetener to the deal we discussed.
Kill him, and we'll call it done."

Daisy had adopted Elaena's feral expression. She was looking forward
to closing the deal.

"With pleasure," she said, stepping down from the platform.

I prepared myself. There was nowhere to run, and I had no artillery.
Two guards were on the door behind me. Two trained assassins—one a pro,
the other mostly mouth so far—in front. I suspected Daisy's reflexes were
faster than mine. I was about to find out.

Daisy spread her arms, and I backed up a few steps. She turned my
spring blade over in her right hand. Great—stuck with my own blade.
There's killing, and then there's just rubbing salt in it. Her jacket fluttered.
Inside her belt, on either hip, I saw my stunner and .38, grips facing me.
One of the oldest tricks in the book. Inviting me to make a grab, get me in
close so she could slide the knife in.

She advanced. I gave ground. Daisy didn't close, instead making a
couple swipes at the air with the knife. That was amateur stuff, showman-
ship, what you did to show off to bosses. Good assassins don't waste energy.
And I knew Daisy by reputation was good. Maybe she was auditioning for
Elaena after all.

Daisy closed in. She lunged, I sidestepped. Her left hand darted out,
grabbed my belt, and pulled me to her. She thrust again with her right
hand, and I tried to deflect but was too slow. The knife sliced the side of my
shirt and past my left hip. She was in close, and I held her there, keeping
the knife behind me and her arm pinned and useless.

"*Grab the fucking gun, you moron,*" she whispered in the clutch.

When life throws opportunity your way, best not to think on it too
much. I yanked the .38 from her belt.

"*I can't kill a woman,*" I whispered back. Never again.

"That's okay. I can." Daisy pushed me away, turned, and threw the knife.
It caught Elaena at the base of the throat, splitting the soft meat between
the collar bones. The surprise on her face was just a little bit sad.

Her guards reacted. They pulled their stunners, moving to protect their Pirate Queen a lot too late. The .38 was loud, but it did the job. The first guard went down. I dove forward, grabbing floor. The second guard brought his stunner up, but he was used to shooting at target dummies, not pros on the move.

Gurgling came down from on high, Elaena's disbelief trying to make itself heard. She coughed and gagged, falling to her knees. Blood ran down the stairs.

The second guard made a sound like a dog whining. I suspected he'd had to think of baseball a lot around his boss, too. Maybe he'd even been in love with her. Or, at least, in lust.

He charged, and that was a mistake. I'd raised my .38 when Daisy's stunner fired once, then twice—that sharp *punk-punk* staccato sound, the catalyzer leaving the barrel. The second guard went down, electrocuted by his own EM field. It'd been a good shot, too. He wore MESH armor, specifically designed to repel stunner fire. Except for his face. Enough of a target for Daisy Brace, boy-o.

The throne room was silent save for the pounding in my ears. And Elaena. She was trying to aim her stunner, but her hand had no strength. The blood gouted out of her now. Clones bleed just like real humans, in case you've ever wondered. It even smells the same.

"Here," Daisy said, mounting the dais. Elaena's eyes followed her up, pleading when she saw Daisy take aim. "I'll put you out of your misery."

Punk.

The First among Three stopped coughing. A few seconds later, the heart powering the blood dripping down the dais stopped pumping.

"You've got some 'splainin' to do, Daisy," I said.

"Later," she answered, angling for the door. "The Hearse isn't far. We've gotta get out of here."

Best idea I'd heard all day.

Then the lights went out.

22

RUBEN QINLAO • LANDER'S REACH, MARS

Ruben traced the texture of Mai's skin with the tip of his middle finger. He focused on the contact, on the supple paleness of her flesh. He admired its softness, full with the privilege of growing up on a planet where water was so plentiful it hung, invisible, in the air.

He drew his fingertip, barely touching, along her right shoulder. Mai gasped with pleasure, the electricity of want arcing through her.

"Ruben," she sighed. She was turned away from him. Her hand reached behind to grasp his thigh.

Her body fascinated him. It held for him an attraction beyond desire, beyond a hunger for sex and the need for orgasm. Beyond even the excitement of discovering anew that which he'd known before with other women. Every one of them alike physically but also unique, one of the universe's fascinating paradoxes. Each time he made love to Mai, it was like Ruben unlocked another secret only he could discover.

He pulled the sheet back so he could see her naked body, then resumed his sketching on her skin. Mai shivered again as he drew a line from the lighter skin of her breast down the narrow of her right side, over the curve of her buttocks. Her head arced upward again as her flesh responded. Ruben pressed against her to extend his reach. She was warm and wet and needful.

"Ruben," she said again, more commanding.

Her hand slipped from his thigh to grip his penis. The hair of his chest brushed her back as Ruben followed her direction. She guided him into her, and his hands encircled her hips. There was a moment of joining, of two human halves making one whole person, and the joy that first moment called forth in each of them. The rhythm of lovemaking took them quickly, a cadence of gasping movement that required no direction, no conscious thought. Connected by a hunger for the connection itself, both driven by the desire for one another like the need for water to drink or air to breathe. Ruben's hands squeezed, holding her fast to him. Mai's pliant skin yielded, the bones beneath giving him purchase.

Tonight was different. Tonight was more. Ruben focused himself on experiencing her, opening his senses. He wanted to feel all he could. He wanted to feel alive and living and loving. Her scent wafted up from beneath the sheets. Her warmth wrapped around him, and being inside her was like discovering the reason for being alive. He tasted the sweat on the back of her neck, and Mai smiled her secret enjoyment of that, turning to watch him over her shoulder. His ears shut out all but her voice as her gasps of "*shì ... shì ... shì*" paced their pleasure.

Their movements quickened.

"*Shì-shì-shì!*"

Mai came with shouts that were almost painful, and Ruben forced himself to hold off for her, to continue thrusting into her until Mai's pleasure subsided. Knowing he neared his own climax, Mai clasped Ruben to her, one human in two halves connected still, and teased the last of his shockwave from him with her body.

When the last of his energy had drained away, Ruben withdrew. Mai turned into him, two bodies folding in to one another, now under an invisible, enveloping afterglow. The sweat of their passion soaked into the sheets beneath them. Mai's breathing began to slow.

They said nothing for a time, neither wanting to break the sacredness of the moment. How many times had they made love in the past week? Ruben wondered. A dozen?

Still new. Still fresh. Still magical.

With Mai it felt like it would always be magical.

"I don't ever want to leave here," she whispered. Lost in his own thoughts, Ruben had almost not heard.

"Mars?" he said. He grunted amusement. "That's unusual for an Earther—"

"No, dummy," she said. Her index finger drew circles in the moist hair of his chest. "*Here*. Now. This bed. This—"

"—fantasy?"

He felt the curve of her smile against his shoulder. "Yes, that," she said. "You're my fantasy man, Ruben Qinlao. I don't ever want to lose you."

"Lose me?" he said. "You getting paranoid?"

"No. It's just that..."

She didn't have to say it. Funerals have a way of reminding the mourners how mortal they are. And wasn't that the point? Ruben thought. Ming's funeral yesterday had been subdued, something she would have appreciated, a solemn affair with a few tears and a few more laughs. Her service might even have pleased her, he thought.

It had been somewhat impersonal, which she would have found funny, with each of the other faction leaders holoing in their condolences. None had made the trip to Mars. Understandable, Ruben decided with grace, given the troubled times. Each had read from a script of amusing anecdotes mixed with earnest memories. Elise Kisaan had been typically cool but respectful. Adriana Rabh's commentary had been short and thrifty, measured out like you'd expect an accountant to count paper money. Trying to channel his father Viktor, who'd loved Ming like a daughter, Gregor Erkennen had spoken thoughtfully of her, the Qinlao Faction, and their place in the Company. But for all his effort, he'd never really known Ming personally, and it showed.

Ironically, only Tony Taulke—the Iron Hand of the Syndicate Corporation—had sounded genuine as he'd recounted her life. It had been Ming's unexpected last request—or a final dig?—that he give a eulogy, and despite all that was happening across the system, Tony hadn't shirked. Maybe he felt grateful for the warning Ruben had passed along after the last board meeting. Whatever the case, Tony had shown a rare kindness in his words, a generosity of spirit for a woman who'd often been his adversary. Whereas the others' speeches had sounded written for them, Tony's had carried idiosyncrasies branding it his own. There had never been love lost between Ming Qinlao and Tony Taulke, but a kind of steely respect, one for the other, had marked their relationship over the years. Tony's generosity in memorializing Ming had given Ruben a newfound respect for the man Ming had once called the Backstabber in Chief.

"Thinking about your sister?"

"Yes."

"She was a great woman," Mai said. She watched her finger twirling his chest hair. "The Company wouldn't be here without her talent, her will. Tony had a lot of regard for her."

"He surprised me yesterday," Ruben said.

"Me too," she said with humor in her voice. Then, more seriously, "Where do you think she is now?"

Ruben thought about it. "I programmed the pod to circle Mars three times. She'll be heading in soon."

Mai nodded against him. "It's nice what you did."

"It was her request," Ruben said. "And I, uh..."

"Yes?"

"I have to go to the bathroom."

"Okay."

"I don't want to get up."

Mai blew out a breath. "Well, you can't pee here!"

Ruben laughed quietly. "Okay. Be right back."

When he lifted the sheet, the cold air hit the sweat still drying on his body. It made him shiver as he rose.

"Nice ass," she said behind him.

Smiling, he walked through the dimly lit bedroom. They'd become so intimate so quickly. But beyond the sex, more than the slaking of new lust, the time they'd spent together had felt like a pair of old souls becoming reacquainted after a long, involuntary separation. Ruben wondered how Mai would feel about giving up her day job as Tony's personal assistant and becoming the new Queen of Mars. Somehow, he suspected, she might like the promotion.

There was a noise in the bedroom. A squeak of alarm.

"Not again," he said to himself. If there was one truism of human expansion—across oceans of water or a sea of stars—there would always be rats. A recent food shipment from Earth had been full of them. Somehow they always managed to stow away in supplies, and once disembarked on the new frontier, they bred like rabbits. The mixed metaphor made him laugh. "Just stay in bed!" he called. "I'll be right there."

He finished up, flushed the toilet, and returned to the bedroom.

"If you liked the back, what do you think of the front?" he asked cheekily. He glanced around for the rat but didn't see it. Already under the bed, he figured. More afraid of Mai than she of it.

She was under the covers, hiding.

"Come on, Mai, it's just a rat," he said. He slid into bed next to her. It was wetter than he remembered. A tribute to their lovemaking, he thought proudly. But the sheets weren't just wet. They felt soaked.

"Mai?"

She hadn't moved.

"Lights: twenty-five percent," Ruben said.

Blood: liquid and dull red in the low light. Blood was everywhere.

"Mai?" he said again, yanking the sheet down.

Mai Pang stared at the ceiling, her throat cut in a half-moon. Blood ran in streams over the skin he'd been caressing just a little while ago. It crested the dam of her collarbones and ran into the crook of her arm pit to pool into the bedsheet. Her jugular notch had filled in as if she'd donned a red broach

"An impressive performance," a voice said from the shadows. "She died a happy woman."

Stunned, still trying to wrap his mind around the warped reality of Mai's beautiful, mutilated body, Ruben began to shake.

"Why?" he whispered.

A light step came from behind. "No witnesses, I'm afraid."

"Witnesses?" Ruben's eyes were filled with the ruins of his lover. Hers were empty.

"The Qinlao Faction is ending," the voice said. A woman's voice, Ruben realized. His senses were waking again. He turned to see the woman who'd murdered Mai Pang, who'd stolen his future. "Stay right there. I'll make this quick."

He turned to find a modestly tall woman wearing a black filter mask. Not from Mars, then. Her black hair was tied behind her head in a fierce bun. Her almond eyes were calm. In each hand she held a katara, an Indian assassin's dagger. Ming had taught him all about exotic weapons, even ancient ones.

"Why?" he asked again. "You could have taken me anytime. Why did Mai have to die?"

The woman was silent as she drew nearer. Ruben's shoulders collapsed. He sat on the bed, holding Mai's hand. The woman in the half mask stood next to him.

"This is nothing personal," she said, her voice sounding hollow and plastic through the filter. "It's just business."

Ruben didn't look up as she raised her daggers to strike.

All business is personal. Ming's lesson came unbidden to mind.

He moved without thinking. His leg shot out from the bed, connecting with the woman's midsection. The air whooshed out of her, and she flew backward.

"Gravity: fifty percent," Ruben said.

The assassin's brown eyes widened as her momentum carried her farther, smashing her into a credenza along the far wall. He'd noticed her skin tone, water fed and flush like Mai's. He'd gambled she wasn't used to operating in low-g environments.

Ruben pulled the top sheet from the bed, shying away from Mai's bloody, naked corpse. He wrapped the sheet tightly around both hands, pulling the red-stained fabric taut in his grip.

The woman had recovered, though she still seemed clumsy in half-g.

"You know how to fight," she said. "Good. I prefer killing wolves to sheep."

Ruben said nothing. He centered his mass, waiting for her attack, planning his response.

Everything is a weapon. Use it.

A fighter's wisdom passed along by Ming in the endless, exhausting hours of combat training she'd forced on him as a teenager.

The assassin advanced again, adapting her movements to the lower-g.

She stepped twice and hopped high, angling for a jump attack from the ceiling, daggers forward like eagle talons.

"Gravity: one hundred fifty percent!" Ruben shouted, preparing his muscles for the dead weight about to drag them down. When it hit, he could barely stay standing.

The assassin's descent accelerated sharply, and she hit the floor hard. Her attempt at rolling out of it faltered, the greater gravity confusing her muscles. She struggled to inhale.

Ruben advanced, powering against the pull of the artificial gravity grid, avoiding her kataras. She tried to turn and meet him but her moves were sluggish, her muscles slowed by lack of oxygen.

"Gravity: Earth normal," Ruben said. Before she could react, he'd moved behind her and wrapped the silken sheet, still shining with Mai's blood, around her neck. One weak hand brought a dagger up and over her shoulder, narrowly missing Ruben's thigh. He pulled up and lifted against her carotid arteries, pressing one knee into the base of her skull. Her hands loosened, one at a time, dropping each katara to the floor. She pumped her feet, trying to gain leverage to flip him over her shoulder.

"Gravity: one hundred fifty percent," Ruben grunted.

A moan of fear slipped from her.

No one stays conscious in a choke hold past ten seconds, Ming said in his mind. *So hold it for twenty.*

Ruben counted slowly. The assassin's struggles diminished. Her eyes fluttered. His gaze wandered to Mai splayed across their bed, staring at nothing. He wanted to kill this woman. To allow air back into her lungs, just enough for her to recover consciousness, then squeeze it out of her again. Over and over.

A moral man.

That's what Ming had named him. She'd handed over their family faction to his care because that, she said, is what it needed now. Not the closed fist of a ruthless founder but the open hand of a compassionate leader.

Ruben didn't feel very moral right now. Part of him hated Ming for hanging that expectation on him. Then he felt guilty for thinking ill of the dead.

How a moral man would feel.

The woman had slumped, seconds ago, against him.

"Gravity: Mars normal."

Her weight and his own lessened. Relief flowed through Ruben as he laid her on the floor. Picking up the knives, he opened his sceye.

"Captain Li, report to my quarters. Bring a squad. And some goddamned gravity cuffs."

A sleepy Li acknowledged the order. Ruben knelt and removed the woman's filter mask. Her young face was dark complected. Indian. And she bore a striking resemblance to a young Elise Kisaan. One of the rumored Three Sisters, Elise's cloned assassins? No one had ever seen them in person before. No one who lived, anyway. No longer mere rumor now.

Ruben recalled the last council meeting, which had ended abruptly when the Regent of Earth had claimed her farms were being attacked. A ruse? Were his suspicions that Elise Kisaan was behind the plot to unseat Tony right after all? She'd sent one of her three cloned assassins to end the Qinlao rule over Mars. Had she sent another to the Syndicate Corporation's Headquarters orbiting high above Earth?

He bound the clone's hands and feet with the sheet, tying the final knots behind her back and out of reach. He was fully clothed and staring down at Mai again when Li rang the door chime. Out of respect he'd covered Mai Pang's body with a fresh sheet. All but her face.

"Come."

The captain and his squad entered, quickly assessed the scene, and encircled the unconscious woman on the floor.

"Sir, I..."

"Medina, I'm leaving Mars," Ruben said, not taking his eyes from Mai. He needed to imprint her vacant eyes on his memory. Their horror would help steady him in the coming days.

"Sir?"

"I'm placing you in operational control of faction business until I return. I would tap one of my cousins, but there's no time. And I don't trust most of them anyway. I'll imprint a seal of authority handing over temporary control to you before I depart."

"Yes, sir," Li said. He was a military man and usually bore the confidence that chosen life required. Now he seemed just this side of dumbstruck.

"Mars is under martial law. Consider us in a state of war. Normal trading will continue until I say otherwise, but all visitors will be turned away from ports of entry. No exceptions. No Martian citizen is allowed off-world who isn't crewing a ship necessary for trade. And ... please have Mai Pang seen to. Place her in the morgue in Wallace Med until I get back. Understood?"

"Yes, sir," Li said again, his voice a bit more solid. "But where are you going?"

The squad was pulling the still-unconscious clone to her feet.

Ruben released a long, slow breath.

"Earth. I have a promise to keep."

23

KWAZI JABARI • ABOARD THE PAX CORPORATUM

The ship's engines no longer hummed through the hull. The *Pax Corporatum* hung in orbit, docked at Regency Station. Kwazi lay on his bed, his eyes closed. He wasn't able to sleep, trying as he had for two days to recreate, through the effort of conscious thought, the fantasy Dreamscape had brought him.

He pictured Amy and her broad smile, which always lit her face from the inside. He made her talk to him about trivial things like how bad the coffee was in Facility 12 and whether or not Mikel and Aika knew that everyone, even other teams, knew that they were dating. Those memories were pleasant, but they weren't Dreamscape. When Kwazi had entered that vibrant world with Abrams and the others, it truly was like stepping into a realm of his own making, a reality painted with dreams he could shape and mold. Amy appeared as her ideal self, the way Kwazi truly saw her, her smile bright, her voice airy and sounding like sunshine felt on cool days. He saw the others there too: Aika and Mikel trading glances they thought no one else saw, a snide Beren who despite his bravado didn't really have a mean bone in his body. Even Max was there, being his strong, silent-type self and clapping Kwazi on the shoulder to encourage his pursuit of Amy. It was like every wish Kwazi had ever wanted to come true was there for the taking, delicious apples to be plucked from a tree and consumed. Kwazi felt happy in Dreamscape, he felt complete—full of life, full of love.

No longer the Hollow Man.

Helena Telemachus had taken Dreamscape away from him. She'd been furious when, after a long search of the ship, he'd been found with the other hackheads, each drifting among their own fantasies. Kwazi hadn't seen Abrams or the others in several days.

"You're lucky I don't throw your ass in gravity cuffs!" Helena had stormed as Milani checked him over.

He'd been missing for more than a day when they found him. He hadn't eaten or even drunk water. He'd soiled himself and had to be cleaned up. Dreamscape made you forget to do those things, the basic rituals of life. But Dreamscape was generous—it gave you so much more in return. It gave you back the dead, more alive than ever. It took away guilt. It made attaining happiness like breathing air.

Half lost in the serenity of Dreamscape, Kwazi didn't say a word when they pulled him out. When you awake from real dreams, good ones, you try to hang onto them, keep them from fading. But they always slip away, becoming ethereal and without substance, until all that's left is the feeling they evoked in you. Dreamscape was different. When you were pulled from Dreamscape—and you had to be pulled, you would never leave willingly— the dreams tried to hold on to *you*.

"Turn it off," Helena had said to Milani while the doctor injected him with vitamins. Telemachus's sharp voice in his head called Kwazi back to that moment in the med-bay.

"Turn what off?" Milani asked.

"His damned implant. Turn it off. Nothing working, nothing to hack."

"*No.*" It was the first and only word he'd said in days. "No, please..."

"Ms. Telemachus, can I speak to you for a moment?" Milani said, drawing her away. Milani whispered, but Kwazi could still hear her.

"Kwazi feels very guilty," Milani said, "guilty for surviving when the others didn't. Dreamscape is giving him solace. Like a prisoner getting time out of his cell. If you take that away from him—"

"Do it, Doctor," Telemachus said. "Kill the SCI. Or I'll find someone who will."

And it had been two days. Two days without Amy, except the Amy he could remember. Less real, less *alive* than the Amy in Dreamscape. Irony nested in irony. He hadn't been able to sleep without Milani's tranquilizers, and even then erratically. Even when he took double the dose.

His sceye flashed. It was almost time. Opening one eye to accept the call, Kwazi said softly, "Yes?"

"Hi," came Milani Stuart's hopeful voice. Her face held an encouraging smile. "How are you feeling?"

"Tired," he answered honestly.

"Did you eat?"

"Not really."

"Kwazi, you need to eat."

"I know."

"Helena's coming to collect you soon," Milani said. Then, again with forced cheer, "Regent Rabh is anxious to meet you."

Reality re-poured its cement over him. They were at Callisto. He was to be rolled out and put on display to smile and wave to the populace and reassure them that all was well.

"I want it back," he said.

There was a pause on the other end.

"I know," Milani said. "You know what she said."

Yes, he knew. Do this event. Make Adriana Rabh happy. Make sure the cameras caught him appearing confident and supportive of SynCorp. Shake workers' hands. Kiss workers' babies. Be a symbol of hope.

What a fucking joke.

"Do this and I'll turn it back on for the trip home," Helena had said.

So what choice did he have? He didn't have the know-how to reboot the SCI himself. And Milani wouldn't do it without Helena's approval.

"I'll see you out there," Kwazi said. Before Milani could answer, he cut the sceye connection.

He rolled out of his bunk. His joints and muscles ached. He took his time moving to the small terminal and the preparation ritual assigned by Helena. Getting ready for the crowd by reading s-mails from admirers. It sounded self-indulgent and narcissistic to him. But she'd insisted it would help him get his head on straight to face the crowds. Reading their messages would immerse him in their expectations. He was an actor researching a role.

Kwazi brought up s-mail and scanned the subject lines, trying to find something new. Anything that made him feel less self-conscious. Less fake.

THANK YOU FOR BEING YOU!

I NAMED MY SON KWAZI AFTER YOU. GODDESS BLESS!

The door to his quarters slipped aside.

"You look like shit," Telemachus said. "Jesus."

She entered, two guards gliding in behind her.

He stared lazily at her with his lack of sleep and constant need for Dreamscape.

"Get up, for Christ's sake," Helena said, pulling him to his feet. "We'll make a quick stop with Stuart, get you a stim. Remember what Tony Taulke said? Don't fuck this up, Jabari. Adriana Rabh is one unforgiving bitch."

Whatever. Kwazi attempted to motivate his tired mind to the role again. *One more time, and then I get it back. I get* her *back.*

Helena led him from his quarters with a firm grip around his bicep.

Please come back, Amy. Please come back.

"So, this is the hero of Mars," Adriana Rabh said from behind her desk. "The man who saved countless lives."

Kwazi stood in front of the Regent of Jupiter, his eyes forward.

"So good to see you again, Regent," Helena Telemachus in her on-camera voice. "Tony sends his regards."

"I don't need Tony's regards," Rabh groused. "I need your expertise shaping public perception."

"Of course, Regent," Telemachus said.

"We're on edge here," Rabh continued. "The rumor mill is churning. It's the one goddamned thing around here that's still working reliably."

"Understood, Regent," Helena Telemachus said. Her voice was restrained, subdued. Kwazi worked hard to stay in the moment. "It's like that on Mars as well."

Rabh grunted. "Elise Kisaan said there was an attack on Earth, too. This little rebellion is spreading."

"That's why we're here, Regent," Telemachus said confidently. "To restore some order. Some faith."

Adriana Rabh appeared dubious. "Good luck with that. Tony sending his flagship here is a fine gesture, but at the end of the day it's just a ship." She looked Kwazi over. "What do you have to say for yourself, Mr. Jabari?"

Awareness returned when he heard his name. "Ma'am?"

Rabh's brows narrowed. To Kwazi she seemed carved from rough marble, the lines of her pallid skin sketched in roughly by time's passing. Those lines deepened now in concern.

"Mr. Jabari, the people of Valhalla Station fancy themselves the modern descendants of Vikings. Do you know who the Vikings were?"

"Yes, ma'am."

"It's a silly notion, but it gives them commonality. It gives them definition as a community," she continued. "Out here on the fringes of settled space, it's important to have a solid sense of who you are. It helps keep at bay the constant knowledge that death is one asteroid strike away." She turned to Helena as if sharing a secret joke. "I don't remind them that Titan is far less civilized, less developed, and farther out."

Kwazi said nothing. It was all he could do to keep his mind focused. It was like his ears were chasing Rabh's words down and grabbing them and tossing them at his brain to catch.

"But the reality is, they're just scared human beings in a fairly new place. They're just people, Mr. Jabari, playacting a role to avoid quaking in fear every day."

"Okay," he said. That was something he understood.

"What they need to hear from you is that the Syndicate Corporation has their back. You're reinforcing a message they've heard all their lives," Rabh said. "Cradle to grave, we're your mother and father. Your nursemaid when you're sick. Your protector when there's danger. Example: it was Erkennen's testudo shield that protected the plastisteel dome after the impact on the orbital ring. Use that. Work it into your speech."

"Yes, Regent," Kwazi said. He was proud of himself for remembering to use her title.

"Go be an icon, Mr. Jabari. Go be a fucking Viking hero," Rabh said, flicking her right hand toward the door in dismissal. "I'll be watching."

"I have to admit, you did well," Helena Telemachus said. Her voice had a cautious respect hiding inside it. "Calling Tony 'the father of us all, the man who provides' was a particularly nice touch."

I was inspired, Kwazi thought. They followed him into his quarters. *I was motivated.*

"You were great, Kwazi," Milani said, squeezing his forearm. He felt it. The genuine warmth from Milani, a contrast to Helena's coldness.

"I kept my end of the deal," Kwazi said simply. "Now keep yours."

Instead Telemachus said, "Adriana was so impressed she's invited us and Callisto's labor leaders to dinner tonight. It'll be a grand thing. Viking themed, no doubt. I'm sure there'll be lots of red meat."

It was her attempt at a joke, Kwazi realized. It wasn't funny.

"Reconnect my SCI," he said. It wasn't a request. His need for Amy braced his courage.

"I don't think you heard me," Telemachus replied. Her voice was a jailer's voice. Only it was inverse jail. She forced him to stay here, outside, in the real world. She kept him from going into Dreamscape ... from Amy. "You need to be on your game just a little bit longer."

"You promised me—"

Helena Telemachus stepped forward. Her eyes held him fast. "Who do you think is running this show, Jabari? You? You're just a walking, talking 3D image, a fiction we created with a tragic backstory. You're an actor hired to stand where I tell him to and read his lines. And when that's done— when I *say* that's done—you'll get your reward. Do you understand?"

He wanted to spit in her face. "Yes," he whispered instead.

She spun on her heel to Milani Stuart, hunched in the corner by the desk. "Make sure he sleeps some before dinner. One thing goes wrong tonight, and I'll hold *you* responsible."

"Yes, Ms. Telemachus," Milani said.

SynCorp's Queen of All Media strode from Kwazi's quarters, the guards following.

Milani moved to Kwazi's side. "Are you okay? God, that woman is so cold!"

Cold hands, Kwazi thought. *Colder heart.*

"I'm fine," he said. "Would you turn my SCI back on now?"

Milani sighed. It was a sad sound. "You know I can't, Kwazi. I wish I could! But it's just a little longer, okay? I promise, then—"

"Okay, then," he said, "do you mind leaving? I'd like to be alone for a while."

I'd like to think about Amy without all these distractions.

Milani placed her hand again on Kwazi's arm.

Still warm.

"Of course," she said. "I'll come check on you in an hour or so. Try to get some rest, okay? Ping me if you need anything before then."

"I will."

With a last look behind her, Milani left his quarters.

Kwazi lay down on the bed and closed his eyes and conjured imperfect memories of Amanda Topulos.

24

STACKS FISCHER • SOMEWHERE IN THE BELT

"Don't worry, I planted a grid bomb," Daisy said. "It's what took out the lights."

Well, that made me feel tons better. Now we were outnumbered *and* blind.

"That was some pretty good shooting back there," I said. "The guard."

"Everyone worth killing wears MESH these days," she said. Then, looking me up and down, "Until they have it yanked off them. You gotta learn to be precise."

I'd lost my longcoat, and I was missing it. Without it, I was as bare assed all over as Guard Number Two's face.

The emergency lighting snapped on. Everything shone with a deep red glow.

"Different grid," Daisy said.

"Uh-huh." I hurried over to Elaena's corpse and slipped the knife from her neck, then cleaned it on her blouse. Her eyes showed utter surprise at being dead. I slipped the blade back into the spring under my right wrist. "Got any .38 rounds?"

"Fresh out." Daisy moved to the only entry to Elaena's throne room.

"Want to take the other side there, grandpa?" she said. "It's called a flanking position."

"The guards are on their way," I said, doing it.

"Yep."

"Is there some reason we're waiting for them?" I asked.

"Because the only guards in the room with us at the moment are dead."

"What the hell does that mean?"

"Fischer, there's a whole escape plan in motion here. Do what I tell you and you'll stay alive."

"Wanna throw some details my way?"

"Not really."

See, this is why I hate working with someone else. People in my line of work like to play it close to the vest. No information is volunteered that isn't needed. Before I could give Daisy my opinion of that in this particular circumstance, alert Klaxons started braying. I hate those things. They hurt my ears.

"Well, they're on their way now," I said. "Tell me where the Hearse is, and I'll lead the way." Standing around waiting for Elaena's pirate army to overwhelm us was getting on my nerves.

"Hold your nutsack, old man," Daisy said. "At your age, that should take both hands."

"Look, you pompous little b   "

Thumps sounded in the distance. The floor shuddered. The thumps thumped closer. Someone was attacking the base. The vibrations in the floor got more vibraty.

"Plan, part two?" I suggested.

Daisy smiled at me. "The fleet. After we arrived, I tight-beamed Galatz as soon as I was alone. I negotiated with Elaena, buying time for him to get the fleet here."

"And here he is," I said admiringly.

"Right on time," she said.

"Well, you sneaky little minx. I take back all those nasty things I said about you. And the nastier things I thought. By the way, where is here?" I asked, moving back into the room. I'd wondered that since we'd debarked the frigate. No one had bothered to tell me.

"Pallas. Where are you going?"

"I'm gonna grab some of that stylish stunner-resistant armor I've heard so much about." Pallas. One of the biggest asteroids in the Belt. But less obvious a base of operations than, say, Ceres. Smart. And properly named for a dead Queen of Pirates, I suppose.

More impacts above.

"No time, Fischer. We're going *now*. While the bad guys are distracted."

She opened the door to the corridor before I could disagree. I hurried after, acutely aware of my stunner-friendly bare ass. The entire asteroid shook with the fleet's bombardment. Guards rushed around us, and I was sure we'd be gunned down. But they were Soldiers of the Solar Revolution —galactic tree huggers with nifty uniforms and a cause that made them feel good about themselves. They might be trained, but they weren't professional soldiers. False advertising! But even professional soldiers don't like bombs dropped on their heads. It's impossible to fight back.

Pallas rocked again.

"Do you know where we're going?" I asked.

"Just a little farther."

We'd reached an upper level. It was starting to look familiar, like maybe where I was marched through on my way to Club Mediocre. There were windows carved out of the rock, with plastisteel holding back vacuum. Outside, there was a pitched battle of warships. The pirates were retreating.

"Fischer, keep up!"

I'd stopped to watch the fireworks. Rookie mistake. She was out ahead of me and nearing a portal I definitely recognized. We were at the slip where Daisy had supposedly betrayed me.

"Hey, slow down! You don't know what's on the other side of that—"

The door slid open, and Daisy barreled through.

I followed her into pandemonium. It looked like some of Elaena's pirates had lost their nerve. Some were trying to evacuate in ordered fashion. Others were pushing past their fellows, desperate to board whatever vessels were still in the hangar. Several were even trying to force their way into the Hearse. But she was my baby and didn't open herself up for anyone but me—DNA coding. Which is why my heart nearly stopped when her canopy popped open.

That girl was cheating on me.

Daisy was halfway across the flight deck.

"Hey, you!" a man shouted. "Stop!"

I moved but not fast enough. It was Officer Friendly, the striper who'd taken me into custody. He and two troopers were angling for Daisy, who was so intent on claiming the Hearse she hadn't noticed.

"Daisy, watch your back!"

One of the soldiers peeled off and kneeled, taking aim with his stunner. I dropped behind the nearest barrel to avoid being fricasseed.

Punk. Punk-punk. Punk-punk-punk.

Stunners were firing all over the place. The idiot on one knee was still in the open. I leaned around the barrel at floor level, raised my .38, and dropped him to the deck.

More stunner fire. Daisy plugged the deserters, knocking them off the Hearse. Then Officer Friendly did for her. She stumbled and went down.

Goddamn it, girl!

She was good as dead if those clothes of hers weren't made of MESH. I hopped out of hiding and ran past the guard on the ground, moaning with a slug in his belly. Officer Friendly was damned near on top of Daisy. She was moving but just barely. He raised his stunner.

"Fucking traitor," he yelled above the bedlam in the hangar. "You sold us out to SynCorp!"

I stopped and brought my pistol up. I had two shots left. Both had to count.

"Hey, striper!" I said. "Point that at someone your own size!"

Friendly turned, and I shot once and missed. He raised his weapon, a smile on his face, and my last bullet plugged him in the forehead. His head snapped back, and he collapsed to the deck. The soldier beside him screamed something obscene and brought up his stunner. I had my own but with all that armor on him and all that distance between us, my odds weren't great.

Then he seized, dropping his weapon, and collapsed to the floor. Daisy had angled her own stunner up his pant leg and fired. Inside the armor, obviously.

Talk about a shot to the balls.

I raced over to her.

"Hold tight, kid," I said. "I'll get you aboard, and we'll blow this rock."

"Nuhn," she said. I stopped trying to move her. That's when I noticed her left side was slack. Motionless. Her right, with the hand that had done the deed on the guard, could still move. Half her face looked like it might slag off any moment.

I'd seen this before. A glancing stunner shot not powerful enough to kill had overloaded her central nervous system. Daisy was paralyzed on the left side. With all the Erkennen med-tech miracles over the years, I'd never heard of anyone who'd ever come back from that.

"Heyah," she said, reaching out her working hand. In it was a micro-drive the size of her little fingernail. "Ahdrianah."

"You can give it to her yourself."

"Nuhn," she said, thrusting her right hand at me. "Tahk it, ash-hole."

I took it. "Look, kid, I can get you back."

"Go," she said from the right side of her mouth. "Whell you shtill cuhn." She glanced up to the roof and the shuddering rock above. Galatz was gonna end this place.

"I can't," I said, and I didn't mean leave. I looked to the stunner in her right hand. She knew exactly what I meant.

"Thash okay," she said. "I cahn."

I blinked once. "You're a good kid, kid. And a damned fine fixer for Adriana. I'll make sure she knows that."

Daisy Brace gave a cockeyed smile that was sad to see. "Goh, ash-hole!"

I climbed into the Hearse and fired her up. No one noticed. As I lifted off, my vector swung the cockpit down toward where I'd left Daisy, now lying flat on the deck. Her stunner was in her right hand, pointed at her head, thumb hooked through the trigger guard.

I raced away from Pallas, losing the Hearse among the laser fire and tracer slugs of warring starships. She was too small for Galatz to worry about. There were bigger fish for his net.

Once I'd gotten away and felt almost safe, I took a breath and wrapped myself in the warm comfort of the Hearse. Then I noticed, on the seat next to me, my longcoat folded neatly, my fedora sitting atop it. A parting gift from Daisy.

There are fates worse than death for people like us, kid. It felt like a half-assed prayer in my head. *Good on ya avoiding yours.*

It was two days back to Callisto. Two long, quiet days. The books I normally lived in to pass the time read like the flat fiction they are. I missed the snark of Daisy Brace, the constant barbs about my age. She gave as good as she got. Just ask the Hearse's would-be hijackers. Ask Elaena Kisaan.

I wondered if this was what parents felt like when a child beat them to death's door. I decided I was just being morbid, selfishly so, and pushed those thoughts away. I had a job to do. Distractions are deadly in my profession.

I'd called ahead and secured a slip aboard Regency Station. Adriana had made that happen, of course. I avoided her desire to speak to Daisy directly. I told the regent she'd get her update shortly and that we should avoid the possibility of someone listening in. It was a slim excuse for silence given the level of security SynCorp runs on comms, but Adriana shouldn't get the news I'd have to tell her that way. I'm not talking about the data on the micro-drive. Some things you should say to people in person. Out of respect.

With the Hearse secured, I made my way to Adriana's office. Rabh security personnel stood guard everywhere. A few of them gave me the fisheye, but I'd already been cleared to make a beeline to the station's core.

When I walked into her office, Adriana stood, nodding to me, then looking past. All she found was empty air before the door cut off her view. Adriana could smell the bad news on me. Did her shoulders slump an inch or two? Did her lips part in silent fear?

I gave her a moment. She cleared her throat.

"Daisy?"

I looked her straight in the eye. This is what you can't do over comms. What you shouldn't do.

"No."

Adriana nodded, accepting the news. She sat down again, a bit too quickly I thought.

"She played it like a pro," I said, speaking slowly. I knew Adriana was distracted. Hell, I was still distracted, and I'd had two days to come to terms. And Daisy and I weren't nearly as close as she'd obviously been to Adriana.

"Of course she did," Adriana said, her voice cracking. She cleared her throat again. "Tell me everything."

And so I did. In the two days' travel back to Callisto, I'd kept the option open in my mind that Adriana might have been playing both sides after all. She'd sent Daisy to the Belt to root out the pirates, sure, but maybe the deal Elaena had mentioned had been real too. But as I detailed what had happened—Daisy's sidling up to Elaena, her tightbeam to Admiral Galatz and the corporate fleet, her making it possible for me to bring the microdrive back—I was convinced Adriana was playing it straight. She was still on Tony's team.

"As far as I know, Tony's fine," Adriana said. "His ship docked yesterday, but he wasn't on it—just Helena Telemachus and that new poster boy from Mars. And Tony's kid, Junior." She turned her mind back to the situation at hand. "I guess I shouldn't be surprised that Elise Kisaan is the trouble. I'll start putting up firewalls to fence off her finances. Once the dollars dry up, the clock will start ticking on how long she can fund this little coup of hers."

I nodded.

"Hand me the drive."

I did. When she took it from me, she held it a moment, stroking it with her thumb. The last thing Daisy had touched. Adriana placed the drive in her terminal.

"Come around here, Eugene," she said. Adriana Rabh is the only one I can stand calling me by my given name. It's how she came to know me, and we'd known each other a long time, ever since the fucked-up Cassandra job. I stood and walked around to look over her shoulder.

The screen was a spreadsheet of dates, ship names, and routes along the Frater Lanes. The Company uses different routes, randomly assigned, to move materiel and resources across the system to prevent anyone getting ideas about hijacking them. The level of detail here was exhaustive: departure dates, lane assignments, last-minute route changes, how much hypercompressed gas was carried down to the milliliter... And there were dollar amounts. Not what you'd think—the value of the cargo—but what that information was worth.

"My own people have been selling them information," Adriana said.

"That fucking pisses me off." When she gets riled, Jupiter's regent curses like a sailor. "I mean, seriously, castrate-somebody-with-my-teeth pissed off."

"Can we find out who?" I asked cautiously, being the only male in the room.

"See this CNP? The address has been rerouted a dozen times. But there should be artifacts in the metadata that'll tell us where it originated."

"Somebody paid top dollar to mask their CorpNet Protocol address."

"They didn't pay enough," Adriana said. She began running her fingers over the console, injecting the drive with algorithms designed by Erkennen Labs to strip away data cloaking. I'd had no idea Adriana was so adept at the technical side of things. I felt more like a fossil than ever. I watched as, bit by bit, the algorithm reconstructed the pathing to identify the actual point of origin for the transaction.

A guttural, triplet chime indicated it had run its course.

"Sonofabitch," Adriana said. "One of my own goddamned miners. And I bend over backward for those fuckers to pay them well, make a life here for them and their families that's the highest standard of living in the fucking system. Ungrateful sonofabitch!"

The screen shone with the rather unremarkable name of the culprit.

"Normally, Daisy would have taken care of this for me," Adriana said, her tone all business now. "I have others I can—"

"Allow me," I said, placing a hand on her shoulder. "For old time's sake."

She nodded and reached up to touch my hand. It was the closest intimacy we'd ever shared. "Daisy died for that intel," she said quietly, and I knew I needed to beat feet soon. Adriana wasn't gonna hold it together much longer.

"She did," I said, squeezing and releasing her hand. "And now it's this asshole's turn." The sobbing started before the door closed behind me.

Time to find a dead man walking named Luther Birch.

25

EDITH BIRCH • VALHALLA STATION, CALLISTO

She didn't stay long at the infirmary after Krys gave her the news.

Edith felt the sudden need to be alone, to camp inside her own head. To weigh the choices of a future that, just a little while earlier, had seemed bright with promise and inches from her fingertips. She wandered the Community Dome. Its narrow corridor-streets were just beginning to come back to life after the colony emergencies. Callistans were venturing from the perceived safety of their pods again.

Marshals patrolled in pairs. Rabh security personnel were posted at every major intersection connecting the districts. In the marketplace, vendors stood behind their bazaar stands vying for the attention of the colonists wandering by. Even the shopkeepers seemed distracted, still on edge as CorpNet's Basement buzzed with speculation about recent events— theories of insurrection and coordinated sabotage and the ultimate downfall of the Syndicate Corporation, whispers of mysterious anarchists called the Soldiers of the Solar Revolution. The speech given yesterday by the Martian had calmed the community's collective nerves a bit, but the air still felt tense, as if charged with a low-yield electricity.

Everything had changed, Edith thought as she walked. *Everything.* Except for her desire to leave Luther—that hadn't changed. But now she questioned whether she should. Maybe hanging on to that dream was just being selfish. Her baby deserved a father. Wasn't any father better than no father at all?

A passing marshal nodded in her direction. Edith offered a thin smile and nodded back. Did she recognize him? Was he the one with the broad shoulders who'd quieted the raving miner in the infirmary? Her brain was only half-working, turning over and over the question: Wasn't any father better than no father at all?

Krys would answer no. A bad father wasn't better than no father.

Go, leave, and good riddance to the bastard, Krys said in her head.

Easy to say from the outside looking in. Easy to weigh the options and reason out the logical solution. But from the inside looking out—decisions had consequences. If Edith left Luther for Earth after she'd made those last few deals with Crow, he'd follow her now for sure. She'd convinced herself otherwise before, that the distance and the effort it would take to bring her back would keep Luther from bothering. He'd find someone else, someone local, and while Edith pitied that future bride-mate, she'd rationalized away any concern for the woman who'd take her place. Edith had her own problems. But now, with his child in her womb, more than ever Luther would want to hold on to her, a prized possession. He'd want to raise the Little Him right—and it would be a *him*, Edith was somehow sure.

The thought of Luther injecting his personality into an innocent child soured her stomach.

Or maybe that's the baby.

Not yet. Surely, not yet.

"Edith!"

But soon the nausea would start. And the cramps and the other symptoms. She couldn't imagine going through that alone. Having the baby alone. Raising it—him—alone. But when she pictured Luther there, it made her want to cry. Thinking about any of it made her want to cry.

Emotionalism. Another symptom? Great! In addition to everything else, now she was getting hormonal...

"Hey, Edith!"

She turned, realizing she'd wandered among the food stands. Reyansh Patel, the vendor of exotic spices from India, smiled and waved her over. The first thing she felt when she saw him wasn't the joy of friendship but the looming specter of Luther, disapproving and jealous. His presence was there even when he wasn't.

Reyansh insisted she come over to the booth. The last thing Edith felt like being was social. But the man had always been kind to her, even when Luther was unkind back. She dug up the smile she'd found for the marshal and approached the brightly colored scarves and fabrics decorating the booth.

"Hi, Reyansh," she said.

"How are you today, best customer?" he asked pleasantly. "Can I interest you in something to dash in your meals?"

"Not today," Edith replied, though she had no idea what she'd make for Luther for dinner. Suddenly paranoid, she accessed her sceye and noted the time. She needed to get home soon. Get cooking.

"Oh come on," Patel insisted in that pushy-with-a-velvet-glove kind of way open-air vendors master. "Business has been slow the last week. Help me out. No coriander? How about some haldi—good for the joints!"

Edith's expression opened up. She felt she owed the man something. Today, a smile was all she had to offer.

"No, thank you," she said.

"Say, what's wrong? You look tired," he said.

Reyansh's attention, she knew, was part of the sales pitch. Make the connection, make the sale. Or maybe he was just being a friend. Friendships seemed to form easier on the frontier, a hint of *we're-all-in-this-leaky-boat-together* about them.

"Oh, you know, it's been a stressful week."

"Hey, some good news—I heard the dome is about fixed. They'll be pulling the testudo back soon. Natural light again! Won't that be nice?"

That *did* sound nice. She was so tired of the unnatural silver of the synthetic lights.

"I suppose so," Edith answered.

"Hey," Patel said, reaching out to touch her left hand. Edith froze. "Is everything all right?"

It took all her restraint to not jerk away from him. She didn't want to be touched. Always in the back of her mind was: what if Luther saw? Forcing her smile to remain, she reached her left hand out and picked up a small bag of cumin, dislodging his touch in the process.

"I think I'd like something after all," she said. "Feels like a chili night."

Patel nodded. "Of course." His tone was tight, uncomfortable. He prepared a receipt and swiped her syncer for the purchase, then handed her the cumin.

"I'm sorry, Reyansh," Edith felt obligated to say. "I'm just out of sorts."

Patel's expression became sympathetic. "No worries, Edith. We've all been out of sorts the last week. Come back anytime. Make it soon, okay?"

She nodded. "Okay."

Luther would be home soon. Edith laid out the ingredients for the chili, organized them, and reorganized them.

Her sceye chimed. Krys was calling.

"Hi," she said.

"How are you doing?" There was concern in Krys's voice.

"Fine."

Krys cocked her head but didn't say a word.

"What? I'm..." The sobbing started somewhere deep inside Edith. In a primal place that her mind didn't know how to control.

Krys took a deep breath but didn't say anything. She let her friend have her space to deal with what she was feeling.

"I don't know what to do, Krys," Edith said at last. Her head kept shaking back and forth. She wiped her eyes. "I don't know what to do!"

"It's okay. We'll figure it out," Krys said helpfully.

We?

Edith's thought was laced with bitterness. It was so easy from the outside to judge, to offer solutions that sounded good. What did Krystin Drake know of her problems? What consequences would there be for Krystin Drake if it all went badly with Luther?

"Edith?"

"Sorry," Edith said, guilty at the negativity railing at Krys from inside her head. Her friend—the only real friend she had on Valhalla Station—was only trying to help.

"Have you told Luther yet?" Krys asked.

"No. He'll be coming off shift soon."

Krys nodded. "So how will it go?"

Edith shrugged and moved to the table to sit down. Her feet hurt. A symptom of pregnancy or just the result of having walked around half the Community Dome today?

"I honestly don't know," Edith said, rubbing her forehead. Was every physical ache and pain she experienced until delivery going to be the baby's fault? "I don't know if he'll be happy or if he'll..."

Her unfinished thought hung in the air, a cloud of uncertainty.

"You don't think he'd hurt you, do you?" Krys asked. "Hurt the baby?"

Of course not, Edith wanted to say. Don't be absurd.

But it was Luther.

There was precedent.

"Will he want the child?"

"I think so," Edith said. Why wouldn't he? An extension of himself, the weight of thousands of years of human genetics pushing itself forward into the future, fueling that same instinct in him. "I—I don't know."

Krys cleared her throat and, in a low voice, asked, "Do you?"

The obvious answer caught in Edith's throat. Didn't most women? Wasn't that her gender's existential reason for being? To create life?

"I—I don't know."

"Oh, Edith." Krystin Drake paused, thinking heavy thoughts. "I suppose ... I mean, you haven't told him yet."

"No," Edith whispered.

"There's always another option."

Edith stared at her friend through their virtual link, not understanding at first. "I don't ... oh, no. No-no-no, I could never..."

Krys raised her hands. "Okay, I was just pointing out the option."

"That's *not* an option, not for me," Edith said.

"Okay," Krys said, "then the only other options I see are: You tell Luther and he's a part of the baby's life. Or you don't and he's not."

Yes, that was the crux of it, wasn't it?

"I know I should be overjoyed," Edith said. "I should be—"

"Quit judging yourself by what you think others will think of you," Krys said. "This is your life to live, no one else's."

Edith smiled at her friend. Maybe she'd been too harsh on Krys earlier. Maybe she'd just been projecting her own fears.

"I'm tired," Edith said. The emotional maelstrom of the last twenty-four hours had put the capper on her recent stress. "I think I need a nap."

"You deserve it," Krys said. "I'll chat at you tomorrow, okay? Ping me if you need anything."

Edith offered a tired half smile. "Thanks, Krys. Thanks for being my friend."

"Back at ya, kiddo."

Laying her head on her arms on the table, Edith promised herself it would just be a quick catnap, the neatly organized dinner ingredients on the counter already forgotten.

"What's all this?"

In Edith's dream, there'd been a shuffling, like a small animal moving through underbrush. She'd been dreaming of Mississippi and playing in the woods. When she opened her eyes, she realized the noise was Luther moving stuff around on the counter next to the stove.

"You've been back to the market, I see," he said. His voice was quiet, establishing a fact. Turning to face her, Luther held up the small bag of cumin.

Edith came instantly awake. "Yes," she said. Her cheeks felt like they'd split open if she smiled any wider. "I thought I'd make chili tonight."

Luther grunted, swinging the cumin like a hypnotist dangling a watch. "A little late for that, wouldn't you say?"

The chrono showed 6:30.

Oh, no.

"I don't ask for much, Edith," Luther began.

Damn it! Why did you have to fall asleep?

The baby? Blame it on the baby.

He cupped the bag in his hand and gave it a sniff.

"I provide for you. I work really hard. All I ask is a little support on the home front, you know?"

"I know, Luther, I'm sorry. It's just that—"

"And yet you'd rather visit Dark Meat in the market than have my dinner ready."

Edith stared blankly. She'd been ready to explain why she'd been so tired. *Luther, I have such wonderful news*, she'd lie, then balance the lie with the truth. *You're going to be a father.*

Luther pulled two pots down from the cabinet and dropped them on the stove. The racket they made startled Edith.

"Do you know how embarrassing it is," he continued, "to know you're flirting with him instead of keeping our home as it should be kept?"

"Luther, I wasn't—"

"How much it hurts me that you do it behind my back, while I'm out *working* to make a home for both of us."

"I swear, there's nothing—"

In one broad, violent motion, Luther swept the ingredients she'd so carefully arranged onto the floor. Spices, rehydrated beef, tubes of tomato sauce ... one tube split, spitting red liquid across her shoes.

In the aftermath of the clamor, there were a few moments of echoing silence.

"Stand up," Luther said.

Edith's feet were like lead. There was a hardness in her belly, a kind of loathing born of experience of what was to come.

"I said, stand up!" He advanced the two steps separating them and grabbed Edith by the arm.

"Luther, please! I've never been unfaithful to you!"

He drew her face up to his, pulling her by the arm. His hand clamped around her forearm like a vise. "That's not what Dark Meat says."

What? What did Reyansh say?

"He gave me some details. About you. Details only *I* should know, Edith."

"That can't be true," she said. Luther was making it up. Reyansh would never say anything like that because he didn't know anything like that. "It's a lie."

"So, now I'm a liar?" he growled, his breath reeking of belched beer.

"No, I just meant—"

"I know *exactly* what you meant," Luther said.

She made the choice in a split second. There was nothing else to do. It would either save her or seal her fate.

"Luther, I'm pregnant!"

Time stopped. Luther's beer breath stopped. Her heart stopped.

His expression was inscrutable. His mouth began to work, like he was chewing his own tongue. His pupils dilated.

Oh, no.

"You get me drunk," he whispered. "You get me drunk and sneak out. You don't think I know what you do?" He yanked her up to stand on her tiptoes, the pain in her arm where he held her flaring hot and sharp. "Then you crawl back into *our* bed…"

"Luther, no—"

His backhand sledgehammered her across the small kitchen. Edith hit the floor hard on her back, the small table where they ate their meals screeching over the floor. The small apartment disappeared in a starburst of orange and yellow spots. Red pain bloomed from the stunned flesh of her cheek. Instinctively, she curled into a ball to protect her stomach.

"Not done yet, slut," Luther said, coming on again. "Not done yet."

26

EDITH BIRCH • VALHALLA STATION, CALLISTO

"I didn't do anything!" Edith cried. Luther bent over her and grabbed her by the same arm. It ached, like it was bruised from the inside. "Luther, I swear!"

"Like I'd believe you. After all the lies."

She stared into his hard eyes and saw them empty of empathy. If she looked deeply enough, she could see her death. The death of her child. The death of *their* child. How stupid was she to think she could get away? That she could outsmart him, run somewhere he'd never find her. She'd never be free of him. Now Edith knew the vicious truth of those words that had seemed like the line from a fairy tale six years earlier.

Till death do us part.

As punctuation to that thought, Edith heard the absurd twinkle of a happy bell ringing.

But the baby ... the baby hadn't bargained for this. The baby was innocent. Luther was right, she'd lied, just not about what he thought. She'd deceived him, mined data from his account, made the deals with Crow. Maybe she deserved this after all—for lying, for deceiving him. Maybe ... she didn't really know anymore. Not right from wrong or up from down or justice from persecution. But the baby didn't deserve it. That was the one anchor of absolute truth in her thoughts, a buoy of clarity Edith clung onto in the storming sea of Luther's rage. And she knew she wanted the child more than anything she'd ever wanted in her life. To bring her child into the universe and love and raise him—or her?—without the fear Edith had lived with every day of her married life.

The happy bell twinkled a second time. No, not a bell ringing—a chime.

"Get up," Luther said, dragging Edith to her feet. She steeled herself for the next blow, her eyes casting around for escape. She could never best him physically. But Luther seemed to relent. "Fix yourself—company calling."

What ... what about the Company?

"I said, fix yourself!"

Luther released her and thrust her against the small table. Rapidly, mechanically, Edith began smoothing her hair, wiping the mucous from below her nose. Luther approached the door to their quarters and engaged the visual display. Clearing his throat, he put on his visitor voice.

"Yes?"

Edith could see an old man on camera, a miner by the look of him. On the front of his coveralls, he wore the double-bar-R of the Rabh Regency. That would give Luther pause. The old man was an official of some kind, maybe.

"Luther Birch?"

"Yes, can I help you?"

"Well, I surely do hope so," the man said amiably. "The Company sent me. Might I have a moment of your time?"

"You've already had several," Luther groused, then more affably: "It's been a long day."

"Ain't that the truth?" The old man smoothed the sparse silvering hair on the top of his head. "I've actually come to talk to you about an opportunity, Mr. Birch. Adriana Rabh has taken personal notice of you." The man brought his hands up in front of him, and he chuckled. "Now, this is a good thing, just to be clear!"

Luther glanced back at Edith. She wiped her cheeks with her fingertips. He pressed mute. "Sit down at the table and stay there."

Edith sat down.

Releasing the lock, Luther pressed a button. The front door slid into the wall. "Come in, Mr..."

"Finn," the old man said, walking in. His brother-in-arms smile beamed at Luther, and the two men shook hands. "Thank you, kindly. I promise not to take up much of your time."

Luther murmured something unintelligible.

The visitor glanced briefly in Edith's direction. She did her best to minimize eye contact, lest Luther notice. The man seemed familiar somehow. Whoever he was, she was grateful for the interruption. Sometimes Luther cooled down when he was interrupted. And now she had time to think of a way out.

"You're a little old for a miner," Luther said.

"Well, that's why I'm not a miner anymore," Finn said. "I'm a member of Regent Rabh's Labor Council."

"You're a biter?"

Finn cocked his head. "We prefer the full 'arbiter,' but yeah."

Luther grunted. "Never had much use for union men. Never saw much point in all that talk. And never saw no dollars come from it, neither."

"Funny you should mention money," Finn said, his tone baiting.

"Yeah?"

"Yeah. Regent Rabh has singled you out for special recognition."

Luther's expression lightened. Edith had real hope that, once the visitor was gone, maybe she could calm Luther down. She glanced at the stove and had the silly notion that maybe she could get dinner made while the two men talked. They'd have to talk a long time for that to be the case. Still, maybe Luther would even invite the arbiter to dinner.

"I'm listening," Luther said.

Stacks Fischer • Birch Living Quarters

I was stalling. I should've popped Birch as soon as the door closed behind me. My line of work isn't like you see in the vids. It's no-nonsense. It's efficient. Anything less begs for trouble.

But the wife complicated matters. If I killed him in front of her, she'd be a witness. Any other enforcer worth what I get paid would have done them both. But I don't kill women.

So I needed time to think. While I bantered with Bubba, I got the lay of the land. Birch was a real piece of work. Not only was he selling out Adriana Rabh for a few SynCorp dollars, but he liked to knock the wife around for kicks. There was still an angry, red gun smoking on her right cheek. She'd tried to arrange her hair, but wild strands gave it away. She had the darting eyes of a mouse cornered by a cat.

Noticing the details prompted my memory. The woman worked in the infirmary. She'd been kind to me there, but her name escaped me. The complications just got more complicated. One thing that was simple, though: Bubba Birch was a bully. A small man in a big body. I hate bullies. Have, ever since I was a kid.

Dealing with him was gonna be fun on multiple levels.

"I'm listening," Bubba said.

"Well," I answered, making it up as I went along, "your whole crew's quota numbers have been up recently. At least they were before the ring problem."

"Yeah. Whoever did that oughta be horsewhipped around the dome."

I nodded. "Glad to hear you feel that way, Luther. We Company men have to stick together. Loyal to the regent, right?"

"Sure. Now, you were saying about some cash bonus or something?"

"You like money, eh?"

Bubba hesitated. Probably sensed the tide shifting a bit. "Sure. Who doesn't, bub?"

"Right." I paced around the small quarters. There was a living area barely wider than a corridor that looked like it led to two small rooms: a bedroom and a study, I guessed. I passed by the wife sitting like a statue at the table. Her right hand was trembling. She noticed I noticed and covered it with the left. "Do anything for a dollar—that sum you up pretty good, Luther?"

He cocked his head. His eyes flicked down to the wife. It was like he was seeing us in bed together. That's the thing about bullies. They're really cowards, so their radar's always pinging red with fear. Always paranoid, looking for the next threat to their bullyhood. I had a penis, so I was a threat. It was that kinda paranoia that forged handprints on cheeks.

"Look, Finn, what's this all about? I thought I was being rewarded."

"Oh, you are," I said standing between the two of them. I pulled my stunner from under my shirt and pointed it at his head.

"What the—Finn, what the hell is this!"

Birch's bulk wrapped around his saucer-wide eyes made him look cartoonish. The woman behind me squeaked. But she didn't move.

"The Company takes loyalty seriously, Luther. And disloyalty? We take that deadly seriously."

"What are you talking about?" Bubba's hands were turned up. "I'm as loyal as they come!"

"Uh-huh," I said, my index finger curving around the trigger. "Selling tanker schedules to pirates doesn't qualify you, boy-o."

His lost look was interesting. I decided he was a good actor. Bullies develop that skill, too.

"I never sold nothing to no pirates," he said, his eyes learning every detail of my stunner's barrel. "I never done nothing but work hard for the regent. Never even called in a day sick I could get out of bed."

The woman behind me shifted. I moved to the side to get them both in view. The last thing I wanted was for her to get in the way somehow. I'd seen it before—a woman, abused, taking the side of the abuser against a stranger. But she stayed put.

"That's not what your terminal logs say," I said. "You did a good job covering your tracks. But you're stupid if you think the Company can't break any encryption you can buy on the black market."

He truly looked lost. Like I'd sped past him and left him the dust of a conversation he didn't understand. Then he turned to the woman at the table.

"Edith?"

That was it. Edith. A flick of my eyes revealed an anguished look on Edith's face. I couldn't tell whether she was about to say something or just wanted me to get on with it.

"It wasn't me," Luther said, his voice full of menace. "It was *her*."

What a fucking asshole. Caught red handed and selling out his wife for the crime.

"That true, Mrs. Birch?" I asked, sighting down my stunner to the center of Bubba's chest. What the hell ... I'd play along.

"I—" she began. "I..." It was like the words wouldn't leave her throat.

Uh-oh.

My eyes made a rookie mistake. I looked her way.

Luther lunged.

Punk!

I'd fired but at empty air. His bulk drove into me, and that sonofabitch was heavy. We crashed backward into the kitchen. His miner's grip slammed my gun hand against the counter, and the stunner went flying.

"Now you'll get what's coming to *you*," he said. His breath smelled like stomach acid and hops. He raised a fist, and I jammed a knee up into his balls. Enforcers don't fuck around. Remember that whole efficiency thing?

Bubba *oof*ed air like vacuum had just sucked on his lungs. His hold weakened on my gunhand but still held it, so I slammed two fingers each into his eyes, digging deep. He screamed and let go, pushing away from me.

Edith was on the floor, her legs pumping to get away from the mayhem. Birch fell backward, and his weight flattened the table to the kitchen floor. I quick-glanced for my stunner but didn't see it. That's okay. I've got backups.

I sprung the blade from beneath my right wrist. Edith made a noise. Encouragement? Terror? Begging me to stop? I couldn't tell.

Luther was clawing at his eyes, trying to clear them.

"Don't bother," I said.

Still blind, he raised an arm. I went in under and uppercut the blade into that soft patch between his collar bones. Like Daisy had done for Elaena, only without the bullseye throw. I struck blood, and it founted out of him like oil in a Texas pasture. No need to draw this out any further. I drew the blade across, severing his left carotid.

Edith screamed, but it was silent. Her mouth was open, and she gagged like she'd forgotten how to breathe. If she'd leaned over, her eyes might've rolled right out of their sockets. If she could've crawled through the cabinets into the next apartment, she'd have done it.

Luther Birch gaped up at me. He was a gas miner, so he'd lived with the possibility of dying every time he suited up for work. But something told me he'd never really believed it would ever come for him. Maybe none of us do. He'd had grand plans of retiring rich. And here it was. Early retirement, sans cash.

That's a life lesson right there. Death doesn't wait for an invite to the party.

Edith Birch • Birch Living Quarters

Edith stared at the horror pooling onto the kitchen floor. She couldn't take her eyes off it. It was like she needed to see it to make sure it was real.

I'll have to clean up all that blood.

Her body felt numb. Her brain had locked up, unable to think. Only a single thought made its way through, repeating, over and over.

I'll have to clean up all that blood.

Luther wasn't moving anymore. He'd clamped his hands to his neck trying to stop the flow. Impossible, of course. And now his hands—his calloused, bear-like hands—lay on the floor at his side. Edith reached up and caressed her cheek with her fingertips. She'd never have to endure their hardness, ever again.

"We need to get out of here, Edith."

The man, Finn, stood over her husband's body.

"I can't," she said. The sound of her own voice surprised her. It was strange in her ears. New, somehow. "I have to clean up all the blood."

"No, you don't," Finn said. "You need to come with me."

"But Luther is dead."

"He is."

"You killed him."

"I did."

Her eyes found his. "I don't know how I feel about that."

"Okay."

"But I'm mostly all right with it," Edith said, her tone less confident than her words. "I think."

"Sounds about right."

Her thoughts had begun to loosen, her brain to work again. Should she tell him the truth? Luther had died for her sins. She'd used his terminal, sold the information to Crow for months. When she'd first heard rumor of the pirates in the Belt, Edith had convinced herself the two weren't connected. But a part of her had known. Had always known. And now Luther was dead.

And I'm free. She touched her stomach. *We're free.*

How could she begin a life with her child born out of such a lie? A new life born of murder? This isn't how she'd wanted things to go. Luther had died for her sins, not his.

"I think I need to tell you something," Edith said.

"I'm pretty sure you don't." Finn reached out his hand and helped her to her feet.

She rose carefully. The floor was red and sticky.

I need to clean up the blood.

"Regent Rabh sent you here to ... kill ... the person who sold the information to the pirates in the Belt," she said. "You didn't come here to kill him, Mr. Finn. You came here to kill *me*."

Sighing, he said, "I came here to put a bow on a situation. And the name's Fischer. Not Finn."

"But, the truth is—"

"Are you planning to sell more information to the pirates?"

Edith shook her head, her eyes again fixed on Luther. Her hand again resting on her stomach. "No."

Luther had insurance, the devil on her shoulder said. *No need for Crow now.*

"Then let me give you a piece of advice, Edith. It's a dirty reality I've learned from a lifetime in a dirty business."

Finn—Fischer—stared hard at her. Like he wanted to tattoo what he was about to say directly onto the gray matter of her brain and didn't want to miss the mark.

"Never let truth get in the way of justice," he said. "You'll sleep better. Now, come with me."

27

RUBEN QINLAO • EN ROUTE TO SYNCORP HEADQUARTERS

Ruben switched off the ship's engines. The Moon panned down in the forward window as he passed beyond the tug of lunar gravity. Earth rose in its place.

Comms traffic was chaotic. Tony's headquarters was under attack. Too far out to spot the space station that served as SynCorp Headquarters, Ruben reached out with antiquated sensors and found energy discharges. Fast-vessel maneuvers that, with their built-in gravity compensators, would fly circles around his little shuttle. Any stellar conflict with those modern ships would come to a quick and predetermined end.

Best to avoid any need for that, he thought.

The hard burn from Mars had taken its toll on Ruben and his old shuttle. The old-fashioned dragsuit had helped him weather the stresses of a full-g burn for more than forty-eight hours, but he'd had to cold-start the engines twice when he'd flipped over to decel burn halfway to the Moon. Three decades before, the model stealth ship had been a cutting-edge example of Erkennen Labs' beyond-the-curve innovation. She'd even broken the Mars-to-Earth speed record, shaving a best-time standard of three days to two, a miracle of technology at the time. The little souped-up shuttle's name now defined the meaning of irony.

But the *Roadrunner* had gotten Ruben to Earth and kept him off the grid doing it. The ship had been Ming's once. In healthier days, she'd take it out when she wanted privacy from Company politics. When a SynCorp law was enacted requiring all spacecraft, private or otherwise, be outfitted with tracking beacons, Ming had quietly ignored the order. That meant the *Roadrunner* wasn't registered on SynCorp's travel network. Avoiding the main Frater Lanes, Ruben had shadowed them like a wolf in the woods striding parallel to a main road.

He was still too far for his human eyes to see anything but stars, so Ruben watched the sensor data coming in from SCHQ—the battle for control of the station raged on. The attack on Taulke's seat of power was the next logical step, given what Ruben had heard on SynCorp's subspace network during the trip from Mars. The daily pabulum of CorpNet propaganda had devolved into rumors of revolution becoming fact. Stories highlighting Kwazi Jabari and the Martian effort to rebuild, of the Corporate Fleet's rout of a group of motley pirates in the Belt, had turned into headlines predicting the fall of SynCorp.

THE CORPORATION IS NOT ALL.

THE FIVE FACTIONS MUST END.

THE SOLDIERS OF THE SOLAR REVOLUTION ARE COMING.

Someone who didn't report to Helena Telemachus had clearly gained control of CorpNet.

Archived footage ran constantly in the Basement, plainly aimed at reinforcing the top level's tombstone headlines. The sabotage of the refinery on Mars. The shuttle crashing into Callisto's orbital ring. Someone was trying to draft the populace into rebellion with anti-Company sentiment. The Undernet had been uploaded to the free-access top level of CorpNet like so much dirty laundry. Now every citizen-worker could pick up, turn over, and examine the unwashed underbelly of the Company's backroom business.

There were no more secrets. No more control of the narrative. There was only informational anarchy. This was more than the Resistance had ever accomplished, Ruben thought. Much more.

Titan was in full blackout—no one had heard from Gregor Erkennen in two days. Channel Black, the encrypted frequency reserved for emergency use by the five faction heads, was silent save for subspace snow. There was even a headline claiming the Qinlao Faction had been ended, which worried Ruben, until he realized the claim referred to him personally. Another headline claimed the same fate for Tony Taulke. Ruben could only hope it too was inaccurate.

He'd almost reached SCHQ, was almost within reach of fulfilling his promise to his big sister. The *Roadrunner* was in visual range. The point defenses of Taulke's headquarters were alive and being answered by the railguns of smaller attack ships. Drones, escorting dropships. Full of SSR, no doubt. They were boarding the station.

It would be tricky threading his way through that chaos, especially with Taulke's point defense cannons targeting anything that moved. Then, all at once, that problem went away. The PDs stopped firing. Someone on the inside had shut them down.

"Well, hell, Tony," Ruben muttered. "I hope you appreciate this."

He pushed the button to bring his engine back online. A red light flashed in time with a harsh alarm.

"Come on, old girl. I'm Ming's little brother, yeah? She'd want you to take care of me."

Ruben pushed again and winced when the power level spiked past orange. He'd been trying to save fuel and minimize his LiDAR footprint, but maybe he should have kept the engine idling.

"In case you're hard of hearing too," Ruben said a little louder, glancing around the small cabin. "Ming was my sister!"

He pushed the start button again. The power spiked again. The level dropped through the yellow and stabilized at the top of the green. Thrust from the *Roadrunner*'s main engine pushed Ruben back in his cushioned pilot's seat. The positioning thrusters steadied her course.

"Thanks, old girl," he said, patting the console the way he'd seen old women pat the slot machines in Vegas-in-the-Clouds. He'd thought them laughably superstitious. Now he got it.

Drawing closer, Ruben saw that most of the action around SCHQ was up top, where Tony's penthouse was. Cut off the head of the snake—that seemed to be the strategy of the SSR. But Ruben knew something they evidently didn't. Assuming Tony was still alive and on the station, he'd be at the opposite end, in a blast-proof bunker equipped for long-term space flight, with a set of state-of-the-art fusion engines. Tony had called it the

Lifeboat in their last conversation, when Ruben informed him of Ming's worries about a coup attempt. From his vantage point in the *Roadrunner*, Ruben could see that the Lifeboat was still attached. Which meant Tony hadn't left yet. At least not via the Lifeboat.

Maybe he really is dead.

The SSR dropships were attaching themselves to SCHQ about halfway down its superstructure, likely with the mission to take over Engineering. That made tactical sense—and was why Tony's Lifeboat was at the ass end of the station.

Ruben dove the *Roadrunner* down and away from the main fighting. No one seemed to notice her small, angular black hull. Old Viktor Erkennen's outdated stealth design continued outliving its warranty. Ruben kissed the cold metal of SCHQ's outer hull with maneuvering thrusters, smiling nervously when the teeth of the airlock meshed between ship and station.

"Okay, big sister, here goes nothing." Ruben stood for the first time in two days, grimacing at the popping in his knees. The drugs the dragsuit had pumped into him in flight—more old tech meant to mitigate the demands of hard burns—swam in his system. He stripped off the dragsuit, strapped a stunner to his hip, and moved to the airlock. Slowly his limbs were coming alive.

The pressure door rolled aside. Ruben drew his stunner and stepped inside SCHQ.

The corridor was empty. With his back against the wall, he advanced toward where the Lifeboat would be: at the very bottom of the station, easily detachable like the useless stage of a rocket in NASA's earliest days of space exploration. He was adjusting swiftly to SCHQ's standard-g. The drugs were doing their job. Ruben walked quickly but cautiously, reconnoitering around corners before moving deeper in, just like Ming had taught him so long ago.

He knew he'd reached the hatch for the Lifeboat by its single symbol over the access controls: the Taulke Faction symbol. The station was full of such images, of course, which helped to hide this one's significance. But down here, on the bottommost level, the symbol was a call sign, a password of privilege. Ruben pressed his fingertips to the Taulke logo rather than the door's controls, just as Tony had told him to do.

The door swept aside. Ruben's eyes narrowed, then focused on the stunner's barrel leveled a foot from his forehead.

"Drop the piece," the man said, his voice smooth and cool. He was massive, his broad shoulders and thick arms testing the resilience of the blue Company coveralls he wore. He looked like an average SynCorp laborer, excepting the weapon pointed at Ruben's head. His thick forefinger wrapped around the trigger. "Or I drop you."

"Ruben!" Tony Taulke stepped from behind the man. "You made it! Dick, drop the stunner. This is Ruben Qinlao."

The big man lowered his weapon on command, aiming a cocked eyebrow at Ruben instead. *One wrong move*, it said. *I don't give a fuck who you are.*

Ruben slipped past. "Why haven't you blasted off, Tony? Those SSR troops are all over the station."

"Yeah," Tony answered as the door slipped shut. "They took Engineering before I could detach. Piece of advice, Ruben: if you ever design a getaway ship as part of your headquarters, be sure any docking clamps aren't tied to the station's main security protocols. Cuz once those are compromised, you aren't going anywhere."

"Good thing I have alternative transportation," Ruben said. He could feel the young mountain looming behind him. His eyes flicked over his shoulder.

"Don't mind him," Tony said. "Name's Richard Strunk. He's an up-and-coming talent in my stable of enforcers. Stacks Fischer can't be everywhere all the time. Would that he could."

"Hi," Ruben said.

Strunk simply stared, crossing his arms. Ruben noticed the big man's stunner was back in a shoulder holster. Near his right hand at the moment, as a matter of fact.

"About that alternative transportation..." Tony said.

"Right. The *Roadrunner*'s just a couple of levels away."

"The *Roadrunner*? You flew Viktor Erkennen's old prototype all the way from Mars?" Tony's wary voice carried a whiff of being impressed.

"She still flies," Ruben said, "and no time to debate. What about your son? And your wife?"

"Sent them away on the *Pax Corporatum* days ago after our little talk. Dick, lead the way."

The door disappeared into the wall. A knife arced into the Lifeboat from the corridor beyond. Strunk's reflexes were good. He slipped aside without thinking, pulling his stunner. The knife buried itself in Tony's upper chest. Ruben caught him as he collapsed. Strunk's stunner fired —*punk! punk-punk!*—as a second knife flew through the doorway and embedded itself in the wall behind them.

Not just a knife. A katara.

The same weapon Kisaan's clone had used on Mars.

Strunk was cursing a blue streak, shooting four-letter words like bullets. He barreled forward into the corridor firing his stunner. There were the sounds of his massive fists hitting flesh.

"We're trapped like rats here," Tony gasped. "Get me out. Get me out!"

Ruben wrapped Tony's arm around his shoulder and moved to the door. The katara in Tony's chest bobbed with every movement. The CEO of SynCorp grunted but held his pain inside.

There she was. Another of Kisaan's clones, ducking in fast motion Strunk's slow and ponderous attempts to lay her out.

Ruben drew his stunner with his free hand and aimed. A blur on the right drew his attention, and he was obliged to send her soldier escort ducking for cover instead.

Punk-punk-punk!

The clone's three escorts fired at Strunk at close range, but it was clear his blue coveralls weren't standard issue. MESH woven, Ruben decided. Of course they were. Strunk was Tony's enforcer. He'd never be in the field unshielded.

The soldiers were wising up to that fact too. They dropped their stunners and moved in, kataras drawn.

"I've got to put you down," Ruben said, not waiting for Tony's agreement. Tony slipped to the floor, unconscious. His stunner knocked from his hand, Strunk had retreated. He was batting away attempts to knife him from two different sides. Ruben drew his own knives, the weapons he'd taken off the clone on Mars.

This clone turned an eye as he advanced, then fell into a defensive stance. She wasn't worried about Strunk, her posture said.

"You're Ruben Qinlao," she said. "I guess Elinda failed, then."

Ruben crouched, turning over the knife in his hand. "And you are?"

"Elissa," she said and lunged.

Ruben stepped back, turning sideways. Her knife slipped past. He grabbed her wrist with his free hand, bringing his own knife down into open air as she counter-dodged and twisted free.

A bellowing stopped them both. Strunk picked up one of the soldiers and threw him hard into his comrades.

Elissa Kisaan debated a moment, turning the odds over in her head. Strunk rounded on her, and without hesitation, she fled the fight.

Ruben blinked. The pile of soldiers was just beginning to disentangle themselves. Seeing Strunk moving in their direction, they seemed eager to follow their leader.

"Strunk!" The big man stopped as the soldiers fled. "Tony's the priority. You carry him. I'll get us to the ship!"

Grunting, Strunk obeyed. He cradled Tony in his arms, careful to avoid the knife still sticking in his boss's chest. Half in and half out of consciousness, Tony moaned as they moved him.

Ruben was less cautious on the return trip. Elissa Kisaan and her bodyguards seemed to be the only enemy on this level. When Strunk stepped with Tony aboard the *Roadrunner*, his disapproval was apparent.

"This piece of shit is gonna get us killed."

Ruben closed and locked the hatch and helped him secure Tony into a cushioned seat. "Feel free to catch the next car," he said.

Strunk grumbled.

Breaking into the first-aid kit under the seat, Ruben pulled a hypodermic out. The meds were so old they were still delivered by needle, not compressed air forced through the skin with a hypo.

"That stuff still any good?" Strunk asked.

"Sure, absolutely," Ruben said. *I think*. He injected Tony, who groused at the pain as the needle entered his arm.

"And it was a lot smaller than that," Ruben said, nodding at the knife in Taulke's chest.

"Get it out," Tony said.

"Can't. When we get where we're going."

"And where's that?" Strunk demanded. He was forced to hunch over beneath the *Roadrunner*'s short ceiling. He looked like an ogre avoiding a canopy of trees.

"The Moon."

"That's crazy," Strunk said. "That's the first place—"

"Short-term solution," Ruben said, moving to the pilot's seat. His fingers punched keys. The ship had never seemed so old, or limited, as it did to him then. "I know a place we can hide. Now, strap in."

"Ruben..."

"Not now, Tony," Ruben answered as Strunk squeezed himself into the copilot's seat. The foam that would help protect Strunk against the g-forces to come squeaked in protest as his bulk settled in.

"Listen to me, goddammit," Tony said, breathing heavily around the pain. "As soon as we're clear, I need you to send a tightbeam. I'll give you the frequency. It's encrypted. To Fischer."

"Okay, but first things first." Ruben detached from SCHQ and fired up the engine. It started in one try. He patted the console, once again sending silent approbation to the old ladies in the orbiting casino. "Here goes nothing."

28

STACKS FISCHER • RABH REGENCY STATION

Valhalla Station buzzed with the news. Ruben Qinlao: dead. Tony Taulke: dead. Elise Kisaan: missing. Gregor Erkennen: gone dark on Titan. The only faction leader still in control of her regency, apparently, was Adriana Rabh.

As we rode the elevator up to Adriana's armored penthouse above Callisto, I thought how strange human nature is. Now and then you'll hear echoes of the Resistance: mankind shouldn't kowtow to SynCorp. We shouldn't sacrifice freedom for security. We should determine our own destiny. I thought it was all bullshit myself. No matter who you are, you're owing to somebody, and the Company seemed as good as any other to collect the bill. Plus, free vacations twice a year: bring the whole family.

But, the Hydra's heads were getting lopped off right and left, and all those downtrodden citizen-workers needing freedom were starting to panic. The bandwidth in the Basement was bloating with personal stories —families wondering where their next meal would come from. Miners on Mars and farmers on Earth wanting to know when their next shift was. They'd had their needs taken care of by SynCorp for a generation. I could see the panic rising like the gorge of an overfed fatman. It was even starting to overwhelm the headlines dominating CorpNet proclaiming mankind's freedom from the evil corporate overlords was close at hand.

Sounded to me like the SSR forgot to ask the populace their druthers first.

People don't like change.

"Where are we going?" Edith Birch asked. She'd come along willingly enough. I guessed she was still smarting from seeing how much blood Bubba's body used to hold.

"To see Adriana Rabh."

Edith waited for me to elaborate. I didn't.

"Why, if I may ask?" There was fear in her voice. Didn't she know if I wanted to kill her, she'd be dead already?

I glanced at the display as the levels flashed by. "Because I need to cinch up that bow I mentioned earlier."

The levels sped by.

"And you need me because..."

"You're part of the cinching."

"Oh." Then, after a few more levels: "Why did you kill Luther? I mean, instead of taking him into custody or something."

"I'm not a marshal," I said. "Custody isn't what I do. And he was a man who needed killing."

My syncer pinged. Since I didn't have an implant, it gave me basic notifications when someone sent a message. It had a black SynCorp five-pointed star attached to it. I hadn't seen that in a long, long time. It never meant good news.

"I'm pregnant," Edith said.

I was preoccupied by the star for a second and a half longer. "Say again?"

"I'm pregnant. I'm going to have a baby."

"Thanks for defining that for me," I groused. It came out harsher than I'd intended, which was not harsh at all. I was focused on the black star. It's a level of encryption I can't decode without the Hearse. Walking around without an implant had its downside. "And ... congratulations."

"Thanks," she said. "I think."

We were almost at the top. I thought through what getting that message meant. Tony must still be alive, or at least he'd been alive when he'd sent it. And if he *was* alive, the rest of the rumors being ground out like hamburger meat from CorpNet's mill might be bullshit too. I wouldn't know for sure till I got back to the Hearse.

"Are you going to kill me?" Edith asked.

"What?" I said, pushing the black star out of my head till I could do something about it. "No. I told you that already."

"Is Adriana Rabh going to kill me?"

"*No.*"

"Okay then," she said. Edith sighed beside me. "Okay."

Edith Birch • Rabh Regency Station

The vator doors parted. Guards dressed in Rabh security uniforms walked in pairs in both directions. Other personnel wearing the Rabh logo on their shoulders moved just as rapidly toward their own crises.

"Come on," Fischer said. "I'm on the clock here, Edith."

She followed, staying close. The man scared her to death. She'd lived in Luther's shadow so long, she'd forgotten what feeling scared really felt like, ironically. When you live with terror every day, terror becomes the norm. Walking beside Fischer, Edith watched the busy bees of Regency Station part before him like the Red Sea at Moses's command. That's what frightened her, the power Fischer seemed to wield without exerting the least bit of effort. And yet, she'd never felt safer than walking in his wake.

Two doors appeared ahead, taller and more ornate than she'd seen elsewhere, and emblazoned with two double-bar-R Rabh symbols. Fischer touched the chime, and the doors slipped into the walls. Edith walked into a room far less impressive than the doors leading into it. Sparse, utilitarian. It was a room an accountant could admire for its lack of waste.

"Eugene," said the old woman behind the desk.

Adriana Rabh!

Edith had only seen her in newsfeeds. Her ivory skin and silver hair made her seem more a living statue than a human being. She was ancient but carried the years with a regality befitting Queen Midas, as some called her. "I trust the contract has been closed?"

Fischer nodded. "Luther Birch is pushing up daisies."

Edith saw a smile tease the sides of Rabh's mouth. A quick glance at Fischer found a sparkle in his eyes. She decided they were sharing a secret joke she'd just as soon not be in on.

"And who's this?"

Suddenly self-conscious, Edith cast her eyes downward.

"Edith Birch, our maverick entrepreneur's better half."

"Mrs. Birch," Rabh acknowledged. To Fischer, and more probingly: "And you've brought her here because..."

"These are dangerous times," he answered, his tone darkening. "I'm looking out for you."

The regent seemed nonplussed. Edith thought Fischer had been talking to her before realizing he'd actually meant his words for Adriana Rabh.

"Do tell," Rabh said.

Fischer shrugged nonchalantly. "You're the keeper of the gold," he said, "the regent who makes sure SynCorp's finances run smoothly. I figured you could use a first-rate bean counter."

Edith's head twisted toward Fischer in amazement. What had he just said?

But Rabh's secret smile returned. It seemed less natural this time. "I see." Turning her piercing eyes again on Edith, she said, "You're an accountant?"

Edith said something under her breath.

"Speak up, dear. The Company is falling apart. I don't have all day."

"I said, yes, ma'am. I have extensive experience with—"

Adriana waved her hand. To Fischer: "I assume this makes us even?"

"Zero sum," Fischer said, winking at Edith. Her cheeks suddenly felt warm. "And now, I have another party to get to."

"Edith, dear," Rabh said, pressing a button on her desk. The elegant doors behind them opened. "I'll have my personal assistant set you up here on the station. We'll talk soon about your duties."

"Um..."

"Yes?"

"I'm pregnant, Regent," she said. "Would it be possible—"

"I'll have my personal physician—"

"I was hoping for a friend from the clinic," Edith interjected. Adriana

Rabh's mouth hung open, ready to finish saying what she'd started. She wasn't used to being interrupted. *Shit*, Edith thought. *Too late now.* More quietly, she continued, "Her name is Krystin Drake. And there's a Doctor Estevez—"

"Yes, fine, whatever," Rabh said. "See yourself out, dear. Mr. Fischer and I need a moment."

Edith turned to go, then paused. "How did you know I'm an accountant?"

"I do my homework," Fischer said. "Part of the job."

"Oh. Right. Well..." She could feel Rabh's eyes on her back, urging her out the door. Edith swallowed, beginning to believe once again in a future that now included raising a child. The thought both thrilled and terrified her. She flicked her eyes at Fischer. Kind of like he did.

Then, quite formally, she held out her right hand. "Thank you, Mr. Fischer. For everything."

The enforcer reached out and took her hand in his.

"For the love of God," he said, "don't name the child Eugene. Even if it's a boy. *Especially* if it's a boy."

Stacks Fischer • Rabh Regency Station

The doors closed behind Birch's widow. I could still hear her light giggle in my head. It was a bright spot of sunlight in a dark place. Adriana's worried expression kicked it out.

"Everything's going to shit," she said.

"So far, Callisto has fared better," I answered. "For example, you're not dead."

"Yet."

"Yet," I allowed. "Whoever's behind these Soldiers of the Solar Revolution, they're running a game."

Adriana sat down again. She seemed tired. Her empire was falling apart. I guess that *would* weigh on a person, all right. "What do you mean?"

"They're using SynCorp's own best weapon against it. Propaganda.

They're directing the narrative, Telemachus might say. And I think it's starting to backfire."

"Don't leave me in suspense, Eugene, you seem to have this all figured out."

"Not all, but some. Maybe." I considered sitting down. My feet were tired. But then my butt would get comfortable, and I needed to move. I had a black star message to open. "Look at the Basement. You'd think the citizen-workers would welcome their liberators, wouldn't you? If you believe the headlines, anyway. And some are. But the Company has taken care of these people for a long time. No one likes not knowing where their kid's next meal is coming from. So far, the Soldiers are all talk and little walk. They're getting cocky. SynCorp's citizens? Just scared."

Adriana considered that. Turned it over in that steel-trap mind of hers.

"Can you hold here?" I asked. "Can Callisto hold?"

"As long as anywhere," she said. Then, amused: "I've got a colony full of Vikings, don't I?"

"Uh-huh," I said, not judging. Very much. "We've taken some short-term losses, Adriana. I'm confident in our long-game chances."

Adriana regarded me. We'd known each other a long time. Could smell each other's bullshit from a long way off, even upwind. She was still sniffing. "And Tony?"

I shrugged. "He's dead or he's not." I didn't tell her about the tightbeam waiting for me in the Hearse. I was pretty sure Adriana was playing for the home team. But these days had been full of unwanted surprises. I'd keep my hole card to myself. "I'm betting on not."

"Your confidence gives me confidence, Eugene," she said. I think she even meant it. "I'll try and contact Gregor on Titan. I'm closest. See if we can't work together, form a dyke against the floodwaters."

I nodded. Made sense.

"It's Kisaan, isn't it," Adriana said with more surety than wonder. "She's finally made her move."

I waggled my head. "Her clones are certainly doing the dirty work. The Soldiers of the Solar Revolution? Just a new-and-improved New Earth Order, far as I can see."

That old cult of Cassandra, the zealots that'd tried to pound mankind back into the Stone Age with the weather a few decades back, one killer storm monster at a time. The Company had saved what was left of humanity by bringing the Neo leader, Elise Kisaan, to heel by giving her the biggest jewel in the system to rule. Now she was biting off the heads of the other four factions. Winner take all.

Took her long enough, if you ask me.

"I never trusted that bitch," Adriana said. "Ming Qinlao should've killed her when she had the chance."

I shrugged. Strategery is above my pay grade. I'm a doer.

"I'll keep in touch, Adriana," I said. Then, genuinely, with zero bullshit: "Stay safe."

"You too, Eugene." A self-assured smile lit up her face. "You too."

29

KWAZI JABARI • ABOARD THE PAX CORPORATUM

Two more days.

Two more days of being rolled out like an organ grinder's monkey, made to dance and sing the praises of the Syndicate Corporation. To reassure the Callistans all was well. Don't believe what you're seeing on Corp-Net. All the way out here, you're safe and sound.

The coup happening in the inner system didn't matter a whit to Kwazi. His sole concern was that the unlimited credit line Tony Taulke had handed him with his medal might be disrupted somehow. Without it, he'd lose access to Dreamscape. No way to pay.

At least Helena Telemachus had finally allowed Milani to turn his SCI back on. Temporarily, each time following a public performance. It was off now, but the occasional hits of Amy's beautiful face had helped calm him down. He'd actually begun looking forward to being summoned to another performance. He knew there was a reward to follow each time. There was another in a couple of hours.

Kwazi sat down at the terminal and pulled up s-mail. Time to prepare for the next performance. He scanned the subject lines.

KWAZI, WE LOVE YOU!

MARTIAN, COME HOME: WE NEED A HERO MORE THAN EVER!

DAVID BRUNS & CHRIS POURTEAU

THE TRUTH IS A NIGHTMARE, NOT A DREAM.

He hard-stopped at the third subject line. That was new.

Kwazi opened the message.

A video file began to play. It was jumbled, the camera schizophrenic. It was loud. Kwazi reduced the terminal's volume. Data readouts appeared. Biometric readings. Heart rate. Pulse ox. The name above the data read *Amanda Topulos*. Two other data sets appeared, one labeled *Aika Furukawa*, the other *Beren Trent*.

The blood pounded in Kwazi's ears. The front-channel of his brain tried to understand what his eyes were seeing. Qinlao emergency medical personnel ferried Amy and his friends from the hell Facility 12 had become. Amy was still in the vac-suit he'd put her in.

They were alive. They'd left the complex alive...

Stretchers ran past the jerky cameras. One bore him next, and his own biometrics appeared onscreen.

The image jumped to a much more sedate scene: the bare white walls of Wallace Med in Mars orbit. Aika and Amy were in beds, side by side, in a room. Their machines beeped and pinged with life.

They're alive!

But how could that be? He'd seen Amy in the hospital morgue.

"I'm afraid Ms. Topulos died," Telemachus had told him while they were still fishing bodies out of the tunnels. "Your whole crew—with so many others. I'm so sorry, Mr. Jabari."

The screen flickered. A new timestamp branded the vid a couple days after the explosions. The beds were empty now. Words typed themselves across the screen.

BEREN TRENT: TERMINATED.

What happened?

AIKA FURUKAWA: TERMINATED.

No. Nonononononono, please don't—

AMANDA TOPULOS: TERMINATED.

A fresh wave of loss swept through him. Kwazi's lungs refused to work. For a fleeting moment, for a short time, the twisted hope that it had all been a cruel joke, that Amy and his friends were alive had bloomed inside his belly. Who could be so cruel as to show him this? To make him think—

KWAZI JABARI.

The words appeared, letter by letter, across the screen.

THE SYNDICATE CORPORATION MURDERED YOUR FRIENDS.

THE TRUTH IS A NIGHTMARE, NOT A DREAM.

The screen went dark.

No, Kwazi thought, standing up from the desk. *It can't be true.*

"You're nothing but an image," Telemachus said in his memory, "a fiction we created with a tragic backstory."

The truth slammed into Kwazi's gut. Helena Telemachus had murdered his family, his future ... just to create an origin story?

The fiction of the hero of Mars.

"I can't believe it, Kwazi. I just can't believe it."

Milani Stuart sat, mouth open, staring at the screen. "It just can't be true."

"Of course it's true." Kwazi spat out the words. Watching the footage over and over the past hour had replaced the lonely depression he'd known since leaving Mars with a new sense of self that lived on hate. "Helena Telemachus murdered Amy. And Brent and Aika. And who knows how many others."

But Milani was shaking her head. "There's so much on CorpNet now, so much propaganda. These SSR claiming to have killed faction leaders... How can you believe this?"

"I believe what I see. Amy's biometrics coming out of the tunnels. The readouts in the hospital." Kwazi's breath hitched in his throat. His hands began to shake. "Her body on that slab."

"I just can't—"

"You have to help me!" Kwazi reached out and grabbed Milani's shoulders, turning her roughly to face him. "I have to get off this ship!"

The look on her face, the wide-eyed fear, made him stop.

"I'm sorry," he said, releasing her. "It's just that—I need your help, Milani. You promised to help me."

"I know, but ... what do you mean? Where would you go?"

Kwazi's face was grim but also held a new kind of determination. "Abrams gave me a contact on Callisto, a guy named Braxton, to re-up Dreamscape for me—a permanent subscription. He can hide us."

Milani regarded him a moment. She was trying to keep her expression neutral. He could tell.

"Oh, Kwazi. Even if what's on those vids is true—"

"It *is* true! Think about it, Milani. Think about what the Company's done. The stories we see in the Basement, all the time. Assassinations between the factions. Tony Taulke himself might have ordered the bombing of Facility Twelve!"

Milani's expression made it clear the thought had never crossed her mind. "Now you're just being paranoid," she said.

"Am I?" Kwazi gestured at the screen. He rolled back the feed until Amy's biometrics were displayed beside the footage of her rescuers hauling her from the ruined tunnels. "Forget the words on the screen. Look at the medical readouts. You're a doctor. Are those fake?"

"I mean," Milani said, "they could be..."

"You're all I've got, Milani," he insisted. "Please, just get me to the surface. I'll disappear. You'll never hear from me again."

"I don't want that," she said, deflating. "I don't want that at all."

"Then come with me! We'll look out for each other. I'll pay Braxton well enough—he can hide us."

Milani breathed in, then out again. She shook her head.

"But, Kwazi, the way we found you before ... a few more days and you'd have died, lost in Dreamscape. How can you ask me to help you do that?"

Kwazi grew calm. He reached out and stroked her face. He hated himself for doing it. But he had to get off the ship. He had to reconnect with Amy.

"You'll be with me, Milani. You won't let that happen. But if you don't come with me, I'll find another way. I'll get off this ship and find Braxton and—"

"Okay, okay!" she said. "But my parents are on Mars. There might be retaliation."

The room grew silent as both of them considered the cost for walking out on the Syndicate Corporation.

"I think they have bigger things to worry about," Kwazi said. "The Company's being pulled apart. And good riddance to the murdering bastards."

"All right, then," Milani said, meeting his gaze. "All right."

Getting off the *Pax Corporatum* had been easier than they'd feared. They were heading to the venue ahead of Kwazi's next speech. This one was going systemwide, Milani explained to the guards. Everything had to be perfect. Would they like to interrupt Ms. Telemachus, who was meeting with Regent Rabh, to confirm?

The guards had demurred.

There was activity in the Community Dome, anemic foot traffic. The asteroid shield had been withdrawn, revealing the newly sealed plastisteel dome overhead. Through it shined the natural amber yellow of sunlight reflected from Jupiter's surface. It felt like ethereal twilight to Kwazi, so used as he was to the rust-tinged haze of the Martian surface.

"When can you reconnect me?" he asked, keeping his voice neutral.

"In here," she said, guiding them toward a doorway with a red cross over it. The sign read *Station Infirmary*. "But you have to promise me, Kwazi—when I pull you out of Dreamscape, you come out—no arguments."

"Sure, of course," he lied. "Whatever you say whenever you say it."

A single tech behind a small reception desk looked up as they entered the clinic. "How can I help you?" she asked. When her eyes found Kwazi, she released her breath.

"I'm Dr. Milani Stuart, and this is my friend Kwazi Jabari."

"Yes," said the woman, a kind of lusty reverence drawing out the *S*. "I know Mr. Jabari." She stuck out her hand. "My name is Krystin Drake. Sir, can I just say how much I appreciate all you've done and ... all you've suffered. You're a true inspiration to us here on Valhalla Station. I mean, truly, when you speak—"

"Thank you," Kwazi said, doing his best to mean it. The handshake was sweaty, so he quickly detached.

"Yes, well, my friend here and I need an exam room for just a moment," Milani said. "I know it's a bit irregular."

Kwazi smiled. "I can pay whatever fee might—"

"Don't be absurd," the tech said. "Haven't had much activity after last week's flood. Take Exam Room One." What she'd just done seemed to settle on her. "Um, if I may ask—you know, in case it comes up..."

"Ah, yeah," Milani said. "Mr. Jabari's implant has been acting up. Some residual disruption after his release from Wallace Med—that's the Martian orbital hospital."

"Right," the tech said, "of course."

"We'll be just a minute."

"Take your time." She stared after them. Or, more precisely, after Kwazi.

"See?" Milani said as she closed the door to the room. "Your celebrity can come in handy."

"These aren't the droids you're looking for," he muttered.

"What?"

"Nothing. Now—please."

"Okay, Kwazi, but listen to me." Milani stood close as he climbed onto the exam table. "You can't dive right into Dreamscape. We have to get safe first, okay?"

"Yeah, of course. My subscription's expired anyway. The sooner we find Braxton, the better."

Milani nodded. From her small medical kit she withdrew a device and held it over his right temple. "Ready?"

"Yesterday."

With a nervous smile, she reactivated his medical implant. A virtual world opened like a flower in Kwazi's consciousness. A second level of awareness was made up of CorpNet headlines, s-mail notifications, and a persistent readout of his own physical condition. And one small, grayed-back capital-letter D.

"Thanks, Milani," he said. "Thank you very much."

"You're welcome," she said, turning to replace the device in her medkit. "But like we agreed—"

Her words cut off with her air. Kwazi's left arm cradled her neck in the crook of his elbow, his right applied forearm pressure to the back of her neck. Milani's hands came up instinctively, clawing at the pressure choking her.

"It's best this way," he whispered into her ear. Her body began to sag. "This will protect your parents for sure. And you." He kindly, carefully lowered her, unconscious, to the floor. "I'm sorry, Milani. Thank you for everything."

After he cried out for help and the staff rushed in, Kwazi slowly faded into the background, then out of the infirmary and into the narrow, sparsely crowded streets of Valhalla Station.

The Entertainment District flashed its bright lights at him advertising all manner of debauched diversion. He was looking for Loki's Longhouse—bar downstairs, brothel up. Abrams had told him to ask for a "trickster's feast," and the bartender nodded and retreated to the back office. A short man, older and a former miner by his build, approached from the same door.

"I hear you're looking for something special," the bulky man said.

"I am."

"Hey—you're that guy. That guy from the vids. That guy from Mars who—"

"I am."

"Well, hell and well met, friend."

"I think that's 'hail and well met,'" Kwazi said, taking the stout man's hand.

"Who gives a shit?"

"Not me."

"All right, then."

Kwazi looked over his shoulder once. "I take it you're Braxton. Abrams from the *Pax Corporatum* sent me."

"Did he now?" The man leaned over the bar. When he whispered, Kwazi smelled the bitterness of poor dental hygiene. "I don't know anyone named Abrams."

Kwazi stayed calm. This man was his best shot at seeing Amy again, and always.

"He knew you. Told me you could hook me up."

The man leaned back and jerked his head at the bartender, who approached from the other side of the bar. The bartender's hand slipped behind his back.

"If you want a hookup, that's upstairs. Nice meeting you, Hero of Mars."

"Please, Braxton," Kwazi said, reaching out to stop the man's retreat. The man's arm was hairy and thick. "Please, I can pay."

"Keep your voice down. And take your goddamned hand off me."

The bartender was close, looming like a second shadow.

"I can pay," Kwazi whispered, picking up his drink. "Whatever you want."

Braxton jerked his head. "Come with me. Nicky, watch the front." He led Kwazi to the office behind the bar.

"These are dangerous times, Mr. Jabari," Braxton said, closing the door behind them. "You of all people ought to appreciate that."

"I do."

"Where's Helena Telemachus? Why'd she let you off the leash?"

"I wouldn't say she let me off."

"What?" Braxton suddenly seemed ready to lay Kwazi out. "You're out without permission? She'll track your SCI. Bring the marshals and Rabh's security down on me. What the fuck?"

Kwazi held up placating hands. "I'll get out of here. I just need you to resubscribe me. *Please.* I can pay whatever you want."

"Resub... Dreamscape? You're a hackhead?"

"Yes."

Braxton burst out laughing. "Well, if that don't beat all! The hero of Mars! A goddamned dreamer!"

Kwazi held up his right wrist. "Take what you want. Just make my subscription permanent."

With a skeptic's eye, Braxton passed his own syncer over Kwazi's. His eyes showed how bad he must be at playing poker.

"Holy shit on a swizzle stick," Braxton breathed.

"Will you do it?"

The dealer regarded him a moment, then opened the wooden drawer of his old-fashioned desk. Out of it he took a device not unlike the one Milani Stuart had used to reactivate Kwazi's SCI.

"Okay, so I'm gonna charge you—"

"Just do it. Take what you want."

Swallowing hard, Braxton held the device next to Kwazi's temple, as Milani had. The grayed-back capital-letter D turned red. It was all Kwazi could do not to activate it, right then and there.

"Done," the dealer said.

"Thank you."

"Now get the fuck out of here, Hero of Mars. And forget my name and forget this place. Understood?"

Kwazi nodded. A tattoo on the underside of Braxton's forearm caught his eye as the dealer replaced the device in his desk.

"What's that?"

"What?"

"That tattoo."

Braxton blanched. Rubbing his forearm self-consciously, he said, "It's nothing."

"It looks like a serpent and its mirror image, looking opposite directions."

"I said—"

"You're one of them," Kwazi said. "You're with the SSR."

Braxton's face set hard. He advanced across the office. Taking hold of Kwazi's shirt, he raised a massive fist. "That's it. Hero or no, you just outlived your own lifespan, son. Sorry it has to be this way—"

"You're taking down SynCorp," Kwazi said, as if conversing over a beer. "You're killing the Company."

Braxton hesitated, fist flexing. "What do you know about the Soldiers?"

The need to retreat into Dreamscape pulled Kwazi like a magnified g-force of emotion. But a breaker had just tripped in the back-channel of his mind. An opportunity presenting itself.

Maybe we could try Polynesian?

That sounds wonderful.

Don't leave her, motherfucker! Aika Furukawa's voice heaved with loss. It echoed off the Martian tunnels in Kwazi's head with a shrill, hopeless desperation. *Don't leave her alone in there!*

"I asked you a question, Hero of Mars," Braxton said. "What do you know of the Soldiers?"

Kwazi stared, unblinking under the threat of the man's massive fist.

"Next to nothing," he said. "Tell me more."

30

STACKS FISCHER • RABH REGENCY STATION

The station was alive like I'd never seen it before. Revolution has a way of shaking people out of their stupors.

I slipped between the Rabh rats zipping this way and that, making my way to the slip where the Hearse was docked. My first priority was to open up that message from Tony. I didn't think it was a last will and testament, but I knew it wasn't birthday wishes.

Unlike the broad expanse of the main docking ring around SCHQ with its bars and fetish diversions, Adriana's VIP facility was much more upscale. The slips were large, meant to cater to overfed corporate types and their bigger-than-need-be stellar yachts. Adriana's own *Staff of Isis* was in the premier slip, of course, closest to the main deck.

I entered the bay with its full-service mechanic stations and air recyclers. There were four slips, and my little sweetie pie was clamped snug as a bug in the third one along. Her blackhull design was spare and necessary for the work she had to do. But in that well-to-do dockyard, she looked like she'd crossed into the wrong neighborhood by mistake.

Two marshals burning daylight near Slip Three woke up when they saw me. They flashed the stars on their belts. Adriana's insurance, I guessed. One looked too tall for his uniform, like he was a teenager still growing and mama overlooked his last growth spurt. The other fella was thicker and wider, the muscle. They looked like a comedy team.

"Boys," I called.

"Stacks Fischer?" the tall one queried across the bay.

He had a tone that made me slow my roll. Maybe I'm paranoid or maybe it's just my gut reaction to badgers. But something put me on my guard. Maybe it was how the mechanics and Rabh staff suddenly scattered into hidey-holes.

"Nope. Sawyer Finn," I said. "Arbiter to Adriana Rabh's Labor Council."

"Uh-huh."

Between them, Too-Tall looked like he did most of the thinking. His stocky partner put some space between them. I noted the crates of supplies to my right. Probably caviar and alcoholic aphrodisiacs to restock the VIP ships that docked here.

Too-Tall motioned to me like we were old drinking buddies. "Adriana sent us along to make sure you got off okay."

"That Adriana, so considerate," I said. "But you're not my type. Wrong equipment."

"I get it." Too-Tall flashed a smile as Stock Boy continued working around to the side. "You're funny."

I didn't have time for bullshit. I pulled my stunner, and up went his hands. They waggled, which was disheartening as hell. It's hard to threaten someone when the threatenee waggles his hands.

"Whoa now, partner," he said. "We're just here to—"

Stocky pulled his piece and fired. I was already moving, diving behind the crates of fish eggs and spirits. Too-Tall was cursing. Sounded like Stocky had jumped the gun. Pun intended.

"You boys should've practiced this dance!" I called from cover. I could hear them moving, finding their own.

"Hey now," Too-Tall said. "Francis here was just a little edgy. It's an edgy time."

Francis?

Now, now, Eugene. Never judge a book by its title.

"Here's the thing," I said. "I've got to be somewhere. My boss doesn't like it when I'm late. So, you boys sheathe your johnsons there and walk away, and we'll forget this little two-step ever happened."

Someone chuckled. Stocky.

"Tony Two-point-oh's dead," Stocky said. "Time to clean up what's left."

"If this is how you want it, this is how we'll do it," Too-Tall said, sloughing off the fiction of friendlies. "Mano a mano."

Seemed more like mano a two-oh to me, but whatever.

I could hear one of them moving. Stocky was repositioning. This was a standoff, a recipe for a shit sandwich, with Fischer as the shit. The longer they delayed me, the more likely they'd get backup. Most marshals will do anything for anyone that pays. I wondered who was paying these two.

On the other hand, if I charged from cover, I was likely to get grabbed up by the loving arms of Mother Universe. I prostrated to floor level and peeked around one of the crates. I could just see Stocky's knee behind a mechanic's station. Too-Tall was a better hider.

Punk! Punk-punk!

I jerked back around behind the crate. *Classic stupid, Fischer.* Stocky was the bait, Too-Tall the marksman. They were triangulating. Marshal's manual, Chapter Fuck-You.

I could retreat into the station. A glance at the door reminded me my legs were too old to cover the distance alive. My longcoat would protect me from the stunner's effect, but Marshal Too-Tall could get lucky. Hit an ankle, or the space between my hat and coat collar. Not likely, but still. As a rule, marshals don't wear MESH uniforms because the general population doesn't have access to stunner tech. I doubted I was that lucky here.

So here we were again: standoff.

I pulled my .38 and stood up. Too-Tall would expect me to stay low, present a smaller target nearer the deck. I decided to be stupid on purpose. That's a one-step process for me.

Stocky was on the move again. I extended an arm.

Punk!

Too-Tall fired once. I felt the stunner blast bounce off my arm, absorbed by my MESH longcoat. Before Too-Tall could see I was fine and fire a second round, I fired my .38 twice. One shot connected, the other sparked off the deck.

Stocky went down, holding his upper thigh, his stunner sliding away. He was cursing and screaming. Lead hurts when it violates the human body.

"Jesus!" he yelled. "He shot me, Ben!"

I told you his partner was the smart badger, right?

Stocky writhed on the floor, trying to crawl back into cover. I took careful aim at his unshielded head with my stunner.

Punk!

Stocky stopped moving. The next time his body moved, Rabh security would be loading him into a long bag.

"*Now* it's mano a mano," I said, taunting Too-Tall.

"You sonofabitch!" the badger yelled. "That was my partner!"

I repositioned behind my boxes again. *Absinthe of the Garden Green*, the side read. Adriana's favorite liqueur for entertaining guests. On a barren rock like Callisto, it helped to remind folks of Earth's greenery. She'd always had good taste.

"Welcome to being single!" I called back. "You'll love watching whatever vids you want, whenever you want. Eating meals for one—"

"Motherfucker, I'm gonna kill you!"

"Not so far..."

He wanted to charge me, I could feel it. It was a smell in the air, fear spiced with hatred. I was doing my best to taunt him into it, but Too-Tall wasn't stupid. Not as stupid as his partner, anyway.

"Francis!" he called, hoping to get an answer. Stocky's answering days were over.

"Doesn't have to be both of you," I said. "Walk away and you can walk away."

"Fuck you, Fischer!"

I sighed. This is what I got for being considerate. I shucked the casings I'd spent on the partner and loaded back full. Then I sprung my knife and worked a latch on the crate storing Adriana's next hangover. It opened, and cool air leaked out. Inside, rows of bottled absinthe made me wish I had better taste. I grabbed a bottle, hunched into a crouch, and lobbed it toward Too-Tall like a grenade. It crashed to the deck, glass and green liqueur splattering every which way.

"What the hell?" Too-Tall said.

Bottle number two, over the river and to the floor.

"Fischer, what the hell are you doing?"

Keep talking, asshole. I've got my own triangulation method. His voice told me he was still beyond the reach of my absinthe grenades. I stood up still in cover, grabbed another bottle, wound it around and around, then let it fly.

"Goddamn it, are you crazy?"

Too-Tall had the tone of a man wiping liqueur off his trousers. Two more of those, then. By the time I was through, my shoulder hurt. I'd have to drink with the other hand for at least a week.

"Last chance, Marshal," I said. "Or join your partner in the arms of Mother Universe."

"Fucking crazy mother—"

I lined up down the .38's barrel through a gap in the crates. The five splattered bottles of *Absinthe of the Green Garden* littered the deck.

I fired once. The deck sparked but that was all. Too-Tall answered with rapid fire from his stunner.

Punk-punk-punk!

He wasn't good enough to thread the gap between the crates.

I fired again. Another spark. Another dud.

"Fischer, you crazy sonofabitch—"

I fired again. Third time's the charm. The floor sparked, the absinthe caught, and for a second all the air in the bay seemed sucked into the space between me and Too-Tall.

Whoosh!

Ever seen a flambé in a fancy restaurant? Well, this was a flame-bay. Marshal Too-Tall was yelling, cursing, trying to get away from the green fire. He forgot all about needing cover. When he looked up, I was standing in the open, artillery in both hands.

He tried to raise his stunner, but my .38 was faster. I was on the move before his back hit the deck. The quick-fire from the absinthe was already burning away. The floor was wet and sticky.

Too-Tall was already dead. He just didn't know it. He thought he'd get in a last lick, but I kicked his stunner away. I kneeled next to him. My knees popped.

I used to be younger.

"Now, who the hell do I have to thank for this little reception?"

But the marshal was gurgling. Not an answer. A prayer, maybe. Then his forearm caught my eye—a tattoo, the mirrored-S of the SSR. So they had marshals in their ranks too.

His gurgling stopped. His eyes flattened.

"Go take care of your partner, Marshal. He'll probably need you over there, too."

I stood and looked around the bay. The locals were still hiding. The deck looked like a war zone for alcoholics with exquisite taste. I should probably explain to Adriana, but I could do that from the Hearse.

She called to me from Slip Three, sitting over there all sleek and sexy and unpretentious.

I'm comin', doll. Just you'n'me for the better part of a week. It'll be like a second honeymoon.

───────────────

Regency Station cleared me without further trouble. Once I was away and on autopilot, I pulled up the message from Tony. Only it wasn't from Tony. It was from Ruben Qinlao. It was encrypted with Tony's black star, though.

"SCHQ is lost," Qinlao said. In the background I could see Tony slumped over in one of the foam chairs of a small ship. His face was pale. Some big mook I'd never seen before was moving around him, trying to make him more comfortable. "Get back to the inner system as quickly as you can."

After all that buildup, the message was a little anticlimactic. I reached to switch it off.

"Oh, one more thing, Fischer. Tony says I should tell you: 'Bravo, Stacks! Bravo!' He says you'll know what that means."

I froze the vid message and stared over Ruben's shoulder again. I had no *idea* what that meant. Maybe Tony had heard about our rooting out the pirates from Pallas. But that had been Daisy's operation inside and

Admiral Galatz's outside. Tony might not even know I'd been there. Well, I had six days of flight time to the inner system to open that particular puzzle box.

I transmitted a quick, encrypted acknowledgment that included the name of a Doctor Brackin in Darkside, the Moon's backwater barrio. The people who couldn't afford to live anywhere else lived there. I did collection work for Brackin on occasion. I told them to mention my name. Maybe he'd give Tony a discount. They could trust Brackin to be discrete.

I settled back and let my mind relax. The Hearse would shadow the Frater Lanes on autopilot. I had no tracker aboard thanks to being the right-hand fixer of the most powerful man in the solar system—until recently, anyway—so I was fairly confident my trip would be uneventful. I'd just gotten comfortable when the world went to shit.

Ain't that always the way?

Ever hear of the Hitler paradox? It goes something like— if you could travel back in time and stand beside Hitler's crib in the hospital, would you smother Baby Adolf? Most people say of course they would. Imagine the tragedy and carnage avoided. Imagine all those tens of millions of lives saved. Then again, how do you know for sure killing Der Little Fuehrer would really bring on a better future? Hell, it might even keep you from being born, in which case you couldn't go back, in which case ... and that's where my brain starts to ache. The point is this: the thousand-million ripples that happened because Hitler walked the world stage would never happen because that one pebble isn't dropped in the pond of time. Also, moustache styles? Totally improved.

I was settling in, comfy in the Hearse's embrace, when a forced message sprang up on CorpNet. If it was slaving the Hearse's comms, the broadcast via the subspace network must've been slaving every comms system in range. Someone had engaged the emergency transmission system, supposedly reserved for systemwide disasters.

I was looking at the former UN building in old New York City, where Elise Kisaan made her regency headquarters. The eye of the camerabot moved up the side of the building until it reached the penthouse, Kisaan's seat of power.

So, here we go. This is where Elise Kisaan declared victory over Tony

Taulke. I wondered if she knew one of her lookalike assassin-daughters was dead yet.

The camera flew in through an open window. A feminine figure with long, flowing black hair rose from behind Elise Kisaan's desk. She moved from the shadows and into the light with an easy grace, movement born of confidence and victory. Her face was still in shadow. In her right hand she held what looked like a bowling ball suspended by straps.

The camera zoomed in on the object. The woman raised her hand for the camera.

It wasn't a bowling ball. It was another woman's decapitated head. Silver-streaked, black locks. Viscera hung from the neck, ragged with saw marks. Someone had taken their time in relieving the dead woman of her noggin'. The wordless mouth gaped open. Her eyes, brown with pupils dilated in death, stared out at the solar system.

It was the head of Elise Kisaan.

"The Syndicate Corporation is at an end," said the woman holding Elise by the hair. The camera eye stayed focused on the former Regent of Earth. "The Soldiers of the Solar Revolution will free those enslaved by SynCorp's shackles. Ruben Qinlao. Tony Taulke. Gregor Erkennen. Adriana Rabh. Every head of the snake will be severed—as I have severed the head of my own mother."

The camera panned up. She looked so much like Elise. Except for the eyes. The golden eyes.

Cassandra, the cyborg child I'd failed to kill thirty years before. Cassandra, returned to take whatever revenge she thought herself due. And she'd started with her own mother, Elise Kisaan. My own personal Hitler paradox made flesh.

Cassandra Kisaan smiled at her audience. "Freedom is worth any price that must be paid."

I should've killed the squealing little shit when I had the chance.

Best enjoy the next six days of flight time, Fischer. After that, it's gonna be a hell of a ride.

Masada's Gate
Book 5 of The SynCorp Saga

The corporate empire is crumbling from within...

SynCorp's leaders are on the run. The Soldiers of the Solar Revolution are closing in.

A desperate Ruben Qinlao hides the injured Tony Taulke in the Moon's rundown barrio of Darkside. Now fighting for the SSR, Kwazi Jabari becomes the face of an insurrection he soon begins to doubt. Seeking total victory, Cassandra Kisaan targets SynCorp's treasure trove of tech secrets held in the stronghold of Masada Station. Only Stacks Fischer, corporate enforcer, stands in her way.

Earth is lost. Mars is under martial law. The outer colonies are the last bastions of Company rule. And what of Sol's billions of citizen-workers? Will they support Cassandra, who promises freedom? Or stand with SynCorp, the devil they know?

Get your copy today at
severnriverbooks.com/series/the-syncorp-saga

ACKNOWLEDGMENTS

Many thanks to our beta readers Jason Anspach, Jon Frater, and Alison Pourteau. Their input helped make *Valhalla Station* a better novel. A special thank you to Nicholas Sansbury Smith, whose wisdom and guidance helped us launch this second SynCorp series.

ABOUT THE AUTHORS

David Bruns is a former officer on a nuclear-powered submarine turned high-tech executive turned speculative-fiction writer. He mostly writes sci-fi/fantasy and military thrillers.

Chris Pourteau is a technical writer and editor by day, a writer of original fiction and editor of short story collections by night (or whenever else he can find the time).

Sign up for Bruns and Pourteau's newsletter at
severnriverbooks.com/series/the-syncorp-saga

United States
Taylor Publisher Services